THE URBANA FREE LIBRARY

TO RENEW MATERIALS CALL
(217) 367-4057

Scamming the Birdman

Scamming
the Birdman

A Thomas Purdue Mystery
by
Larry Karp

A Write Way Publishing Book

5002495

Write Way Publishing
PO Box 441278
Aurora, CO 80044
writewy@AOL.com / www.writewaypub.com

First Edition; 2000

ISBN 1-885173-84-9
1 2 3 4 5 6 7 8 9

Dedication

This one's for Peg Kehret
for all those years of help
and encouragement.

Scamming
the Birdman

1

Blistering mid-August day, coming up on noon. New York's a cauldron of bubbling road tar. Hugh Curtis and I wait on the sidewalk in front of Goldfarb's Confectionery, directly across Broadway from the eight-story, gray stone Rigby Building. Shading my eyes, I squint up past a row of leering gargoyles to second-story windows where gold-block letters proclaim the location of LoPriore Importers, Inc.

I nudge an elbow into Hugh's ribs. "Don't forget, I've never seen this guy. Soon as you spot him, holler. We'll follow him up the street to Union Square Park; when he turns into the crowd at 14th we'll get right behind him. Be careful in case he looks around—*he* knows *you*, too. Keep the gun inside your jacket; when it's time, just shove the barrel square against the back of his chest. I showed you where the heart is, right?"

Hugh nods. "Yeah."

"Okay. Quick two shots, that's all, clean hit. He'll go right down on the sidewalk, not make a sound. By the time anybody bothers to stop and check him out we'll be halfway back to my place."

Another muttered, "Yeah." Hugh's voice is as grim as his gray eyes. In the ten minutes we've been at our watchpost those eyes haven't come off the entrance to the building.

I rock back and forth on my heels. Without relaxing his vigil Hugh works a cigarette out of his pocket, slips it into the right corner of his mouth, flicks a match into flame, lights up. He blows a cloud of smoke toward the street.

"Where's the gun?" I whisper.

Hugh pats his jacket pocket. "I know where it is," he hisses without moving his lips. "I know where to point it. I know how to pull the goddamn trigger. Now would you shut the hell up."

I clasp my hands behind my back, lean gently against Goldfarb's window. People move past, a steady stream along the sidewalk, their chatter a band of white noise. I check my watch. 11:54.

Hugh grunts. "There. White turtleneck, white pants. Vincent LoPriore, the fuckhead."

LoPriore the Fuckhead is roughly my height, an inch or so short of six feet, with olive skin and a small, dark mustache. Stocky, solid, a walking tree trunk. He turns out of the building entryway and starts uptown on Broadway, bowling along as if he were angry at someone. It occurs to me blood will show too well against that white shirt. What if Hugh has the same thought?

"Let's go." Hugh's voice is hoarse.

He drops his cigarette, stubs it out with the toe of his shoe. Not taking his eyes off LoPriore, he wings along the sidewalk toward 14th Street, keeping pace with his quarry across the street. I stay close at his side.

At the corner the lights are with us; we trot across Broadway, go west on 14th. LoPriore's curious white outfit makes it easy to keep him in sight. The noontime mob at the southern end of Union Square is horrendous, but that's part of the strategy. LoPriore needs to go down in the short block between Broadway and University because past University the crowd will thin out to the point where someone might notice the shooting. Or LoPriore might turn around and catch sight of Hugh.

It's no easy thing for two men to work their way through a surging mass of lunch-bound New Yorkers—particularly when those men don't want to attract attention. Hugh and I angle toward the street and snake-hip single-file along the curb, taking care to avoid the swooping crosstown buses and zipping taxicabs.

My heart drums. With the back of my hand I swipe water off my forehead. University Street is coming up fast. Above his orange-red mustache, Hugh's face is scarlet, gray eyes like ice. The man in white is now just a step ahead and a couple of paces to the left.

Suddenly Hugh veers away from the street, into the thick of the pedestrian traffic. I have to struggle to stay with him. We can't get separated now, not unless I want to be face-to face with a first-class disaster. I elbow my way past an elderly woman with a shopping bag on her arm. "Bastard!" she shouts after me. "Hoodlum!" I ignore her. No choice. University Street is less than three yards ahead.

Once again the New York traffic gods smile on Hugh Curtis and Thomas Purdue. The corner light goes amber, then red. A few pedestrians scurry across; the rest pile up backward from the curb. I set my feet against the reverse human wave.

LoPriore is directly in front of us; I smell his musky male cologne. He's not a man who likes to wait: back and forth he shifts, from right foot to left to right again, all the while running fingers through his slick, black hair. I edge past Hugh so if LoPriore happens to turn around he'll see a stranger, not a sworn mortal enemy.

I glance at Hugh.

Hugh nods, almost imperceptibly.

As I watch the traffic light I silently rehearse the upcoming scene. The instant the light goes green I need to shove to the right. Then Hugh can come forward, take his shots. No way can we let LoPriore get into the street and become visible in the rapidly expanding crowd. He's got to go down right on the curb, as if he tripped or slipped. The mob of New Yorkers will just charge past and over him, trying to make up the ninety seconds they lost standing in wait for the light to change.

Talk about hair-trigger timing and split-second operations.

The light flashes green.

The crowd surges. As I shift my body to the right, Hugh moves up smoothly to fill the breach. His right arm bends at the elbow. Right hand slides inside his jacket.

Waves of heat rise from the blacktopped street. The blazing sun sends streams of perspiration flowing behind my ears and down my neck. The crowd jostles me in every direction.

A huge delivery truck roars into life, starts across the intersection. Through a shimmering haze of exhaust I watch in fascination as Hugh pushes his hand forward toward LoPriore. Hugh's arm jerks rigid once, twice.

Vincent LoPriore, a.k.a. The Birdman. Big-time collector of things that go chirp in their flight. Odd duck, this Birdman: flew his own course; never seen in any flock. Everyone in NYMBCA—that's the New York Music Box Collectors Association—knew *of* him. But no one *knew* him. Myself included.

Considering how low a profile LoPriore kept, it's amazing how many people in New York hated him. I could have made my fortune selling lottery tickets for the privilege of pulling that trigger.

Edna Reynolds would've jumped at the chance. In New York's antiques circles Edna's known as The Doll Lady, but there's nothing doll-like about her. She's a large woman with steel-gray hair and eyes to match, and when she sets her feet and speaks her mind—often in language salty enough to conduct electricity—the earth trembles. Edna's nickname comes from the fact that she collects automata: elegant dolls and whimsical furred animals which move in charming and funny ways to musical accompaniment. Edna's also an accomplished repairer and restorer, even creates her own original musical automata.

One of Edna's friends was sweet, dotty, blue-haired Carolyn Marcus, who collected modern musical trinkets. A few pathetic bars of "Raindrops Keep Fallin' On My Head" from the 18-note musical movement inside a little porcelain girl with an umbrella over her shoulder, and Carolyn was on the express train to hobbyist heaven. But strange things happen. A few years back, Carolyn was making her way through the Armory Antiques Show, and what should she stumble upon but a magnificent singing mechanical bird by Bruguier, circa 1830. Carolyn thought it was adorable. Even better, the dealer was clueless. As Carolyn handed him her check, who should dash up to the booth but Vincent LoPriore. One of his scouts must have tipped him. He turned on the charm full-blast, offered Carolyn twice, then three times what she'd just paid, but no deal. "No thank you, young man," Carolyn told him. "I appreciate your offers, but I'm going to keep my new birdie."

Don't try to picture LoPriore's face.

That evening he went to Carolyn's apartment, offered her what must have seemed like enough money to buy every singing bird ever made. Poor old lady, it made no sense at all—but she just didn't want to sell. Finally, LoPriore lost patience. Carolyn's cat, a gray-and-white striped butterball as round and as old as its mistress, was snoozing on a chair. LoPriore snatched it up, wrung its neck, and tossed the corpse onto the floor at Carolyn's feet. "Bad idea to keep cats around birds," he sneered as he pulled a wad of bills out of his pocket and thrust them into Carolyn's shaking hand. Then he grabbed the Bruguier bird off the table. Carolyn pushed the money back at him and started to scream. LoPriore slapped his hand over her mouth, told her if she didn't shut her yap and keep it that way, there were going to be *two* dead old pussies on the floor. With that he left.

Carolyn staggered to the telephone, called Edna and somehow managed to get the story out. Edna said sit tight, she'd be right over, but Carolyn must have been too scared and addled to think straight. East 72nd Street was sixteen stories down. By the time Edna pulled up, puffing and snorting, the area was cordoned off, cops all over the place. For nearly an hour she watched the blueboys do their thing; then when the Roosevelt Hospital meat wagon left with its bagged load and the doorman started hosing down the red grainy splotch on the sidewalk, she walked quietly away.

Edna didn't talk to the cops. Not that she was afraid—perish *that* thought. But Edna was seventy, had been around every block in Manhattan. She knew what the outcome would be once LoPriore mobilized his team of lawyers. Better to wait. She wouldn't forget.

Neither would Frank Maar forget Vincent LoPriore. Frank owns Wind Me Up, a hole-in-the-wall shop on West 12th crammed with some of the finest music boxes, automata, clocks and phonographs to be found in the world. NYMBCAns know Mr. Maar as Frank the Crank, partly because of what he sells, partly because he's as striking a manic-depressive as you'll ever see. To Frank's singular mind, drugs are chemicals and chemicals are poisons, so he careens through his days unmedicated. Never mind that his own body chemicals rage madly out of control: at least they're *his* chemicals. He'd as soon swig a glass of Drano as swallow a lithium tablet.

Frank's best friend used to be Paul Burleigh, who ran the Londontown Antiques Shop up on the West Side and was a high-ranking officer in Vincent LoPriore's bird-scouting army. The two bachelor antiques dealers talked to each other by phone at least once a day, had dinner together three or four times a week, and directed endless lines of buyers and sellers to each other's shops.

One afternoon Paul called Frank to tell him he'd found a spectacular early-nineteenth-century mechanical singing bird in a hand-carved wooden case, and no, in answer to Frank's question, he hadn't yet called LoPriore. Frank told his friend he had a customer for such a treasure, a wealthy collector who'd pay a high price and would then be good for *beaucoup* followup sales.

At dinner that night Paul gave Frank a big cardboard box, not altogether willingly. "What if LoPriore finds out?"

Frank laughed. "How's he gonna find out?"

Frank's question was never answered but Paul's was. First thing next morning Frank called his customer, sold him the wonderful singing bird, then tried to call Paul to share his manicky joy. But no one answered the shop phone. No answer at Paul's home either. Later that morning a browser found Paul on the floor in the back of his store, a hole placed with surgical precision midway between his eyes. No merchandise seemed to be missing and the cash register was closed, so the cops signed it out as a botched holdup: perp must've got scared and run.

For more than a week Frank sat at his desk in his locked shop, a pile of money in his safe, the Ancient Mariner with the albatross hung 'round his neck. Frank knew he owed Paul Burleigh a lot more than half the dough from the sale of the bird. How the hell was he ever going to pay off *that* debt?

***

My friend Broadway Schwartz also had a major account to square with LoPriore. Schwartz, a small man in his fifties with intense dark eyes and a long pointed nose, is an antiques picker, earns his living spotting diamonds in mountains of coal. Like athletic ability or artistic accomplishment, Schwartz's talent is an endowment, the outcome of a fortunate ripple in the gene pool. It's definitely been fortunate for me: the best music boxes in my collection have come thanks to the little man with the ever-present black fedora and the unparalleled eye and ear for quality.

Not long ago Schwartz uncovered a particularly good estate: an old woman died in her East End apartment, leaving an only daughter to dispose of sixty years' worth of accumulated goodies. Schwartz spent hours checking and listing the items. Next day he made rounds among dealers, taking enough money down to cover his purchase price. The rest—his profit—would come on delivery of the goods. But when he went back to close the deal and pick up the merchandise, the daughter wasn't alone. There was a man wearing a white suit and a cruel smile. "I think maybe you oughta split," the man said to Schwartz, and pointed at a beautiful mechanical bird in a cage, all gold and enamel, with a porcelain-dial clock on the bottom. "Mrs. Orbach sold me this already."

Schwartz thought Mrs. Orbach looked frightened.

"And she sold the rest of the stuff to a dealer, a good friend of mine—guy put me on to the bird here. *I* think he oughta get a good reward for that—don't you, Shorty?"

Schwartz looked at Mrs. Orbach. No question, she *was* scared, and not just a little. He'd heard about this Birdman; now he'd met him. Great.

No one's more street-savvy than Schwartz. He knew in any business there comes a time when you're smart to cut losses. He didn't say a word, just tipped his hat to Mrs. Orbach and left. The rest of the day he spent returning money. Didn't make him look good, but what could he do? "Me and her had a definite deal," he said to his disappointed customers. "But somebody else got in, paid her a bundle, and cut me out." Over dinner that night, his companion, Trudy, told him not to worry. "What goes around comes around," she said. Schwartz nodded grimly, more in hope than faith.

How do I know these stories? One: the antiques circle is a tight little world. Two: people are accustomed to telling doctors what they'd never say to anyone else. Three: I'm a doctor who collects antique music boxes. Simple.

Then there's Mr. Espinoza, whom I did not meet until the game was already underway. Espinoza's a round little teddy bear with a shy smile, big brown eyes, and a softly-accented voice like a warm bougainvillea-scented breeze at dusk in his native Puerto Rico.

Espinoza had as much reason as anyone to wish poachers on The Birdman. He owned and operated a small hotel on Madison, next door to the Church of Our Lady of Perpetual Life, which happened to be the sanctuary in which Vincent LoPriore worshipped God. After LoPriore's mother died it occurred to him to give the parish a priest's house in Mamma's name, adjacent to the church. Not *just* a house—it would be on a full lot, fenced off from the street, with gardens and a little central fountain. A place of repose for body and soul; a refuge where parishioners could find peace in quiet contemplation. That's how LoPriore's attorney explained his client's idea to the TV news reporter. But to build this boon to Manhattan's mankind, Mr. LoPriore needed to acquire the lot next door and demolish the hotel that stood on it. And the owner, Mr. Espinoza, didn't want to sell. Would, in fact, *not* sell, despite having been offered a very reasonable price, more than double what the place was worth.

Espinoza's refusals were courteous but firm. He appreciated Mr. LoPriore's generosity, but this was his home. He'd run the hotel for nearly a quarter-century, first with his wife and for the past four years since her death, by himself. Sure he could take the money and open a new place somewhere else in the city, but aside from sentimental considerations he had built up a large and loyal clientele over the years. They liked the accommodations, they liked the location; how many of them would follow him? "No, thank you, Mr. LoPriore, but I do not want to sell."

The TV reporter interviewed the priest. Picture the Army's newest second lieutenant being asked his views on a dispute between the Secretary of Defense and the dovish chairman of the Senate Armed Forces Committee. The poor young man kept tugging at his collar and looking away from the camera as if hoping to spot someone who might rescue him from his inquisitor. Well, certainly, yes, it *would* be lovely to have such a facility, and it is *very* generous of Mr. LoPriore, and of course it *would* be a fitting tribute to his late mother ... but on the other hand, he could definitely understand Mr. Espinoza's feelings. Mr. Espinoza was also a member of his congregation; he would *never* want to see Mr. Espinoza coerced ...

Vincent LoPriore, though, seems not to have been quite so tenderhearted about coercion. Unpleasant things started to happen. In twenty-five years no one had seen a rat in Espinoza's hotel, but all of a sudden guests were finding large rodents in their rooms, some alive, some dead. Men with ugly scars and flaming tattoos stood on the sidewalk in front of the hotel, telling prospective customers they didn't really want to stay there. Then one afternoon two men checked in for overnight. In the morning Espinoza asked them how they'd enjoyed their stay. "Terrible," one of them said. "All the furniture's broken up, there's two smashed windows, the toilet's running water all over the place, and shit's smeared on the walls and ceilings. I think I'll register a complaint." Whereupon he reached across the counter, grabbed Espinoza by the throat, and punched him in the eye. As the little man fell, his assailant said, "They shouldn't let crummy places like this stay open."

As usual, LoPriore had no public statement but his attorney expressed dismay when the TV reporter followed up with him after interviewing Espinoza in the hospital. "Mr. LoPriore still wants to acquire the property," the mouthpiece intoned. "But he deeply regrets this terrible act of hooliganism; in fact he asked me to convey his best wishes for a speedy recovery to Mr. Espinoza. It's a disgrace, how unsafe New York has become. Something ought to be done about it."

My wife, Sarah, sitting next to me, shouted, "Oh, what a liar!" Nurse-social workers go heavy on indignation.

I looked up from my book, studied the TV screen.

"That poor little Mr. Espinoza," Sarah crooned. "*I* think something ought to be done about people like Vincent LoPriore!"

Better lucky than good. Not only did Sarah mention LoPriore's name, but at the moment I focused on the TV the reporter was standing in the entry to Espinoza's hotel. THE REGINA, said the gold letters above her head; I chuckled. The Regina was a lovely disc-playing music box, manufactured a hundred years ago in Rahway, New Jersey. Doctors have good memories. When it came time to do something about Vincent LoPriore I remembered the Regina.

2

So many candidates, able and willing. How was it Hugh Curtis came to own the lucky trigger finger?

Here's the story.

Last summer, a hot mid-August afternoon. Classes at Manhattan Medical School don't start until after Labor Day. I'm at my workbench, dripping sweat onto a music box—a Regina, in fact—whose goddamned dampers just *won't* behave, when my friend Fitzhugh Curtis bursts through the open doorway and bellows, "Thomas! Maddy's in the hospital."

Maddy is Hugh's wife, an all-time all-star ditz. Next to Madeleine Curtis, Gracie Allen is Sadie Sobersides. I drop my tools, swing around in my chair, ask Hugh what's wrong with her.

"Dunno." Hugh shrugs, extends his hands. "They're saying heat stroke but ..." His lip starts to shake. "Thomas, I think she's gonna *die*."

"Where is she, Hugh? Which hospital?"

"Man Med. Emergency Room."

Loud, clear bugle call to action, the only sound capable of drowning out the squawk of diseased music box dampers. Thomas Purdue, MD, third-generation physician, professor of Neurology at Manhattan Medical School, is on his feet, moving toward the door. "Come on, Hugh—we'll find out what's going on."

Hugh is a big man, six-four, 220 pounds, with red hair and a flaming mustache. Any hot dispute, Hugh Curtis is first in, fists in motion. Looking at him now, though, I think of the Cowardly Lion. He shakes his head. "No—you go, Thomas. I'll wait here ... if that's okay."

The bigger they are, the harder they fall. "Sure." I smile, pat Hugh's arm. "Make yourself at home. I'll get back to you soon as I can."

Halfway to the door Hugh brings me up short. "Thomas? Is Sarah ... I mean ..."

My wife and I are a bit unconventional in our living arrangement. Home is a fourth-story walkup loft on West 16th Street partitioned into a custom pad for the couple who can't stand living together but can't bear living apart. The Great Wall of Purdue runs north-south, separating Sarah's tidy bandbox living room and bedroom from my disorderly music box repair shop and sleeping area. A small vestibule at the southern end of the wall leads through one door into Sarah's living room, through another into my shop. At the northern end of the wall is a common kitchen and dining area, the sole east-west border crossing. Usually there's free passage but occasionally in response to misbehavior by the King of the Eastern Territories, the Empress of the West closes the border.

I point at the wall. "She may come out; she may not. Don't worry."

I'm out the door, down the stairs.

Manhattan Medical School Hospital, Emergency Room, Cubicle Twelve. Frantic activity.

In contrast to what's going on around her, Madeleine Curtis lies as if in a deep sleep, no hint of suffering on her face. Her luxuriant blonde hair frames her face on the pillow like a halo. She's forty-five but looks a good ten years younger, despite the little portable respirator on the floor near the side of the bed, rhythmically puffing air into her lungs through an endotracheal tube. IVs drip slowly into each arm; a yellow rubber catheter drains clear urine. One nurse, a slight black woman, checks and charts vital signs; a stout white nurse whose bun of a cap looks faintly ridiculous atop her bouffant hairdo injects the contents of a syringe through a rubber cap on the left-arm IV.

The black nurse looks up over her stethoscope. "Sixty over thirty-eight, Dr. Loomis," she calls out. "Going down."

Meyer Loomis, Senior Resident, acknowledges the information by saying, "Ummm," and stroking his chin. "You gave her the Levophed? All of it?"

The nurse nods.

"Maybe that'll help."

Loomis turns to face me. "You said you're a friend of the family, Dr. Purdue?"

"Uh-huh." My eyes don't move off Maddy. "Her husband and I collect antique music boxes; we've been very close for more than twenty years. You said she was found unconscious? In Central Park?"

"Yeah. Some guy noticed her lying on a blanket with an empty bottle of wine next to her; he tried to wake her up, but ..." Loomis points at Maddy as though unwilling to waste needless words on a drunken woman. "So he called a cop."

"You figure—"

"Heat stroke, probably. Lying out in the full sun, over a hundred degrees, dehydrated herself on alcohol—"

"But her temperature's not elevated—how does she have heat stroke with a temp of ninety-eight? It ought to be one-oh-five, six, seven. Let alone that heat strokers are generally agitated, not comatose."

Loomis strokes his chin again, a gesture I'm beginning to find irritating. He sizes me up: am I going to swallow his story? "Well, actually, I think it's pretty clear, Dr. Purdue. She probably *did* have an initial hyperthermia and agitation—but then, considering her dehydration, she must have suffered a major intracranial thrombotic episode. That's my working diagnosis."

He glances at the nurses as if for confirmation; they both manage to be looking in other directions. I want to punch him. He's Meyer the Buyer, a good-looking guy but lazy as hell, thinks he can get by on his pretty face. "Is there evidence of a lesion on the EEG?" I ask. "CAT scan? MRI?"

"We, uh, haven't had time ..."

The black nurse jumps in with telling alacrity. "Would you like an EEG, Dr. Purdue?"

"Dr. Loomis is managing the case," I say quietly.

Loomis's forehead begins to shine. "Even if we request an EEG as an emergency it'll take probably an hour. Longer than that for a CAT."

"You've got an emergency machine down here," I remind him. "I can run it if you'd like."

Loomis flashes teeth. "Sure, go ahead, Dr. Purdue."

The nurse is out of the room before Loomis is done talking. Less than a minute later she's back, wheeling a small machine trailing several wires. I bend over Maddy's head to apply the leads. Once they're on I gently lift her eyelids and murmur, "Hi, Maddy" into her ear.

Loomis snickers, the piss-whiz. "I don't think she can hear you, Dr. Purdue."

I don't answer him. Maddy may be paralyzed but from the expression in her eyes as I uncover them, there's no doubt she's fully conscious. She *did* hear me, recognized my face and my voice. And she's scared positively silly.

"Let's get things moving," I say, and flash Maddy a wink before I release her eyelids. To my surprise, her eyes stay open. They're terrified, motionless as the rest of her body, but clearly imploring me to help her. "This'll give us some answers, Maddy," I say softly.

I push the switch on the EEG machine; paper begins to roll. The room is silent: everyone but Madeleine Curtis staring at the lengthening ink line.

After a couple of minutes, I turn to Loomis. "What do you think, Doctor?"

Scratch chin, knit brows. Meyer Loomis's best Young Dr. Kildare face. But this is no goddamn TV show. "Well?" I snap into his gorgeous phiz.

"Looks like a normal tracing," he mumbles.

"No focal patterns, no slow waves? No sign of intracranial hemorrhage? Thrombosis? Ischemia?"

Loomis straightens his posture, fixes me with an arrogant stare. "No, Dr. Purdue, none of that. But it could be a midbrain infarction—they often present with *coma vigil* and a normal EEG."

"Right and wrong, Doctor. *Coma vigil*, yes; someone with a midbrain infarction *can* look a lot like Mrs. Curtis, awake but not able to move or communicate. But the EEG patterns would *not* be normal. It's brainstem—not midbrain—infarctions that may present with normal EEGs."

Loomis licks his lips, swallows hard. "Perhaps this is a psychiatric problem, some sort of hysteria producing profound catatonia ..."

I shoot a glance at the respirator, puffing away on the floor next to Maddy's head, then begin to ask Loomis whether he thinks a shrink would be at all likely to tell him respiratory paralysis is a common hysterical symptom. But my eye catches a change in the EEG squiggles. I grab Loomis's arm. "Look at that. Seven-cycle-per-second synchronous discharges with non-specific high-amplitude spikes."

Which brings a sneer from the resident. "That would indicate grand-mal seizures, Dr. Purdue." Magisterial sweep of the arm toward Maddy. "Does she *look* like she's convulsing?"

"She's paralyzed, you ninny," I snap, and quickly bend down to look into Maddy's eyes. Dark windows. A fish at the market, lying on a bed of ice.

The EEG pen is now tracing a flat line.

"Dr. Purdue ..." says the white nurse, pointing at the electrocardiogram, which has also gone flat.

I grab Maddy's wrist. No pulse. Give her CPR, call a code? No. *Primum non nocere:* if I can't reduce someone's load of pain, at least let me not increase it.

Poor Hugh.

Poor Maddy. I lower her eyelids and mutter, "Hysteria lethalis," at Loomis. "Maybe she was scared to death."

"Guess we'll just have to wait for the post," Loomis chirps. The bastard actually looks relieved: one less problem. "Better contact the family," he tells the nurses. "I'll go check out the chest pain in Cubicle Three."

The white nurse follows Loomis out the door. The little black nurse turns off the respirator, EEG, and electrocardiogram. As she leaves the room she gives me a sad smile.

The instant the door clicks shut behind her I turn around, yank open the top drawer in the steel supplies table, grab a 20cc syringe and an 18-gauge, four-inch-long needle. "Sorry, Maddy," I say softly, then pull back the hospital gown and plunge the needle into her body, just below the breastbone. Dark blood begins to flow into the syringe. Bull's-eye, left ventricle.

When the syringe is full I cap it, stick it into my jacket pocket, and pull the needle out of Maddy. Then I grab another syringe, and a long, clear plastic tube, which I feed through Maddy's nose, down into her stomach. Cloudy fluid rises in the tubing. I apply suction with the syringe, then cap it and put it into my pocket along with the blood. Finally I yank the tube free, toss it into the covered waste container. The whole process doesn't take two minutes.

I'm at the sink washing my hands when the white nurse comes back to prepare the corpse for its gurney ride to the morgue. She says she can't find the patient's husband. "He was here a little while ago; we called him when she was admitted and he came right over." Her expression turns curious. "He was incredibly upset."

I drop my used paper towel casually into the waste container so it hides the nasogastric tube. "People do get upset when they find their wives paralyzed and on life support in a hospital emergency room."

"Oh, Dr. Purdue." The nurse almost giggles. "You know what I mean. He was ... well, like *really* upset. Like I was wondering whether we'd have to call Security. He was making Dr. Loomis really nervous."

"Good. Dr. Loomis could use being made nervous. The more really, the better."

"Dr. Purdue!" The nurse looks as if she's on the verge of reading me Section 1A of the Riot Act. "You said you're a friend of the family—do *you* know where her husband is?"

I smile and move toward the door. "Can't say."

The nurse's eyes narrow. "Can't say? Or won't?"

"A fine linguistic point," I call back over my shoulder. "One that neither of us has time to linger over."

Leaving the ER, I make my way through the subterranean passageways of Man Med to the Department of Pathology, past rows of unoccupied secretaries' desks, into the office of Dr. Arthur Forbes, Laboratory Pathologist.

Art rolls my two syringes in his hand, looks at them with suspicion. Then he looks at me with even more suspicion. "Just why do you want me to do these on the QT, Thomas? Why don't you just run 'em through the regular lab?"

"They don't have patient ID tags," I say mildly.

That wins me a prize fish eye. "You *could* have put tags on. For that matter, you still can."

"But then I'd have to run them through the lab. And I want you to do them on the QT."

"Jesus, Thomas!"

"Be careful, don't drop those tubes. They're important."

"Thomas, this isn't reasonable. You have to tell me more than that."

I turn toward the door. "Did *I* say life's reasonable? But actually, it is ... sometimes. You got the tenure you deserved last year, didn't you?"

Art Forbes's tenure hearing was a major thrash. His list of publications was skimpy, and he was on the verge of being denied when I gave the committee a good twenty minutes of what-for over the possibility of losing the best young chemical pathologist in New York—who by the way had already won two Teacher of the Year Awards. That swung the vote.

The heat from Art Forbes' brown eyes could melt steel girders. "So it's IOU time, Thomas? Is that what you're saying?"

"Not at all." My voice is honey and treacle. "It's just that right now *I'm* the one who needs help and you're who can give it. Don't worry; I'll explain. Later."

"But for now I should trust you, you're a doctor?"

Art's tone is noticeably softer. I smile to myself. "You could put it that way. What you find out is going to tell me how good—or bad—a doctor I am."

3

Back in the workshop I see my company has increased by two: Sarah and a Scottish fellow by the name of Johnnie Walker. Johnnie is sitting on the end-table next to Hugh Curtis, clearly having his customary bad influence on my friend.

Sarah catches my look, flips it right back at me. "Hugh found refreshments," she says. "Right after you left."

The effort of trying to give her a nasty glance nearly sends Hugh sprawling. I eye the bottle: Johnnie's looking a bit drained. That's not going to make my job any easier. I draw a breath, blow it out. "Hugh, I'm sorry. Bad news."

Sarah lowers herself into a chair. After twenty years with me she knows. Hugh regards me with the puzzled eyes and open mouth of the anguished drunk.

"She died just a few minutes after I got there," I say. "A cop found her in Central Park, unconscious on a blanket with an empty wine bottle next to her. Completely paralyzed, heart and respiratory failure. Maybe heat stroke with extensive brain damage; I'm not sure. But no sign she was in any pain."

"So she finally drank herself to death."

The bitterness in Hugh's voice sets me back. Maddy drank a lot, sure, but consider the intimate company she kept. Hugh and Maddy Curtis, the Scott and Zelda of the New York Music Box Collectors Association. Before I can think of a reasonable reply Hugh lurches to his feet, yanks a handgun out of the pocket of his blue blazer, starts waving it around like Wild Bill Hickok gone amuck. "Goddamn it, Thomas," he yells. "I'm gonna kill that son of a bitch, Vincent LoPriore."

Sarah bounds out of her chair, cuts loose a scream that could shatter goblets in the kitchen.

Under almost any other circumstances, I'd be laughing. Hugh Curtis is forever promising to blow some mug or other into the next world. But like as not if you walk into one of the theater-district watering holes that same night, there'll be Curtis and the mug, arms around each others' shoulders, sharing their troubles over a pint of brew. Interesting, though, who this particular mug happens to be. The Birdman.

"Hugh," I say, very gently. "That thing is loaded, isn't it?"

Hugh gives the gun a quizzical look, then tries to focus his eyes on me. "Well ... yeah. Of course it's loaded. What do you think, I can kill LoPriore with an empty .45?"

"Good reasoning," I say, careful to keep Hugh's eyes locked on mine. "But whether little Betsy there is a forty-five or a seventy-eight or a thirty-three and a third doesn't matter. What *does* matter is if she decides to go off she'll blow a hole through me big enough for Hudson River rats to crawl through. Now put her away. Please. You're scaring Sarah to death, and frankly I'm not feeling all that comfortable myself."

Hugh looks wounded. His hand is shaking something fierce. He gives Sarah a semi-apologetic nod and slowly slips the gun back into his pocket.

Sarah sighs, sinks back into her armchair.

"That's a good fellow," I croon as I take Hugh by the shoulder, move him the few steps back to the sofa, push him down into it. "Now, tell us." I sit down next to him. "Why are you so unhappy with Mr. LoPriore?"

"Vincent LoPriore ..." Sarah mumbles. "That name sounds so familiar."

Curtis stifles a sob; it comes through as a rude snort. "How would *you* feel, Thomas," he bawls, "if some son of a bitch bastard ran off with *your* wife—and your whole music box collection?"

Thick scotch clouds perfume Curtis's words. I wonder as I often do how this thundering booze detoxification plant ever managed to turn his old man's dinko shoe store in Hackensack, New Jersey, into the Curtis Shoes chain, hundreds of shops world-wide. Probably pure power of will. When the Prez and CEO of Curtis Shoes is of a mind to play irresistible force, no object in his path ever stays nailed down. I suppose if cars can run on ethanol so can Hugh Curtis.

"That's hard to imagine," I venture. "This LoPriore character ... and *Maddy*? Together? Made off with all your musical snuffboxes? You're sure?"

Curtis lays hold of the bottle of whiskey, takes a long swallow. He's far beyond such pleasantries as drinking glasses. He glares at me, slams the bottle down. "*Yeah*, I'm sure. The two of them ripped off my whole bloody collection. I was in Japan on business, got back two nights ago, and first thing I see is the snuffs are gone. At first I thought it was robbers—ordinary robbers, I mean—but then I started thinking, where the hell is Maddy? I opened the safe and guess what: my inventory's missing. Descriptions, pictures, the works. What second-story man's going to do that, Thomas? Open a combination safe, take out just the inventory of my snuffbox collection, then close the safe and not leave a scratch. They cleaned me out—Maddy and Vincent LoPriore."

"But why Vincent LoPriore?" asks Sarah. "Was he ... oh, I'm sorry, Hugh. "Were he and Maddy having an affair?"

Curtis bites his lip white. "Don't think so," he mumbles. "No, I figure he just decided to get at my collection through my shit-for-brains wife. It started with that goddamned article about me in *New York Pleasures*. Remember?"

I nod. *New York Pleasures* is a slick, glossy monthly that focuses on sports, entertainment, and hobbies in the Big Apple. Each issue features a pictorial on the fun-time activities of some interesting New Yorker. Fitzhugh Curtis was the February subject, he and his world-class collection of musical snuff boxes. Hugh's little treasures dated from the late eighteenth and early nineteenth centuries, and included some impressive constructions of burl wood, tortoise shell, and precious metals. Many were adorned with jewels and/or elaborate miniature paintings on ivory or silk, or elegant micromosaics in metal, bone, ivory, and wood. Each box was fitted with a miniature musical movement in airtight quarters beneath the snuff compartment. With cylinders not longer than three inches, these mechanisms played elaborate arrangements of selections from operatic overtures and arias. To this day no one understands how the craftsmen of that time, working only with hand tools, were able to slit blocks of hardened steel so finely as to end up with eighty or more teeth on a three-inch-long musical comb. Wonderful to see and hear, the finest early musical snuff boxes bring prices comfortably up into the five-figure range. And Hugh Curtis had only the finest.

Hugh brings his open hand down onto the coffee table; the nearly-empty bottle of Scotch dances a little jig. "LoPriore saw that article, the bastard. Damn near three months he drove me nuts, wanted to buy one of my boxes. Couldn't seem to get it through his fat head what no means."

Now I'm puzzled. "You have ... sorry. You *had* more than a hundred snuffboxes. And you couldn't sell him *one*?"

"Don't be a goddamn idiot!" Hugh puts poor Johnnie out of his misery, then slams down the bottle as though he's insulted at its limited capacity. "LoPriore didn't want just any old snuffbox I might be willing to part with. He wanted my Leschot double bird."

I have to snicker at my own stupidity. "Okay, Hugh, sorry. Now I understand."

"I'm glad *you* do," Sarah says.

"You know about singing bird boxes," I say. "Push a lever and a little feathered bird pops up, moves around, sings a little tune? You've seen them."

Sarah nods.

"Well, this one of Hugh's is the ultimate. It dates from right about eighteen hundred, made in Geneva by a genius named J. F. Leschot. Case is tortoise shell, decorated with enamel-painted miniatures, and it has *two* birds inside. When the birds pop up, a little comb-and-cylinder mechanism starts playing a tune from 'The Magic Flute.' The birds sing accompaniment while their heads and beaks move, and their wings and tails flutter. It's like watching magic. Amazing they didn't burn Leschot at the stake."

Hugh stares accusingly at the empty bottle. "My prize piece," he mumbles morosely. "Irreplaceable."

"If Hugh *did* want to sell it," I tell Sarah, "he'd probably be talking in the hundred-thousand dollar range."

"Huh!" Hugh clears his throat. "LoPriore's opening offer was a quarter of a mill."

Sharp insuck of breath from Sarah. Hugh looks just this side of amused.

"*Opening* offer?" I say.

"You heard right. And every time I said no, up it went. A week later it was half a million; by May we were into seven figures. Finally he sent me a check, registered mail. As if I'd agreed."

"For how much?"

"It was blank, Thomas. Except for his signature."

Sarah's eyes go glassy.

"He sent you ... a blank check?" I stammer. "My God, Hugh—I've heard about this guy. They call him The Birdman, he collects high-end bird-related antiques. The only people he ever seems to talk to are the ones between him and something he wants, and money never seems to be any sort of consideration. But still—"

Hugh stops me with an outstretched palm. "At that point I thought I might be smart to do some checking so I put a dick on him. Vincent LoPriore, age forty-six, unmarried, lives by himself in the Carroll Parkside—that's a twenty-four-carat, five-star residence on Fifth between East Sixty-Second and Sixty-Third, facing Central Park. He owns LoPriore Importers, down on Broadway, just below Fourteenth Street. Just what it is he imports I can only guess at."

"With the kind of cash he has to toss around I'd say the guess might be pretty well educated. But what happened, Hugh? When he sent you the check, I mean?"

"Hah!" Hugh comes perilously close to smiling. "I pasted his freaking check onto a roll of toilet paper. "Sent it back to the jerk with a note saying I thought he could figure out what to do with it."

Sarah and I exchange glances. "I don't suppose that struck him very funny," I say.

Again Hugh looks in danger of being mildly amused. "Not quite. Next thing I knew, there he was on the phone. I thought I was listening to a Jimmy Cagney flick." Hugh twists his face into a sneer, spits growled words out of the corner of his mouth. "'Yer makin' da mistake'a yer life, m'friend. When Vin-tzent LoPriore wants a thing, Vin-tzent LoPriore *gets* it. Kapeesh? I figure I been pretty generous, pretty patient wit' ya, but if ya wanna be unreasonable—' That's as far as I listened. I told him to piss off—the Leschot wasn't for sale, not at any price, and if I ever got another letter from him or another phone call, I'd make sure he heard lots of birds singing. I told him hell would freeze before he ever got his scuzzy hands on my Leschot. 'Oh, yeah?' he said. 'Is that a fact? Try an' remember that when you're readin' in the papers about how they're ice skatin' on the River Styx.' The son of a bitch! Then he hung up the phone, right in my ear."

"Educated son of a bitch," I muse. "Skating on the Styx. That was the last you heard from him?"

Hugh nods grimly. "It was seven weeks ago—June twentieth, if you want to be exact. I'd forgotten all about him, but the other night when I saw my place cleaned out I remembered in a hurry. I got my ass up to Central Park in nothing flat—but LoPriore wasn't home. So I went across the street to the park side, sat down on a bench and waited. And a couple of hours later, here comes this greaseball, all dressed in white, and who's with him but Maddy, chirping like a bird"—Hugh winces at his own choice of words—"and gabbing away sixteen to the dozen. They went inside the lobby."

"And you?"

"I started up after them." The red stubble on Hugh's cheeks stands out like tiny blood spots on library paste. "But then I thought about Russ and Lucy ... my kids. Jeez, Thomas—to have them find out all at once their mother's a whore and a thief, and their father's in the can for using some scumbag's head for a soccer ball? Uh-uh. I turned around, went home, and that's where I've been the last two days. Sitting and thinking, sitting and thinking."

And drinking, I say to myself, but I know better than to say it out loud.

"Didn't even go in to work. And then today I got the call from the hospital ..." Hugh's voice trails off.

I let the silence build for a moment. "She didn't die of a

stroke, Hugh," I say, very softly. "Not heat stroke, not any kind of stroke."

I pause just long enough to check my audience. No question, I have Hugh's attention *and* Sarah's. "My best guess is she was poisoned."

Sarah's hand goes to her throat. "Thomas ... then, the bottle ... that wine bottle you said they found next to her on the blanket. Can you test it for—"

I shake my head. "Between when Maddy was found and the cops and medics got there, the bottle vanished. But I took samples of her blood and stomach fluid. Point is, what Hugh's just told us puts a whole new twist on the situation. Maddy helped LoPriore make off with Hugh's snuffboxes but then she outlived her usefulness—literally. LoPriore must have taken her into Central Park, right across the street from his place, a little picnic on the grass. Glass of wine or two or three to celebrate their success. Only there was something in Maddy's glass that wasn't in his. Once she was down for the count he took the glasses and walked away. Who was to notice?"

"Not necessarily."

Sarah's obligatory black to my white. I cue her with a smile.

"If LoPriore didn't need Maddy any more, maybe he just threw her out. She couldn't go to the police, could she? *Or* go back home. Maybe she went to Central Park by herself, put the poison into her own glass, drank it down, and waited there to die."

I start to say when people are serious about suicide they don't usually lie out in the open where they might be found and resuscitated, but a sudden movement of Hugh's arm cuts me off. I lurch sideways to grab my friend's hand before it can get inside the jacket pocket. "Lemme go, Thomas," Hugh roars. "Now I really *am* going to kill the bastard."

If big, strong Hugh were sober he'd pitch me across the

room into the metal lathe and go on his way. But drunk as he is, the advantage is mine. I twist his wrist; he lets out a howl. "Sit back down," I snap, then reach inside his jacket pocket, remove the gun, put it down on the end table out of his reach. For reward I get the drunkard's hurt, reproachful glare.

"Hugh, don't be a horse's patoot," I snap. "You were right to think about your kids; you still need to do it. Their mother dead and their father up for Murder One? That'd get you how many months on the front page of the *Daily News*?"

"Thomas is right." The concession is plainly painful to Sarah. "Let him get his test results, then he can notify the police."

"I didn't say anything about calling the police."

Hugh and Sarah stare at me, one in confusion, the other in dread anticipation.

I'll get the tests," I say. "But no point calling the police. Even if Maddy *was* poisoned, how are they going to prove who gave the stuff to her? You said it, Sarah. Maybe she took it herself."

Bad enough I got the upper hand in debate with my wife, worse, I hoisted her on her own petard. She flashes me her best watch-it-Buster-I-know-what's-coming look, but I decide to damn the torpedoes. "I don't think LoPriore ought to get away with it—whether he actually gave her poison or drove her to take it. But you and your kids shouldn't get hurt in the process, Hugh. Wait 'til you get rid of some of that booze, then I'll tell you what I've got in mind."

Hugh's bloodshot eyes shimmer. "I knew you were my friend, Thomas."

"Oh, sure." Sarah knows she's beaten, if only for the moment. "Your friend! With friends like Thomas ..."

Hugh manages a crooked smile.

"Take off your shoes," I tell Hugh. "Stretch out on the

sofa there, take a nap. You'll feel better when you wake up." I bend over, swing Hugh's feet up onto the sofa, pull off his shoes, pat him gently into place. He's making sawdust before he hits full horizontal.

"Poor guy," I say *sotto voce* to Sarah. "He's exhausted."

Sarah of the gimlet eyes. "You're hatching one of your plots, aren't you?"

"Got to run a couple of errands," I say over Hugh's phlegmy snore. "Be back for dinner. Talk to you then."

Big roll of the eyes from Sarah. "I know what you're going to talk about, Thomas. I also know I'm not going to like it."

4

Hugh Curtis lives on Pringle Way, a little alley tucked into that peculiar area of Greenwich Village west of MacDougal where no-parking streets run off in every which direction. The same key that lets me through the gate in the brick wall, into the courtyard, also admits me into the house. No alarm system. According to Hugh an alarm only tells burglars you have something worth stealing.

Oh, by the way, that key is on Hugh's keychain, which I fished out of his pocket while I was making him nice and cozy on the sofa. If she'd seen me do it, Sarah would have used some pretty blunt language to question the propriety of my behavior. Which is why I made sure she didn't see.

I lock the door and walk slowly into the living room, cram-jam with Danish modern, Maddy's last biennial makeover. Light wood, white cushions. Spotless beige carpet. In each corner, wrought iron floor lamps stand like dysmorphic storks. On the far wall are the narrow, glassed-in shelves that held Hugh's fantastic snuff box collection, and Hugh wasn't kidding: they're empty. But the massive sideboard on the opposite wall is still loaded with Hugh's *karakuri*—clever Japanese automata, mostly carved in wood, some dating back as far as the 17th century. Still hanging on the east wall above the sofa is a huge 18th century Japanese noble's cape in the shape of a giant bat, all silk and heavily embroidered, worth a fortune by itself. So the theft really wasn't for money; it was a matter of unrestrained covetousness, a green-eyed monster running savagely amuck. It was also meant as a punishment. Leaving the Japanese items was LoPriore's and Maddy's way of rubbing Hugh's nose in the pile of shit they'd dropped on his living room floor.

But why? LoPriore, sure, but Maddy? All the money she wanted, all the freedom. She brought up the two Curtis kids, went to P.T.A. meetings, dabbled here and there in neighborhood art galleries, redecorated the house every couple of years, went a-docenting up at M.O.M.A. every Wednesday afternoon. So why all of a sudden this nutty caper? Raging menopausal hormones? Fear of fading looks and a bit of judicious flattery by LoPriore? Did she wonder just what Hugh did at night on his business trips to Japan? Did she *know* what he did and not like it? Or after all those years of basically proper matronhood, did she simply grab at a chance for a little adventure? Twenty years in a doctor's office has long since put me past being surprised at what people say and do, but the curiosity remains. More often than not it also remains unsatisfied.

As I think about the happy afternoons and evenings I've spent in this room my mood goes further and further south. When Hugh got a new musical snuffbox we'd sit here and listen to it, the sun through the big front windows warm on our backs. On summer evenings, breezes carried in scents of the flowers Maddy cultivated in the courtyard. By reflex my hand reaches for a music box; Rossini's what I need right now. But all Hugh's glorious musical mademoiselles are singing their songs for Vincent LoPriore. No solace for me here any more.

Move, Purdue.

I snatch up the phone, punch Broadway Schwartz's number.

Schwartz doesn't even say hello. Just, "You sound like something's up."

No way to keep the smile off my face; I can practically see his nose quivering. "Right as usual, Broadway. Something is up. No time to go into details now, but I need two things. First, can you make a phone call for me in the morning? I'll give you the number, tell you what to say."

"Fine by me, Doc; easy enough. What's the other thing?"

"Where can I go—right now, with no questions asked—and buy a gun?"

I hang up the phone, stroll into the master bedroom suite. What a mess. Shirt carelessly draped over a chair; gray, short-sleeved cotton pajamas on the floor; piles of underwear everyplace. The bed looks as if someone gave it a going-over with an eggbeater. I quickstep over to Hugh's dresser, take a set of fresh underwear, a clean white shirt, a rolled pair of socks. Then I go to the clothes closet and select a pair of gray, summer-worsted trousers, belt to match, and a nice gray-and-red tie. In the bathroom I grab Hugh's little Norelco from the sink and his toothbrush out of the holder. A quick open-and-shut of the medicine cabinet and I'm on my way out, Hugh's clothes and toilet articles rolled up under my arm.

Before I can shut the door, the phone rings. Once, twice ... I count to sixteen, then twelve on the immediate second try. Probably Man Med Hospital, trying to notify Maddy's next of kin. It'll be a while before they find him.

I hoof it over to Seventh Avenue where I hail a cab. The driver's a mouse-faced little man named Morton Coleman, at least according to the license which is prominently displayed as prescribed. Mr. Coleman does not look overly happy about the address I give, and who can blame him? I don't much care for it myself.

The address is in the East Village between Avenues A and B, a dingy stone walkup with a concrete stoop painted red to hide the crumbles. For New York the street's unnaturally quiet. No kids playing stickball, no stoopsitters. A man walks past the cab, looks fitfully from side to side, then nervously checks behind himself. Evening shadows spread over the pavement, wider and longer by the minute.

"Wait here," I tell the cabbie. "I'll be right out."

"Hey, Mac—you kiddin' or something?" The driver is indignant. "Maybe you want I should just go stand on the sidewalk and hold out my wallet in front of me? And say thank you when they cut my balls off because I only got ten bucks?"

I pull out a fifty, slap it into the cabbie's hand. "Here you go, Coleman—instant balls. Lock your doors, keep the motor and meter running. If anyone hassles you, go around the block. But take off on me for good, count on seeing me later. I've got your name, your license number *and* the number of your cab. Am I being clear enough?"

Silence. Coleman's face says okay-but-I-don't-like-it.

I open the back door of the cab, step outside, lock the door, take a second to aim a warning finger at Morton Coleman. Then I trot across the sidewalk and zip up the red-painted stairs to the stoop.

Door buzzers are set into the cracked wooden panel to my right. Two columns of four buttons: two apartments per floor, four floors. S. Kleinfelt is in 3F: that'd be third floor, front.

I push the button.

A window opens above me and a man leans out, cupping his hand above his eyes. "Yeah?"

I call one word up to him: "Schwartz."

He disappears back inside. The window closes. The entry buzzer sounds and I go in.

The hallway smells like cooked cabbage and used diapers,

wall plaster dulled near-brown by eighty years of exposure
and abuse. Near the foot of the stairwell is a bit of marker-
pen graffiti: CORA SEMWORTH BITES THE BONE FOR
FREE, with a phone number underneath, presumably Cora's.

Sooner I'm out of here, the better. I start up the stairwell,
three steps at a clip.

On the third landing I run into the man who opened the
window, a tall rattlebones in his sixties. Yellow light from the
globe above him reflects off his long corrugated forehead. He's
got a birthmark the color of red wine on his left forehead, and
a large wen above his right eyebrow. Wouldn't be difficult to
pick him out of a lineup. He looks me up and down, then
hands me a paper bag, surprisingly heavy. "That's five hundred, right, pal?" he says through a dense cloud of garlic.

I pull five hundreds out of my wallet, give them to Kleinfelt.
"Schwartz didn't tell me the price—but you're the doctor."

Kleinfelt's little smile is one of weary cynicism. He riffles
the bills, counts them slowly, one ... two ... three ... four ...
five ... "Okay, pal. Thanks."

I start to open the bag. Kleinfelt's already on his way back
upstairs, but as he hears paper rustle he looks around. "It's
there, pal, don't worry. Just exactly what you ordered. Damn
if I know what you want it for, but frankly I could care less.
Just get the hell outta here with it."

I tuck the bag under my arm, go back down the stairs, out
to the street where Morton Coleman is sitting in his cab with
eyeballs the size of flying saucers. Good thing he doesn't know
what I'm carrying in the brown bag. The idea of mouth-to-
mouthing him doesn't do much for me.

5

Back in the loft Sarah greets me by pulling a lemonsucker face and pointing at Hugh on the couch. "He hasn't moved since you left. If it weren't for the way he snores I'd worry he was dead."

I laugh. "I could hear from two flights down. Let's just let him sleep. Best thing for him right now."

Sarah looks at me with suspicion. Go on, says her face. Where was it so important for you to run out to?

"I stopped by Hugh's, picked up some fresh clothes," I tell her. "And his razor and toothbrush." I don't bother to mention what I've got wrapped in a paper bag at the core of that roll of clothing. It'd only upset her.

"How did you get into Hugh's apartment?"

I pull Hugh's key chain out of my pocket, dangle it in front of Sarah's face. "I took it before I left."

Her expression tells me just how unkosher she considers that to have been.

"He wasn't going to want it himself, now, was he?" I lay the keys on the coffee table. "He'll feel a lot better in the morning with some clean clothes and a shave."

Sarah apparently decides this particular line of questioning has reached a dead end. "Where else did you go?"

"I needed to talk to Schwartz."

"I should have known."

Sarah's estimation of Schwartz's character has softened a bit since his performance last winter during what we all started calling "the Music Box Murders." Before that he was the bad boy from the wrong neighborhood who was forever leading her husband into questionable activities. Now she grants me equal responsibility. She looks me up and down. "You're not carrying a music box."

"No music box buy this time." I make a show of looking toward the kitchen. "How about some dinner? I'm hungry."

"Not so fast, Purdue."

Full alert. Sarah's voice is up an octave from normal, and when she addresses me as Purdue the situation is serious.

"You're up to something, aren't you? Getting involved in a situation that's really none of your business."

For Sarah the social acceptability of a disaster is in direct proportion to both the number of people who are up against a wall and the distance of that wall from her. "If this were a massacre in Bosnia you'd tell me it was my business," I say. "Or a famine in India. But when my good friend gets clobbered it's none of my concern."

"Thomas, I'm not going to let you sidetrack me with your warped logic. Just tell me: what are you about to do?"

"Help Hugh through this mess. Keep him from doing anything he might later regret. Maybe manage to get his snuffboxes back. Exactly how, I'm not sure yet. When I am, I'll tell you."

Sarah often accuses me of diddling truth, but please take note that at no time during our entire verbal exchange did I pitch a lie. I *did* go to Hugh's place to pick up clothing and toilet articles. I *did* talk to Broadway Schwartz. I *did not* buy a music box. And I *am* going to keep Hugh from doing anything he might later regret, as well as try to help him get back his rightful property. The truth and nothing but the truth, that's what I told Sarah. Maybe not the whole truth—but two out of three's not bad. I didn't mention anything about Klinefelt and the gun, nor did I come out and say I was going to help Hugh settle his score with Vincent LoPriore. All in good time. Once I have the plan scoped I *will* tell it to Sarah. Not that she'll like it—but I'll deal with that when I need to.

"Thomas, I know you. This is one of your stories."

"Now, Sarah, you know my regard for truth."

She stamps her foot, hard. For an instant Hugh goes silent, then as he picks up where he left off in mid-snarfle, Sarah whispers harshly, "*Damn* you. That's just another story—a one-sentence story."

My wife's come a long way. Not all that long ago she'd have flat-out called me a liar; now she'll at least acknowledge a story for what it is. None of us—not you, not me, not even Sarah Purdue—pass a day of our lives without going out of our way to avoid having to gaze upon the repulsive nakedness of Truth. Some of us admit that, others don't. If you can't tell the difference between a story and a lie I feel sorry for you, even sorrier for those whom you love and who love you.

I give Sarah my best disarming smile. Truce. Time out. She shakes her head, grimaces like Hattie McDaniel, disapproving of Miss Scarlett's outrageous behavior but unable to do a thing about it. "Okay." Sigh. "Dinnertime."

On my way to the kitchen I pause long enough to lift the lid of my big Nicole variations box and push the start lever. The air fills with golden trills and cascading arpeggios. "Carnival of Venice." Hugh doesn't miss a beat in his snoring but I swear the corners of his mouth flicker upward. Sarah's expression as she turns and looks at me goes rapidly through surprise into grudging but unmistakable sympathy.

6

A few minutes after nine next morning I'm at my workbench, fitting a replacement tooth into the comb of a fine
Henri Metert forte-piano overture box, when I hear an ugly
groan. I look around: Hugh is trying to raise his head from
the sofa.

"Think you're going to make it?" I ask over my shoulder.

Hugh shelters his eyes from the sun flaming through the
skylight. Another hot day in the works. "Not sure," he mutters. "I finished all your goddamn scotch last night; don't
even have a hair of a dog."

"Settle for coffee, then."

I stand up, stretch my back. Hugh follows me into the
kitchen. "What the hell time do you wake up?" he moans.

I pour him a cup from the coffeemaker. "About seven,
even during vacation. Force of habit."

"Bloody uncivilized is more like it." Hugh takes a tentative
sip, then coughs. "Christ Almighty." He studies the coffee. "What
the hell is this? Mud off the bottom of the East River?"

I give him a little shove. "Drink up, let's go. We've got
stuff to do."

A half hour later, Hugh is shaved and dressed, sitting with

me at the kitchen table over second cups. He listens to my story, looks thoughtful. Then he growls, "Friggin' LoPriore! Got Maddy to help him rip off my snuff boxes, then offed her when he didn't need her any more." Hugh extends his arms in helpless supplication. "Goddamn, Thomas! Why didn't you just let me shoot him last night? The whole world'd be better off."

"Not quite, Hugh. For one, *you* wouldn't have been. For two others, your kids."

Hugh's face screws into an expression of reluctant agreement. "I still wish I could kill him," he mumbles.

"I didn't say you couldn't."

Hugh's face goes blank. "But you said—"

"Whoa. Listen. I only said you shouldn't blow airholes through the bastard with your own traceable handgun. Use a little common sense ... wait a minute. I'll be right back."

I go to the workshop, open the supplies cabinet, grab the heavy, brown paper bag. Then I go back into the kitchen. As I dump the contents onto the table, Hugh whistles.

"Right, Hugh. This gun they can't trace." I point at the little cylindrical extension on the end of the barrel. "Silencer. Sounds like a cough. Now here's the deal. Sarah's at work; we're clear all day. In just a few minutes LoPriore's going to get a phone call about a bird box for sale—an irresistible bird box. He's going to be climbing the walls."

Hugh looks dubious. "Who's making the call? You? Me? He'll probably—"

"Ask me no questions, harbor no doubts. It's all taken care of. To see the bird, LoPriore's going to have to go to Mangiapane, an Italian restaurant on Sixth, near Seventeenth Street. Close to where he works. He'll go up Broadway to Union Square, then across Fourteenth Street to Sixth. Lunchtime, it'll be mobbed the whole way. You'll take your friend here"—I pat the gun on its black barrel—"and we'll wait across the street from LoPriore's office building. He shows, we follow him. When we get him in the middle of a big crowd, you put the gun behind his heart and pull the trigger. Bang! Except it *won't* be bang. It'll be just a little fart, no one'll hear a thing. While he's falling, we just keep on walking. Swing past the West Side docks, drop the gun over the rail into the Hudson. Then you go home and wait for Man Med to call you about Maddy. After that you call your kids. How does that sound?"

Hugh chuckles, shakes his head. He reaches out to touch the gun lightly, then grabs it by the handle and shoves it into his jacket pocket. "I can't believe you're doing this for me."

"What are friends for?"

"And you're even coming along."

"I wouldn't miss it for anything."

Sometimes the best story is undecorated truth.

Talk about hair-trigger timing and split-second operations.
The light flashes green.

The crowd surges. As I shift my body to the right, Hugh moves up smoothly to fill the breach. His right arm bends at the elbow. Right hand slides inside his jacket.

Waves of heat rise from the blacktopped street. The blazing sun sends perspiration flowing behind my ears and down my neck. The crowd jostles me in every direction.

A huge delivery truck roars into life, starts across the intersection. Through a shimmering haze of exhaust I watch in fascination as Hugh pushes his hand forward toward LoPriore. Hugh's arm jerks rigid once, twice.

Vincent LoPriore walks into the street, across University, onward toward Fifth Avenue.

Taking advantage of Hugh's confusion I wrestle him off

the corner, start pulling him downtown on University Street. People stare but that no longer matters.

It takes Hugh less than a dozen steps to recover. He spins free of my grip, moves as if to pull the gun back out of his pocket, but fortunately thinks better of the notion. Instead he grabs my shirt in his huge fist. "What kind of a lousy gun did you get?" he hisses into my face. "The freakin thing jammed."

"No it didn't," I say, bland as butter. "It was set so it couldn't possibly be fired."

Hugh looks at me in the way I imagine Jesus regarded Judas at the Last Supper.

"And besides," I add, "the bullets are blanks. Just in case."

Now Hugh loses it big time. Right in the middle of the Lower Manhattan lunchtime sidewalk crush he whips out the gun. What he proposes to do with it I don't know, nor do I care to find out. I snatch the pistol out of his shaking hand, stuff it away into my own jacket pocket. Then I take him by the arm. "Cool it, Hugh. Keep walking; listen to me."

Hugh plants his feet. I sway from side to side, ready in case he decides to take a swing. "Hugh, don't be a schmuck—listen to what I have to say. If you don't like it you can still wipe up the street with me."

I start downtown again, walking slowly. Grudgingly, Hugh gets off the dime, swings in at my side. "This better be good," he growls.

Thank God Sarah's not with us. I can just hear her. "Good? From Thomas? *That* you can be sure of, Hugh."

As we work our way down the sidewalk I'm careful to keep eye contact with Hugh—but with no show of irritation, no hostility. Gaze level, face relaxed. The line between a good doctor and a successful con artist is as fine as they come.

Just a minute or two and Hugh's stare softens. *Then* I start talking, softly, gently. "That son of a bitch is still walking,

Hugh, but he's a dead man. Play it right, his face can be in the gutter for you to step on whenever you'd like. *That's* what he deserves for ripping off your collection and snuffing Maddy. Sure you could shoot him, but face it: you're an amateur, you're probably going to get caught. Then the story's all over the tube, on the front page of every newspaper. Your kids'd lose their mother *and* their father."

Hugh's eyes are weighted with bitterness.

We cross Twelfth Street. "Hugh, there's no reason to give this bum a quick, easy ticket out of the world. Make him suffer. *Watch* him suffer. Every day a new pleasure for you. And in the bargain you get back all your snuffboxes. The whole collection."

Magic words to a hardcore collector. Now Hugh's listening for sure. The last time I saw that light in his eyes was a few months earlier when we were walking through a midtown antiques mall and he spotted a gorgeous silver snuff box with a very early platform-type musical movement below the snuff compartment. "That's the ticket." I smile, punch his arm gently. "We'll scam the shit out of your Birdman friend. Leave him with no bird boxes, no snuff boxes, no money, no dignity, no nothing. Except misery."

"You've got an idea? An actual plan?"

"One that'll work like a charm."

Hugh stops, as if it were too much effort to simultaneously move his feet forward and keep up with my line of thinking. He shoots one cuff, then the other, then narrows his eyes and aims a finger at me. "Let me get this straight. You and I are going to strip LoPriore clean. And I get back every one of my snuffboxes."

I tap the side of my head. "I've got it all thought out. We'll need operating capital. Can you fill a suitcase with green paper in, say, three days?"

Hugh looks uncertain. "How big a suitcase?"

"One that holds two hundred-K. That ought to do it."

"Two hundred thousand dollars! Thomas, are you crazy?"

A small gray-haired woman going past turns and looks with mild curiosity. Hugh lowers his voice, leans to speak directly into my face. "How the hell am I supposed to put my hands on that kind of dough?"

"You've got three whole days." The smile I turn on Hugh could bring pigeons fluttering up off the hot asphalt to perch on my shoulder. "You can do it. Take it from your stock accounts. Do a little short-term creative accounting in your business. Don't worry, it'll all come back. We're going to snatch LoPriore's birds, remember? Then we're going to sell them. Everyone in the game is going to walk away with a pocket full of money. *After* repayment of all expenses."   H u g h doesn't look convinced. "Two hundred thousand dollars? And I'm supposed to just believe your plan's going to work. I should take it on faith you've thought of everything."

Emphatic nod. "How long have you known me, Hugh? When I say I've thought of everything, what're the chances I really have? Besides, you know what they call a con man who doesn't think of everything?"

Hugh shakes his head.

"A corpse."

Hugh laughs nervously, but he laughs. Then he swallows hard, takes a deep breath. "Okay. Something tells me I'm nuts, but all right. I'll get the money. And if the scam works, frankly, I wouldn't even care if I didn't get it back. Scamming the Birdman, huh?" He flashes a smile of unalloyed enthusiasm. "Be worth it at twice the price."

Hugh extends his hand. In spite of the August heat it feels like ice.

"I'll get right to work," I say. "Go home now, wait for

the hospital to contact you. They'll want you to identify the body ... can you manage that?"

Hugh swallows again, sucks at his lips. "Yeah. I'll just tell myself she had it coming."

"Whatever works. Call your kids, get past the funeral. Right after that we roll."

7

When Sarah sails in from work a little after five that afternoon, I'm in the shop hunched over a cylinder box comb. Sarah slings her bag onto the sofa, stands over me, purses her lips. "You're humming 'Onward Christian Soldiers,'" she says.

I put down the comb, slide my magnifying visor off my head, wipe my soggy face with a shirt sleeve. "You make it sound as if that's an odd thing for me to be doing."

"It *is* an odd thing for you to be doing."

I point toward the musical mechanism, brass shining in its polished wooden case. "Hymn box, plays six pieces of sacred music. OCS is one of them; it's running through my head."

Sarah's expression says maybe that's true, maybe not. But with the comb off the mechanism there's no way she can demand proof and she knows it. The Empress of the West withdraws, if reluctantly, then decides to test the vulnerability of a different flank. She sweeps the room with her eyes. "I don't see Hugh."

"That's because he's gone home. He was sober enough this morning to go identify Maddy and call his kids."

"And you've been here all day."

"Except for when I walked Hugh partway back and stopped for lunch."

Perfectly true, every word. No, I don't bother to mention Vincent LoPriore or a nonfunctioning gun in a paper bag casually dropped from the West Side Piers into the Hudson River, but why should I? No point. She wouldn't understand.

"What about that little cannon Hugh was waving around here last night? I don't like to think of him carrying it around. It frightens me."

"Frightens me, too. But we don't have to think about it, either of us. I hid it last night after we ate dinner."

"Thomas—"

I hold up my hand. "There won't be any accidents. The gun's in one place, bullets somewhere else. You know how I feel about guns."

How I feel is that every congressman who votes against gun control should serve time as a target in a shooting gallery. Which Sarah knows.

"What if he gets another one?" she asks.

"He won't."

"Why not? How can you be so sure?"

Moment of truth.

"I told him my plan and he really likes it—thinks it's a much better idea than shooting LoPriore." I wipe my face again, lean back in my chair.

"Your plan ..." Sarah's voice fades out. She walks the few steps to the sofa and plunks herself down, back poker-straight, face as severe as her voice. "All right, Thomas. Talk."

Give Sarah this: she listens. Sits quietly on the sofa, legs folded, bare feet tucked beneath her. Only when I stop does she let out a little sigh and say, "Thomas, why are you doing this? Do I really have to tell you you're a doctor? This is a matter for the police."

"What do you mean, police? Where's the evidence of a crime?"

"You could start with the fact someone stole Hugh's snuff boxes."

"But they also stole his proof of ownership. The insurance company'd have a field day. And if he decided to go through the courts, for every witness he could find—like me—to swear he once owned those snuff boxes, LoPriore'd find one to swear *he's* had them for years. In fact, I'll bet LoPriore's already got forged documents of sale, maybe even some nice faked glossy photos of buyer and seller smiling and shaking hands. The case would drag on for years, endless countersuits and appeals. And with Maddy dead—"

"Yes—'with Maddy dead.' If this LoPriore person did kill poor Maddy, don't you think *that* should be left to the police?"

"Same problem: No evidence of a crime. It was a hot day, she had a lot of wine to drink, she died. At least, that's the way it looks."

"But you took blood and stomach samples for toxicology studies."

"Anything that shows up, she could have taken herself. *I* don't think she did—but how am I going to prove it? Should I just let a murderer walk away? Hugh's my friend, Sarah. Can't you understand that?"

She nods an unwilling yes. "I've got to admit, loyalty to your friends has always been one of your more admirable traits. For that matter, so is your sense of justice, even if I do think it's a bit skewed by any reasonable criteria. Yes, all right. I can understand you'd like to help your friend and see a murderer punished."

"So?"

"So it just happens you have some character traits that are a little less admirable."

Well, no one's perfect. "Like what, for instance?"

"Like I can't help thinking there's something in this for you."

"Something like what?"

"I don't *know*. But if I have to make a guess, I'd say a music box."

"Do you see any music boxes up for grabs here?"

Her expression says no she doesn't, but she doesn't trust her eyes and she certainly doesn't trust me.

"Sarah, listen. My plan's going to work only if LoPriore is as greedy and unscrupulous as I think he is. If he's not I'm going to fall flat on my face. But if I'm right he's going to give back Hugh's collection and pay a stiff penalty. Don't you think that's reasonable?"

Sarah thinks as long as she can stretch it out. Finally she says, "Yes, Thomas, when you put it that way, of course it sounds reasonable." The words ring flat, as if she were pulling them out against their will. "But I know there's more than you're telling me. And something else." Her face turns even more serious. "Damn it, I worry about you. This Vincent LoPriore sounds very scary; you think he's already killed somebody. If you fall on your face I'm afraid you won't be able to get up."

I walk over, kiss her on the end of her nose. "Thanks," I say, "I appreciate that. But I'm not going to fall on my face. Trust me."

"Thomas, I hate it when you say that. I don't trust you and you know it."

I smile. I know it. I love it.

Once Sarah's gone to change clothes I call Art Forbes. He's got the results of the tests on Madeleine Curtis's blood and stomach contents. Yes, she was poisoned. I thank Art, tell him I'll take it from here. No written report, please. Slowly, I lower the receiver into its cradle.

Just as slowly I lower myself into a chair. Instant through-the-wringer exhaustion. This has been some kind of wild twenty-four hours ... and it's all just begun.

Time for a little emotional transfusion.

I push the start lever of the lovely inlaid Lecoultre aria

box on the table next to the phone and what comes forth but
"*Vieni! la mia vendetta*" from "Lucrezia Borgia." Can a music
box have a sense of humor? Golden chords wrap around my
chest, tighten, pull me up out of my slouch. A sudden transi-
tion to a minor key fires tone into my quaggy muscles. A
stark anticipation note jolts my spine. The succeeding silvery
arpeggio slings me onto my feet. I'm a flat tire, patched now,
air hose open full blast.

The music fades gently to silence. I walk quickly back to
my worktable, slip on my magnifying visor, set myself back to
the hymn box comb. "Onward, Christian sol-ol-diers, march-
ing as to-oo waw-err," I sing softly as I slide a honing stone oh
so carefully against the tips of the teeth.

All through Madeleine Curtis's funeral at the midtown
Marcuse Memorial Chapel Sarah keeps a tight grip on my
arm. A minister who first met Maddy in her coffin drones
away in a maple-syrup voice about wifely and motherly vir-
tues, now and again glancing heavenward as if he suffers from
some sort of holy tic. A sniffle arises from this side of the
chapel, a loud honk from over there.

Hugh Curtis listens, stone-faced, in the front row, an arm
draped around each of his children. Son Russell tries to main-
tain the dignified demeanor of an up-and-coming Washington corporate lawyer but it's too much for him; he keeps
taking off his frameless glasses to dab at his eyes. The girl,
Lucy, a pretty young woman with dark eyes and cascades of
brown hair, is frankly a mess. By the final amen she's satu-
rated a full box of tissues.

Afterward, the crowd gone outside, Sarah marches me up
to the three mourners. She expresses her sorrow to Hugh with
the lightest of kisses on the cheek, then moves aside to talk to
the children.

"You all right?" I half-whisper to Hugh.

"Yeah." A growl, then a light shrug. "I'm fine. Kids're having a rough time, though." He glances over his shoulder, sees Sarah earnestly chatting up Russell, Lucy snug under her wing. "I told them you said their mother died of a heart arrhythmia from too much sun on top of a little too much wine. An accident."

"Best story you could have told them. Also the best cover for our game."

Hugh scratches absently at the side of his nose. Russell walks over, hand extended. The boy's grip is firm but his hand is like a trout just pulled from the stream. "I want to thank you, Dr. Purdue. For trying to help my mother."

"Sorry I couldn't do more than try, Russell."

"And I also appreciate everything you're doing for my father."

"Russell means how kind you were breaking me the news," Hugh says quickly. "And all the time you've spent talking to me ... listening to me. It's helped more than you know."

"I'm available any time." I say. "How long are you and your sister going to be here, Russell?"

"The end of the week—I'm going back to D. C. Friday. Lucy's got a Saturday evening flight back to Boston."

"Life goes on." I look back to Hugh. "Tell you what. I'm going to be pretty busy this week anyway... got a lot of things to take care of. How about I call you Sunday morning?"

Hugh nods. "Fine."

8

Next morning smack on ten o'clock Schwartz knocks, then cruises into the workshop. He rubbernecks the hymn box from over my shoulder. "Looks like you're just about done."

"Pretty close." I push the play lever. As we listen to "The Sicilian Mariner's Hymn," Schwartz wrinkles his nose. "Nice music—but it sounds like it's all full of, like tiny little crickets. You hear?"

I pick up a rectangular piece of glass in one hand, a small can of oil in the other. "That's dry cylinder pins, Broadway. You've got to oil them so they slip nice and quietly off the tooth tips. Watch."

When the music stops I smear a drop of oil over one side of the glass, then set the mechanism running again. As the cylinder rotates I pass the oiled glass lightly over the moving pins. Schwartz's eyes light up. "Hey, shazam. All those little noises are gone."

"Just have to oil the pins."

I put down the glass, point toward the kitchen. "Let's go inside, talk a little."

"Uh-*huh*." Savvy Schwartz, always right there with the goods. "I said something was up, didn't I?"

In the kitchen I put prune Danishes on two plates, pour a

couple of cups of coffee, motion Schwartz to a chair. "I've got an idea I think can make us a bundle," I say. "Interested?"

Schwartz gnaws his Danish, nods slowly. "Seein' it's you, Doc, yeah. Sure I'm interested. But if it was anybody else, I'd probably be askin' some things about that bundle. Like there's big bundles and little bundles; there's bundles that're easy to carry and ones that keep slippin' outa your hands. There's—"

"How about a bundle of green paper? Big enough to add up to about a half-million tax-free dollars. And you won't have to carry it at all: it'll be in a bank account for you."

Schwartz stops eating. He pushes his fedora back on his forehead, takes a moment to stare at me. "Like I said, Doc: seein' it's you, I'm sure everything about the deal is jake. But if it was anybody else, I'd sure be askin' what I gotta do to walk away with this five hundred-K in a bankbook. And"—he works his tongue around inside his lips—"whether it could be maybe, well ... just a little bit dangerous?"

"Fair enough. If I were somebody else I'd say if you do your part and I do mine and everybody else does theirs, it should work. Then I'd tell you the plan."

By the time I finish we're halfway through our second coffees and Danishes. Schwartz shakes his head. "Doc, I don't know where you come up with these ideas from."

"Neither do I, Broadway. But what do you think of it?"

"Mmm." Schwartz hums mild conditional approval. "I got a question."

"Shoot."

"This guy you want to do the number on. He wouldn't happen to be the character you had me call up a few days ago? Vincent LoPriore?"

"None other, Broadway. Why?"

Schwartz looks like a parachuter about to take his maiden jump. "He's a funny guy, Doc, and I don't mean funny-haha.

Just hearin' his voice over the phone gave me the creeps. What the hell were you doin' there, a dry run?"

"Call it more like a warmup. And it worked just fine."

"Whew!" Again, Schwartz shakes his head. "Me, I wouldn't go anywhere near Vincent LoPriore with a gun. Especially if the gun was jammed and loaded with blanks."

"He never saw the gun, Broadway; he was never supposed to and he never will. It's gone now, on the bottom of the Hudson. I'm talking about a clip game, not an armed robbery."

Schwartz's doubts are clearly short of being settled. "That's fine and dandy, Doc—but who's gonna tell LoPriore *he* can't use heat? Case you don't know, this ain't no cream puff you're going after. Word is what LoPriore Importers imports is different kinds of white powders and such that you sniff up your nose or shoot in your arm. A guy like that is not a person to go and cross without thinkin' about it."

"I've thought about it, Broadway," I say quietly.

Schwartz tries to smile. "Well then, okay. You're in, I'm in. Long as you know the facts." His face goes pensive. "That reminds me— Wait a minute."

I wait.

"One other thing about LoPriore. Weird stuff. Only person he was ever close to was his mother, and she, uh, died a few years ago—"

"She 'uh, died.' Broadway, what exactly are you trying to tell me?"

"Just that she didn't die of natural causes. She got shot. Drive-by—"

"A drive-by shooting? On Fifth Avenue in New York?"

"Gimme a minute, hey, Doc? She lived in Jersey, Weehawken. Got shot right outside her house on her way back from supper one night with her son."

"Any particular son?"

"Only one she's got. Sorry, had. One story is they were aiming for LoPriore but nailed his mother by accident. The other word is they did the mother on purpose, right in front of LoPriore. Whatever, LoPriore wore black for a year, black suits, coats, turtlenecks, shoes, socks. Winters, he still wears black, but now he goes to white on Memorial Day, just like Mamma did, then back to black after Labor Day. But whether it's black or white, his shirt's got to have a pocket on the left-hand side so he can always keep a picture of his mother in the pocket, right over his heart. You know what was his mother's name, by the way?"

"Mrs. LoPriore?"

"You're a comedian, Doc. Her name was Birdie—Birdie LoPriore. How do you like that?"

"Birdie's son The Birdman, huh? Guess our boy's got a few emotional wrinkles. But how the hell do you know all this, Broadway?"

Shrug. "Grapevine, Doc. No big deal."

No big deal. Depending upon your particular political mindset, you can either tip the C.I.A. to the antiques informational grapevine or hope and pray they never hear of it.

"Interesting—that bit about the picture in the pocket. Gives me an idea; listen."

Schwartz listens, then looks at me reproachfully. "Jeez, Doc. How does stuff like this come out of a doctor's head?"

"Figure it didn't. It's August; I'm on vacation. Good old Thomas Purdue, R. F. Regular Fella."

Schwartz eyes me with as much suspicion as he thinks he can get away with. "You're on vacation, okay. So why're you wearin' your white hospital coat, which I *never* see you do outside of your office? And why's your doctor's bag sittin' out here on the table?"

"Because I'm going to play doctor—and you're in the game. You've got that ID for me?"

Schwartz extracts a small plastic-laminated card from his pocket, puts it into my hand. We look at each other. We both smile.

"I think I'm startin' to get the picture," Schwartz says. "Hey, Doc, knock knock."

Quicker and less painful to go along. "Okay, I'll bite. Who's there?"

"Earl."

"Earl Who?"

"Earl de Pinza—"

"Broadway ..."

"—or your music box'll squeak."

I roll my eyes, then slip the ID into my wallet and get up from the table. Schwartz, yukking it up for all he's worth, follows me.

The Carroll Parkside is a tall apartment building dating to the 1920s, with a façade of marble and gray stone. By tilting my head I can count twenty-six rows of windows below a wide marble ledge. Probably a rooftop garden behind the ledge— nice touch. Nice place. When Carroll Parksiders want to go for a casual, inexpensive dinner I suspect it's the Russian Tea Room, and I don't imagine many Carroll Parksider ears have ever heard the words, "Attention, K-Mart Shoppers." Nothing jazzy at the Old CP, just lodgings for people with money but no need—or desire—to flash it to the world at large. A perfect place for a Vincent LoPriore.

The skinny doorman wears a maroon wool uniform that must be murder on a day like this. Enough gold braid on his shoulders and around the border of his cap for him to pass as a three-star Army general. Above his left breast pocket is a nickeled name tag: Marvin. As Schwartz and I walk up to him, he shows us a mouthful of nicotined teeth and says, "Gentlemen."

I tell him we've come to take some samples; we'll check with the Lobby Attendant.

"Ah, Sir, the concierge. Yes. Inside the lobby, just this side of the elevator." He practically falls over himself swinging the door open.

The lobby is small but made to look larger by mirrored walls edged by graceful art-nouveau swoops of frosting. A huge cut-glass chandelier with sphinx-heads spaced equally around its frame hangs from the center of the high ceiling. Halfway back on the north wall are two small chairs on either side of a floor lamp. Curious: a narrow passageway runs between the elevators and the far wall.

The concierge is a black man, about sixty, with an impressive white woolly beard and suspicious eyes. He sits imperiously at a small wooden desk just this side of the elevators, doesn't take his eyes off Schwartz and me for an instant. "Yes, Doctor?" he says, as we come up to his station.

Silently begging Schwartz not to ask whether he's chopped liver, I make a small ceremony of showing my recently-acquired laminated card. "I'm Dr. Theodore Perkins," I intone as if I were The Lord announcing my own second coming. "New York City Board of Health. This is Mr. Schultz, one of our chemists. We're here to take samples. Air, carpet scrapings. The usual."

"Samples ... carpet scrapings ..?" The poor concierge looks like a child in need of emergency adenoidal surgery. He glances at Schwartz, then looks back at me.

"Routine health monitoring," I say. "Buildings chosen at random: commercial shops, restaurants, at times a major apartment building. Now, a place like this"—grand, sweeping gesture of the arm—"won't have any trouble at all. Unless, that is, they don't comply voluntarily and we have to obtain a court order to do our job, Mr ..?"

"Ross," the concierge mumbles into the question. "Charles Ross."

"Right. Mr. Ross. Thank you for your help. We'll just take the elevator up, check out a couple of hallways, won't disturb a soul. Then we'll be gone and I'm sure you'll never hear from us again."

Charles Ross's face says few things would please him more.

Everyone's got perks; you need to know what yours are, and use them when you can. Pulling rank as a doctor is not something I like to do but it was the best way I could think of to check access routes and security in the Carroll Parkside. I stride into the nearer of the two elevators, Schwartz in my wake. The door closes behind us.

Schwartz pushes the button for the third floor. "'V. LoPriore, Three-oh-One,'" he says. "Buzzers were on the wall there behind Ross's desk."

A moment later the elevator lets us out on the third floor. Apartment 304 comes up first, to the left. We walk slowly down the corridor, past 303 to 302 to 301 at the far end. The eastern wall to our right is just that, a bare wall; no back-alley lodgings here. A view of Central Park for each occupant. At the Carroll Parkside, every man a king.

More important, I don't see video cameras anywhere, not in the hall, not downstairs in the lobby. But something's bothering me. The elevators. "Funny," I mumble. "Three doors here, two in the lobby. And the elevator we got off here is in the middle, but downstairs it was on the left."

"Easy, Doc." Schwartz grins. "One on the left here's the service elevator. It opens to the rear on the first floor, behind the lobby. From there you go out into the alley next to the hotel. Front's plastered over so the lobby should look nice. Guys like me, don't have a white coat to wear, we need to know stuff like that."

"What a team." I clap Schwartz on the shoulder, then point down the narrow passageway between the elevators and the eastern wall. "That door at the end is an emergency exit?"

Schwartz nods. "Yep. Bet it leads down to the service entrance."

"Perfect!" I give him a big hug. "Let's go take a peek."

One step toward the emergency exit, I hear a door open, then shut behind us. "Hey!" calls a rough voice.

We keep walking. No Lot's wife bit here. But no dice. Another "Hey! You guys! You lookin' for someone?"

I turn around and look into the accusing eyes of Vincent LoPriore. He's dressed as he was four days earlier, all in white, but his face is black with suspicion. Mouth a crooked gash, great big wolfy teeth, hawk-beak nose. Black hair slicked with musky-smelling oil. Up this close he looks a whole lot more threatening than he did from behind, in a pack of Broadway foot traffic.

"You guys lookin' for someone?" LoPriore says again. The set of his head states clearly the question is not going to be put a third time.

"Health Department," I say, very lightly. "Just taking some routine samples.

I start to turn away but LoPriore reaches out and grabs my arm, not gently. I wheel around to glare at him but if he's the least bit intimidated he doesn't show it. "Routine samples, huh?" he snarls. "What kinda routine samples? You want to know the truth, I think I smell a little bullshit on your breath. How about showin' me an ID."

Sure I'll show him an ID. I take the card out of my wallet, extend it toward LoPriore. He makes a grab; I pull it back.

"Look all you want," I say, chiseling a sharp edge onto each word. "No touching."

A sneer spreads across LoPriore's face as he squints to study the card. "Dr. Theodore Perkins, huh?"

"That's right."

"Who's the little kike, Doc? Your sidekick there."

Time to end this. I shove the card roughly back into my pocket, stick my nose in the air, and say, "I think we're through talking, sir."

"Maybe *you* do," says LoPriore. "But maybe *I* don't. "How about you show me a Visa card ... Dr. Perkins." He extends his hand.

"I'm not showing you anything else," I snap. Dr. Perkins, high on his white horse. "We're going to take our samples now, and leave. If you have a problem with that, call the manager."

"Hoo-*hoo*." A cruel smile oozes over LoPriore's face. I've seen that look before. Bad Bobby Maxwell, the seventh-grade bully at Cornwell Junior High, at the point of telling me what his father or brother did with my mother or sister. What came after that, I remember too well.

I watch LoPriore's hands but only his mouth moves. "Somebody's feelings gettin' hurt? Okay, go ahead, take your samples. I'll stand here and watch. Maybe I can learn something useful."

Nothing for it but to go ahead. I open my doctor's bag, take out a roll of tape, a metal spatula, a Petri dish full of agar gel. Then I get down on my knees. Schwartz follows my lead. LoPriore, radiant as Lucifer in his white outfit, bends from the waist to study us.

He watches intently as I sniff and paw at the carpet runner, scrape the carpet with the spatula, inoculate the culture medium in the Petri dish. "That should do it," I say as I hand the dish to Schwartz. "Label it Third Floor, Carpet—"

LoPriore interrupts my instructions by bringing his white shoe down with a stamp onto Schwartz's hand. Broadway screams, drops the Petri dish, collapses to the floor. He writhes in pain, waves his injured hand in the air.

I spring to my feet swinging.

"Hey, hey, hey." LoPriore is pointing a handgun at my chest, wiggling it ever so slightly as if the fanning motion might cool off any violent thoughts in my head. "Sorry, Doc— just a little accident. What you were doin' was so interesting I was tryin' to move so I could see it better."

The elevator door opens with a clang. LoPriore flashes me a wordless warning, then slips the gun back inside his jacket. A Pekingese dog at the end of a leash trots off the elevator with a tiny, wizened snow-topped woman in tow. As the Lilliputian pair pass us, the woman eyes Schwartz with gentle curiosity. "Good morning, Mr. LoPriore," she says in a voice like a cracked reed. "I hope you're having a nice day."

"Thanks. I always have a nice day, Mrs. Carver." LoPriore smiles ever so slightly in my direction. "Hope you're having the same."

Mrs. Carver and her dog disappear into Apartment 303. LoPriore bends over Schwartz, who by now has recovered sufficiently to give him a white-faced evil eye. "You're okay, ain't you?" LoPriore croons. "Sure." He looks back at me. "Takes more'n a little step on a hand to put away a mockie; they're worse'n rats to get rid of. Six million in gas chambers and still you see 'em every place you look. But, hey, Doc, I want to tell you something. I think this ain't a very safe business you're in—all those deadly germs you got to mess with. Maybe you and your buddy ought to get into a less dangerous line of work ... before one of you happens to get seriously sick."

With that he turns sharply away. Schwartz and I watch

him march down the corridor and disappear into Apartment 301.

As the door clicks shut Schwartz lets out a whispered, "Jesus." He looks with concern at his hand.

"Everything move?" I ask.

Schwartz wiggles first fingers, then wrist. "Yeah. Some of them don't feel the greatest. But they all move."

I bend down, palpate his hand carefully. "I'll bet it hurts— but I don't think anything's broken."

By now most of Schwartz's color is back. He grins, if weakly, then points at the floor. "Good thing they got expensive carpet, nice and thick." He climbs to his feet.

We move, more quickly this time, toward the emergency exit. "Let's go get you some ice," I say.

Schwartz shakes his head no. "Better we should get finished here; we sure as hell don't want to come back any time soon. Anyway, I been hurt worse on my job—happens all the time. Like last week over on the west side, I dropped a full bookcase on my foot. Sweet guy, though, ain't he?"

"I'd say he's living up to his press notices."

We go through the emergency exit door, start walking downstairs. The wide concrete steps are limited by a removable iron railing. I look all around, as if for discoloration and growth of mold spores, but in fact I'm checking for another species of bug. I don't spot it.

We go past the second-floor emergency door, down to the service entry. Schwartz was right on. There's the service elevator door, opening from the rear of the elevator into a small vestibule. Directly opposite, the outside door can be opened by a push-rail, no doubt for fire safety considerations. Nice that the Carroll Parkside was built before security paranoia in New York became a diagnosis of psychological normality.

Schwartz nudges me. "We're golden, Doc," he whispers. "No cameras anywhere, no recording devices."

"Looks that way. And if we do our job right they'll never know they need any."

As I open the service door Schwartz puts his thumb and forefinger to his nose. "Pee-*yew*," he groans, and points at the garbage cans to the street side of the door. "Not exactly Nosegay City here, Doc."

"More like Fat City, I'd say. Those cans are a wall between the door and Fifth Av."

I lead Schwartz out into the alley where we stand and watch the door slowly swing closed. It stops short of lock engagement. I give it a little push, then peer at the lock. "It's a Sarti. Remember that."

Schwartz snickers. "Yes, Doctor. Thank you, Doctor."

"All right, enough. We know they've got a doorman, a lobby attendant ... excuse me, a concierge, and no video cameras or sound recorders anywhere. The service door has a Sarti lock, needs a key from outside. Let's look back in the alley."

Walking along the alley toward the rear of the Carroll Parkside is like going down the entryway to Carlsbad Caverns. Behind the building, midway between Fifth and Madison, the corridor bifurcates into a right-left path, running uptown to 63rd and downtown to 62nd. Unlike the Carroll Parkside, the buildings facing onto Madison have apartment windows in their rear walls.

"Okay, Broadway," I say. "Now to get us a base headquarters fit for a queen. Hail, Regina!"

Schwartz gives me an odd look, then follows me up the alley back to Park Avenue.

9

On Madison, a block over from Central Park, the neighborhood is still fine but considerably less posh. People stream along the sidewalks, going into and out of the little specialty shops and ethnic restaurants which occupy ground level in most of the buildings. Above the commercial establishments, space is about evenly split between offices and apartments.

At the corner of 62nd, Schwartz and I turn uptown. We walk past one apartment building, then a second, then come to the Church of Our Lady of Perpetual Life sitting primly on tree-speckled grounds behind a black, wrought-iron fence. Just past the church grounds I see what I'm looking for. Black sign with gold-painted letters spelling REGINA; in smaller print underneath, A LITTLE HOTEL.

I grab Schwartz's arm, point at the sign. "Good thing Sarah watches so much TV news. Couple of weeks ago there was a feature about how LoPriore's trying to muscle out the owner so he can build an addition for the church next door. Nice that the hotel backs on the alley, isn't it? Almost directly behind the Carroll Parkside."

Schwartz glances at his sore hand, then flashes teeth in a nasty grin. "What if they got no rooms, though?"

"Then we're screwed. But I'm betting they will ... at least by the time I'm done talking."

I pace Schwartz up the five worn gray stone steps, into the lobby. Clean, if a bit to the Spartan. Speckled marble floor with red carpet running from doorway to registration desk at the back of the room. Leather-covered chairs and sofas straight from the '30s arranged around floor lamps to make three scattered seating groups. One is occupied by four young Orientals with maps spread in front of them, jabbering away with lots of arm and hand language. A mid-ceiling speaker is treating us to a fine jazz piano rendition of "I've Got You Under My Skin."

From behind the counter a round little man with café-au-lait skin watches us approach him. Mid-fifties, I'd say, with lustrous black hair going gray over temples and ears. His bright blue shirt, lavishly decorated with orange flowers, hangs loose over the top of near-phosphorescent green polyester trousers. More gaudy than the clothing, though, is a mass of purple and yellow bruises around his bloodshot left eye and down his cheek.

"Help you gen'lmen?" he asks.

This is one jittery little man, and with good reason. Schwartz and I need to get off on the right foot. I smile, point to the speaker. "Art Tatum, right?"

The little man's face relaxes into bright cheer. What hitman would greet him this way? "Hey—you like good jazz pianos," he says, as if this point confirms me as a good person.

"Sure do." I point at his injured face. "I saw the TV show, Mr. Espinoza. Somebody should sock it to that bastard LoPriore. Make him pay, with a ton of interest."

Espinoza's chummy expression zips back to highly suspicious. He glances toward the young Orientals who are gathering up their maps and heading toward the door, groundwork apparently laid for a day of sightseeing in the Big Apple.

"I don' have nothin' to say to no more reporters," Espinoza says. "Or lawyers. I t'ink maybe you oughta go. Nothin' personal, jus' ... you know."

"Take it easy," says my mouth; trust me, I'm a doctor, says my smile. "I'm on your side—and so is my friend here." I take Schwartz's left arm at the elbow, lay his hand and forearm gently on the registration desk. "Little swollen, see. Bruised. It came off second-best to LoPriore's shoe. Not as bad as your face, but still."

Espinoza's chocolate eyes widen. He rests a hand lightly on Schwartz's injured fingers, feels the pain, looks up into my friend's face. "He step on you' han'? Why?"

Dismissive chuckle from Schwartz. "He doesn't like Jews."

Confusion and anger push back the sympathy in Espinoza's eyes. "Just 'cause you Jewish he step on you? I t'ink he no like *any*body. Me, he call crummy little spic. When I no take what he tell me is his final offer, he say, 'You no want to be reasonable, fine. But one way or another you gonna be outa here. Vincent LoPriore don't take a no from some crummy little spic.'" Espinoza jabs a finger toward his face. "Then his men do this to me."

"We want to do something to *him*," I say and reach across the counter. "My name's Thomas Purdue; this is my friend, Broadway Schwartz."

The little man's smile makes a partial comeback. His handshake is tentative. "Espinoza," he says. "But people call me Nozey."

Schwartz laughs. For an instant I'm concerned, but Espinoza's smile broadens. "Yeah, is funny. When I firs' come to New York and meet the girl she become my wife, she no could say my firs' name, Guillermo. Kep' comin' out Goo-ah-mo. So she start callin' me Nozey. Then ever'body does."

Schwartz looks around. "Your wife work here, too?"

Nozey's eyes are suddenly lakes of melancholy. He shakes his head. "My wife, she die four years ago. She work here with me twenty-two years—that's how long we were marri'. Our two kids, they work here too, 'til they grow up and move. One in Jersey, th'other in California."

Schwartz coughs and nods sympathetically. "Sorry."

"Is okay. She had cancers. Nothing nobody could do. Now I work here myself; is my home. That sumbitch LoPriore—he want me to go away, jus' leave my home. Twenty-six years, my whole fam'ly ..." Espinoza's voice trails off.

"You won't have to leave," I say. "Not if you go in with us. You can get rid of Vincent LoPriore forever ... *and* make yourself a little money while you're at it. A little of *his* money."

Espinoza looks up, rubs his chin. He studies my face, then stares at Schwartz. Finally he says, "Who *are* you guys, anyway?"

"Purdue and Schwartz," I say. "Two guys who've had it with LoPriore and want to clean his clock just as much as you do. The shoe's about to go on the other foot. Want to do some kicking?"

Poor Espinoza wriggles in temptation's fond embrace. "How do I know you're not more of LoPriore's guys? Doin' some new trick, tryin' to get me out of here?"

"I guess you don't," I say. "But from what I heard on TV and the way your face looks, you might as well take a chance with us. How much worse can you do? If we win you get to keep your little hotel—and just for fun step on LoPriore's face in the gutter."

Espinoza picks up a toothpick from the counter, jabs absently at a back tooth. He sighs long and slow, then turns a rueful smile on me. "I guess I not doin' all that good myself, huh? An' how much longer I wanna go on livin' like this? Yeah, sure. I take the chance. What I gotta do?"

"Rent me a room on the second floor, in the rear. Or better, if you've got it, a suite."

"You want a suite ..." Espinoza picks up his ledger. "From when 'til when?"

"Starting tomorrow, for not more than a week."

Espinoza studies the ledger, taps the eraser end of a pencil on the counter. Then he draws a line through a row of boxes. "Okay, Mr. Purdue, you got it. Second story rear suite. Lessee ..."

"Book the room under ... hmm. De Pinza," I say.

"De Pinza?" Schwartz explodes. "Hey, Doc, what—"

"*Evelyn* de Pinza. What's the rent?"

Espinoza puts down his pencil, regards me as if I've made an indecent proposition. "Hey, wait—you' gonna get rid of LoPriore an' I'm supposed to charge you rent?"

"Sure. Sounds like your business hasn't been too good lately; we can't have you go bust before the big payoff. Come on. What's the rent for a week?"

"Well, is a back suite." Espinoza gnaws on his toothpick. "They go for one-thirty-five a night, nine hundred a week."

I count nine hundreds out of my wallet onto the desk top. "There you go, rent. If it makes you feel better, call it an advance. By the time Mrs. de Pinza checks out you'll have roughly a half million to go with it, courtesy of Mr. Vincent LoPriore."

Espinoza's toothpick falls to the ground. "*How* much you say?"

Schwartz lunges forward as if to keep the round little man from following the toothpick.

"Five hundred thousand dollars, Nozey, and don't forget, no taxes. There'll be a little work involved, but nothing I think you won't enjoy."

"Haysoo-Christo, *es demasiado*," Espinoza mutters tonelessly, shocked back into his native tongue. "*No puedo comprender.*"

I reach across the counter, pat his shoulder. "Be surprised

how fast you'll get used to it. Now let's have a look at that suite."

It's the 'fifties: living room with blond sofa, tables and chairs; kitchen all chrome and red vinyl; two rooms in the back, each with blond bedframe and dresser, a small bathroom between them. Very clean, no torn fabric anywhere. In the living room three right-angle fissures in the far wall adjacent to the kitchen. Overflow sleeping facilities. *I woke up one morning standing on my head, stuck in the wall in a Murphy bed.*

Schwartz and Espinoza follow me through the living room into the larger bedroom, then watch as I unlock the back window and throw it open. Leaning on the sill, I crane my neck to look first right, then left. When I draw back inside I'm smiling all over my face. "Take a look, Broadway."

Schwartz replaces me at the sill. "Out onto the fire escape landing, down the ladder, easy jump to the ground," I say. "Down the alley, around the corner, maybe ten yards to the Carroll Parkside service door—which you can't see from Fifth Avenue because of the garbage cans. We couldn't ask for better."

"I sure hope you guys know what you're doing." Espinoza looks as skeptical as he sounds.

"Trust me," say my smile and my mouth. "I'm a doctor."

Espinoza rolls his eyes. The tiniest grin cracks the left corner of his mouth, giving him the appearance of a mischievous little animal. "*Vay iz mir,*" he says softly.

Schwartz and I look at each other, then at Espinoza. Everyone starts laughing. Espinoza shrugs. "I live almos' thirty years in New York now. I speak the language pretty good, no?"

Schwartz is beside himself. "*Very* good," he finally manages to get out. "Okay, I'm sold. What now, Doc?"

"Now, we get the rest of the team aboard. Costumes and

makeup are going to be critical; we need the best in the business."

"Who you thinkin' of, Doc?"

"Evelyn de Pinza, of course."

Schwartz's puzzled look cracks me up. "Call her Edna Reynolds if you want."

Schwartz's face goes crafty, then dissolves into pure amusement. "Ho-ho, Doc—Edna Reynolds. You think she'll do it?"

"I might have to be a little persuasive but I think so."

"Boy, Doc, I don't know." Schwartz glances at his swollen left hand. "Edna the Doll Lady. If that LoPriore wasn't such a son of a bitch, I think I'd be startin' to feel sorry for him right now." Then something seems to occur to Schwartz. "But what's with the de Pinza bit?"

"Most of us can't use our own faces, Broadway; that's why we need Edna. And none of us better use our own names. So it's Evelyn and her son Earl de Pinza—you remember him Knock knock?"

Poor Espinoza looks from Schwartz to me and back again. "Get used to it," I say. "You ain't seen nothing yet."

Schwartz's face tells me he's put it together. "Earl and Evelyn, huh? And I bet I know who's Earl."

"Bet you do."

10

Edna Reynolds lives on the fourth floor of a comfortable old apartment building with thick plaster walls on Lexington between 69th and 70th. She's been my friend for two decades, my patient for the past three years. As I tell her my story she sits at her workbench, fixing the broken arm of a hundred-year-old French drummer-automaton. From the back of the table her next case, a mechanical white rabbit inside a green silk cabbage, seems to be sizing up her surgical skills. He's got nothing to worry about.

All through my spiel Edna doesn't say a word, but when I stop talking she rolls her chair away from the workbench, and takes a minute to size me up. Then she says evenly, "You live a step over the line, Thomas; it's part of your charm. But this? I think you've fucking flipped out."

Schwartz coughs.

"I thought you'd like my idea, Edna," I say.

"Christ Almighty, Thomas! I haven't heard anything like it since I went to see *The Sting*. Are you going to hire Paul Newman to play opposite me?"

"Sorry, can't do. I know you'd like that but unfortunately Paul doesn't know shit from Shinola about music machines. You'll have to settle for me as leading man."

"Huh!" Wry smile. "Life's just one goddamn compromise

after another." Edna's face goes serious. "Thomas, you're not just pulling my chain, are you? This is for real?"

"Believe it, my dear. Hugh Curtis has been your friend as long as he's been mine, and he's gotten as dirty a deal as you'll ever see. If we don't help him now—"

"He's fucked. I'm not stupid, Thomas."

Schwartz covers his mouth, coughs again.

Edna turns sharply in his direction. "What's the matter, Broadway. Got a cold?"

"Allergy attack." Schwartz stands up. "Can I have a glass of water? To take a pill?"

Edna points toward the kitchen. "Help yourself. You know where everything is."

Schwartz is through the doorway in nothing flat. Edna's gray eyes twinkle.

"You love to embarrass him, don't you?" I say.

Edna chuckles. "Can't help myself. He's a riot—hears an old woman say a naughty word and he gets like a beet. Oh, honestly, Thomas, the dumb things people do. Maddy Curtis. I'd never have imagined ... It's a dirty trick, Thomas."

At first I think she's referring to what LoPriore did to the Curtises but then she says, "You're going to ruin a man's life. That's not something to do lightly."

"No argument, Edna. But if anyone deserves a one-way trip to the gutter, it's Vincent LoPriore—"

The expression that comes over Edna's face puts whatever else I was going to say on hold. Schwartz, on his way back from the kitchen, actually stops, then backs away from Edna. "Vincent LoPriore ... *he's* the mark, Thomas? Oh my. That's not someone you want to mess around with casually."

"People keep telling me that. But I don't intend to be casual."

Schwartz holds his injured hand out for Edna to see. "We

were checkin' out his building, before we came here. Guess he
didn't care for the idea; he stomped my hand."

"So he's seen you both," Edna says. "Won't that be a
problem?"

"Not if you do *your* job," I say. "Make me up so he won't
recognize me. Schwartz, he shouldn't ever have to see again."

"Hm." Edna looks away. She seems to be considering a
large Turkish gymnast-automaton on a table against the far
wall.

"Scared?" I ask her.

"A little." Edna smiles tightly. "But only a little. If you're
not scared, Thomas, why should I be? I'm seventy years old;
I've got high blood pressure, had a stroke. You're how old,
forty-five? You've got a lot more to lose than I do. Sure, let's
take out this Birdman bastard. For what he did to Carolyn
Marcus alone, he deserves it."

A crooked smile spreads over her face. "Maybe you could
at least get Marvin Hamlisch to do the music."

Frank the Crank is just as easy. When Schwartz and I get
together with him it's like a Marx Brothers movie: the Return
of Shyster, Flywheel, and Meshuggener. According to Sarah,
putting us in a room together should be considered an act of
criminal irresponsibility.

We sit around Frank's desk behind the counter at Wind
Me Up. The unshaded bulb hanging from the ceiling gleams
off Frank's pate, accentuating the hollows in his cheeks. When
I deliver my punch line, Frank chortles, "Ho-ho-ho. Vincent
LoPriore, huh? You don't do things by halfways, do you, Doc?
Mess up and you're food for the fishies. If they can chew
through cement, that is."

"Do I hear you saying you don't want to play, Frank?"

"Not play? Me?" With his scooped-out cheeks, closely

trimmed salt-and-pepper beard, narrow face, and gleaming little brown eyes, Frank looks like an amused, highly intelligent fox. "No, that's not what I'm sayin'. Number one, I figure if you're willing to do it I'd be a damn fool not to come aboard. Number two, for a sack of potatoes as big as you're talking about I'll listen to almost anything. And Number three, I figure it's come-around time for what Mr. Lo-P did to Paul Burleigh. Worst kind of human being, Vincent LoPriore. Treats people like dirt, but let St. Vinnie's Hospital need a new wing and bango—there's a couple million up front for the Birdie LoPriore Pavilion."

Schwartz's chuckle is clabbered. "Maybe he thinks the hospital was named after him."

Frank sniggers. "Birdie and her Little Birdman. You could make a lot outa that."

"I already have, Frank," I say. But before I can go on about the picture LoPriore always carries next to his heart, an old, old song pops into my mind. I start to sing. "*I know a very wicked man, I knew him when a lad. I never met his equal telling lies.*"

Cackles from Frank and Schwartz.

"*And though he takes delight in doing everything that's bad, he thinks he'll go to heaven when he dies.*"

Raucous laughter.

"*When but a child he robbed his dear old grandma in her sleep, he stole two golden teeth out of her jaws.*" I pause, just long enough for effect. "He kills, he steals collections, he's a menace to us all ..."

Schwartz flings an arm around Frank's neck; Frank does the same to me, and they join in, loud, off-key, *con mucho brio.*

"*But the neighbors think that he's all right becau-au-ause..*

He goes *to* church *on* Sun-*day.*

He passes round the contribution box.

But meet him in the office on a Monday, he's as crooked and as cunning as a fox.
On Tuesday, Wednesday, Thursday, Friday, Saturday
He's robbing everybody that he can.
But he goes to church on Sunday, so they say that he's an honest man."

"Count me in, Doc," Frank crows through the backslapping and laughter. "Hell and high water. Hot and cold. Rain and sleet. Feast and famine. Horn and Hardart. I'm with you all the way."

Look out, LoPriore. Flywheel, Shyster, and Meshuggener are rolling.

Sammy Shapiro stands in the living room of his swish Second Avenue pad, making no attempt to conceal his interest as I spin my yarn. With his shiny black hair, gleaming red cheeks, wide lapels, and trademark black-and-white wing-tipped patent leather shoesies, Sammy looks like a refugee from a Roaring Twenties movie set. NYMBCA members joke about never buying a used car from him, but motor-impaired Chevvies and transmission-challenged Toyotas are not Sammy's line. He specializes in top-quality music machines, Hupfeld Phonoliszt-Violinas and Nicole Freres grand format overture music boxes, always cash on the barrelhead and no receipt. Sammy is slick, sharp, utterly unencumbered by anything resembling a conscience—New York mechanical music's wonder boy, the child of P. T. Barnum by Ma Barker. His skill at buying low and selling high is the stuff of legend.

At the mention of Hugh Curtis's name, sixty watts blaze in each of Sammy's eyes and he lets out a low whistle. "So *that's* it, huh? Hot damn! I'd'a never figured."

"Figured what, Sammy?"

"That Maddy Curtis ..." Sammy covers his mouth with

his hand, lets out a snicker of sudden enlightenment. "Hey, I knew it had to be, well ... *some*thing. But I never figured Maddy."

"That's twice, Sammy. You want to tell me just what you figure had to be 'well ... something'?"

"Sure thing, my man." Hands come together with a clap. "Week and a half ago I found the ultimate snuffbox, twenty-four carats pure. With enamel work like you never saw and a cylinder by Henry Capt that played like to make the angels come in their robes. Right away I say to myself, this has Hugh Curtis written all over it."

"With a nice five-figure number written right underneath."

"Well, hey, my man!" Sly Sammy Shapiro turns the bent eye on me. "I didn't exactly pull it out of a wire trash basket on Eighth Av. Sure, five figures. So I call Hugh; he says he's on his way to Japan, business; can I hold it for a few days 'til he gets back? Well, for Hugh, sure, you bet I'll hold it. I'd be crazy not to. We make a date for the next week. But when I go over there, guess what? Not only is he not interested, he doesn't even want to see it. It's hello Sammy, goodbye Sammy, and I'm out the door. And talk about somebody looking like shit. Weird: Hugh Curtis won't even take a quick gander at the world's greatest snuffbox? Like I said, I figured it had to be something big, but ..." Sammy waves his hand as if it had suddenly caught fire. "Whew! Go on, my man, do go on. I am pure ears."

Pure Ears listens attentively, then delivers a sharp slap to my arm. "So we're talkin' big money, my man! Great, great, great! Always knew you had it in you, Thomas; it was just a matter of when. Glad you finally decided to come play with me in the bigs."

I try hard to keep my disgust under wraps. While Schwartz and I were walking crosstown from Frank's I told him I hated having to deal with Sammy Shapiro. "But we need someone with solid brass balls who's bought and sold a lot of mechanical music. Somebody who can pull LoPriore's chain to the point where he stops thinking. You know anybody better than Sammy?"

Schwartz shook his head. "Nobody beats Sammy in the Chainyankers' League—but this ain't a guy I'd even trust with five bucks to go around the corner and buy a bag of bagels. I just hope he doesn't decide to try both ends against the middle."

"You're right," I said. "But there're three things in our favor. One: Sammy ought to see that any way he cuts it, it'll be tough to beat a half-million bucks for a few days' work. Two: he's got to know the kind of medicine LoPriore can dish out, and I don't think he'll want to open wide for a dose. And three is that all the time the game's on, there's going to be another, little game going too. One called Pin the Tail on the Donkey. What do you think?"

Schwartz laughed. "You're the doctor."

The doctor swallows his contempt, gives Sammy his best chummy smile. "So half a million dollars for dangling bait sounds pretty good to you?"

"Sure isn't something to walk away from." Sammy sneers. "Who's the fish?"

"Vincent LoPriore," I say as casually as I can.

Sammy backs a step away from me, his glowing cheeks gone abruptly pasty. "Shit," he whispers. "*Him* and Maddy Curtis? You've got to be kidding. The friggin' *Bird*man ..."

"Not kidding," I say. "But for once that frigger's going to be the friggee. Still interested? Or is it getting too gamey for your taste?"

Sammy picks a bit of lint off his trousers, flicks it onto the floor. "Nah, don't be silly. Sure I'm interested." His tone projects considerably less conviction than his words. "For a half a mill ... yeah, you bet. But just so you know, this is one fish I'm not about to pull into my boat unless I'm good and goddamn sure he's dead."

"You won't have to pull him in at all; that part's my job. You've just got to make sure the hook's set."

Sammy recovers himself at least to some extent, pushes forward a reluctant smile. "Okay, my man. Figure I'm in. I just hope you got your insurance policy paid up. You're not careful, you could be playin' canasta with Jimmy Hoffa."

Back in the '40s and '50s, Linden Boulevard, a major thoroughfare in Flatbush, was rock-solid middle class, the heart and soul of Dodgerland. That was then. Now the big old frame houses with their spacious front porches look old and tired, ready to throw it in. Roofs sag as if in despair. Wide strips of paint peel off siding. You climb rickety wooden steps at your peril.

An hour after leaving Sammy Shapiro, Schwartz and I are in the torrid living room of one of those poor, discouraged houses and I'm pitching the occupants about getting rich quick.

"They're a great two-fer, Doc, good as we can get," Schwartz told me as we sat in the steamy Lexington subway car, clattering our way past South Ferry through the underwater tunnel into Brooklyn. "Mick and Sandy McFarland. She's an actress, plays bit parts on those afternoon TV soap operas, can wrap any man right around her pinky finger. Also, she's a twenty-one-jewel dip."

I gave Schwartz a curious look. "I don't know if being Looney Tunes is a plus, Broadway. We've already got Frank the Crank to deal with."

"No—hey, Doc, you got it all wrong." The lights in the subway car blinked off for a few seconds, then flashed back on to show Schwartz's gut-ache expression. "Not dip-*nutty*.

Dip-*pickpocket*. That's what you said you wanted, right? And Mick's a private detective, not overly picky about his clients if you get my drift. Knows every angle there is."

"Hm." I smiled. "Soapy Sandy and Mick the Dick."

Schwartz laughed, his customary good humor back in force. "You'll love 'em, Doc."

I watch my audience watch me as I talk. Mick the Dick is about thirty, a hunk with dark hair, shining appleskin cheeks and smiling blue Irish eyes. He wears a plain white T-shirt that can't begin to conceal the biggest pair of biceps I've ever seen. As he listens he leans slightly, protectively, toward Sandy on the sofa next to him. She's a slim young woman, about Mick's age, with cascades of light curls framing big green Betty-Boop eyes, and skin a Georgia peach would kill for. In a fetching white-and-blue cotton summer dress, she makes it plain to the most casual observer that humans are mammals.

"What do you think?" I ask them.

Sandy grins at Schwartz. "Hey, Broadway. I didn't know you had thinkers like this for friends."

"The Doc's in a class by himself," Schwartz says. "We listen to him, we're all of us gonna have an address on Easy Street."

Mick and Sandy glance around the room, taking in the Salvation Army Reclaim furniture, the dingy plaster walls, the cracked front window pane. Mick wipes sweat off his forehead with the back of his hand. "Sounds like a better address to me than Linden Boulevard," he rasps.

"I'll say." Sandy is no less enthusiastic. "Bet we could get us a nice condo, right in the city, midtown. Then I wouldn't have to ride that subway back and forth every day. And besides—it'd be a lot more fun than living out here in Brooklyn." She nudges her husband. "Profitable, too. We could go out every night, walk along Broadway in the theater district. We could stop at the Carnegie Deli for cheesecake when we're done. Bet I could get every month's mortgage payment in just a couple of good nights."

Soapy Sandy and Mick the Dick, traipsing the Great White Way for fun and profit. I can't help smiling. Schwartz pokes me. "See, Doc, I told you. Sandy Stickyfingers, she's the best in the business."

"She'd better be," I say. "Or else she'll be lucky if it's only her sticky fingers that get cut off."

Instantly, Sandy's in my face. "What do you mean, 'she better be,'" Sandy shrieks, Brooklyn-outraged to a deep crimson.

Before I can say a word in reply, Mick is on his feet. "You tryin' to insult my wife?"

Neurologists often have to deal with aggressive people; the idea is to keep the situation from escalating without letting them think they've got you on the run. I rest an open hand lightly against the chest of Mick's soggy shirt. "Hold on," I say, evenly but firmly. "No insult intended. You both just have to know if we're not careful on this job, we're going to end up in jail if we're lucky and dead if we're not. Now come on. Cool it."

I'm ready to duck if Mick swings, but instead he slides into a progressive grin. Soapy Sandy's face relaxes into a broad smile; she brushes my cheek with her fingers. "O-kay," she says. "I accept your apology."

I'm about to say I was explaining, not apologizing, but before I can get out a word Sandy adds, "And just so you know I don't bear grudges"—she waves a wallet under my nose—"here."

I grab for my left pants pocket. Empty. "Jesus," I whisper, pat the pocket again. It's still empty.

I take back my wallet, slip it into my pocket, then shoot a wink sideways at my snickering pal. "In Schwartz I trust."

By all appearances the elderly man in the seedy little apartment on West 48th between Eighth and Ninth is a Slob First Class. He wears a faded grease stain like a medal above the pocket of his open-necked white shirt, and his shave suggests he goes to a palsied barber. Uncombed gray hair, eyebrows bushy enough to win a Scotty dog big points from an AKC judge. Brown seems to be his color: baggy brown suit, scuffed brown shoes, muddy brown eyes. But according to Schwartz, Cleveland Gackle is the best lockcracker in New York or anywhere else, so here we are talking to him. In Schwartz I trust? I'm trying.

At no point in my pitch would I bet Gackle is listening. He lounges in a spring-sprung overstuffed chair with a faded red-and-gold floral-pattern cover, eyes noncommittal, giving nothing away. His mind could be anywhere. When I finish talking there's no response. I look at him for a few seconds, then say, "Interested?"

Gackle hauls himself upright, giving the impression I've caused him a major inconvenience. "I might be," he says. "Then again, I might not."

"Excuse me," I say, just a bit sharply. "But I think I need a better answer than that."

Gackle points a gnarled brown finger at me. "A person oughtn't to move too fast," he says. "That's a mistake. A wispy smile curls the corners of his mouth. "'Course, you don't want to move too slow, either."

"He's interested, Doc," Schwartz says quickly. "That's just how he talks. Don't worry about it."

Over the years I've learned to pay Schwartz heed. "Fair enough," I say to Gackle. "We'll move the plan along at just the right speed, everything nice and smooth. Then you can walk away as fast or as slow as you like with your half-million tax-free dollars."

Gackle turns a mild drop-dead look on me: I can go to hell if I want and if I don't, well, that's all right too. He sweeps the room with his hand. "Listen, Sonny. I've lived in this place for close to forty years now. Rents's low, I got whatever I need. Not that I'm gonna turn the money down, understand, but that ain't your hole card with me, uh-uh. Hole card's the job." He leans forward as if to discuss a highly confidential matter. "Schwartz says you're a doctor."

I can't make a connection, but I'll play along. "That's right."

"Well, then. I bet ninety-five percent of your patients're just crap, right? Checkups, little bit of a sore back, can't sleep nights—that kind of thing. Maybe one time a month you see a person who gets you to thinkin' hey, wait a minute now: this is actually interesting. Well, it's the same with me. The goddamn bread-and-butter jobs in my line could put a man to sleep just thinkin' about them. Open up a door for a guy to get inside and trash hell out of his ex's new place. Or go through his business competition's records. Or his partner's files, try and get something on his own partner to turn him in to the IRS. That's the whole balla wax, big deal. But this idea of yours ... I gotta admit I really like it."

He actually was listening to me. As Mel Allen would've put it: How about that! "Not to offend you," I say, "but you're going to have to look ... well, just a little sharper than you do now. New suit. Fresh shave. Clean shirt. You up for that?"

"I might be." Again the wispy smile. "I don't suppose *you* put on a soup and fish just to sit around in your house, do you? You came to me, remember? I didn't ask for any job interview."

I feel as if my smile might harden into a permanent set. "Just one other thing. From the way it smells here I'd say you have a pretty serious relationship going with Mary Jane. While you're on the job I don't think you ought to see her. Not with the risks we're going to be taking."

Gackle doesn't come close to blinking. "Mary Jane's been

my sweetheart for longer than you've been on this earth," he says, as sharply as I've heard him say anything to that point. "She calms my nerves. She clears my head."

Years ago I had a patient, a young trucker, who pushed himself too hard to make miles. A marijuana cigarette, he insisted, kept him alert and sharpened his reflexes. I couldn't persuade him otherwise. When he crashed his sixteen-wheeler, it was on the main street of a small southern town; he went through a red light at three times the speed limit and demolished a Suburban station wagon carrying a young mother and her little girl. The trucker walked away from the accident—or would have had not the husband of the woman appeared at the scene, heard the story, saw the trucker was higher than a kite on Mt. Rushmore, and pulled out a gun and shot him dead.

"I don't know," I venture. "I still think it'd be best if you give MJ a nice little three day vacation while you're working with us. Can you do it?"

"Maybe I could." Gackle shrugs lightly. "Then, again, maybe I won't."

Our next stop is the alpha to Cleveland Gackle's omega. The tiny studio apartment on Third Avenue in the Fifties smells more like a hospital than Man Med. The light is bright to the point of painfulness. You really could eat off the floors, also off the walls, ceilings, or any of the gleaming, polished hardwood chairs or tables in the room. The only fabric I see anywhere is a brown, tightweave blanket on the neatly-made single bed against the far wall. I smile to myself but don't say anything. Not until I can get a better read on the occupant.

Who seems to be yet another brand of nutcase. Fenton Dassidario, as Schwartz introduces him, is probably in his mid-forties, not more than five foot seven, with a fringed bald head disproportionately large for his body. Below a bulging forehead, his close-set dark eyes, pug nose, and pursestring

lips are crammed together in the middle of a face that tapers
sharply south of his floppy ears. Smiling blandly, bobbing
his head ever so slightly, he puts me in mind of a fetal Humpty-
Dumpty. "Pleased to meet you, Doctor," he says primly.

I offer my hand but Dassidario makes no motion to take
it. He's wearing white cotton gloves; by reflex I look for signs
of skin disease, but aside from a bit of flaking around his
hairline I see nothing. "The pleasure's mine," I say, and re-
tract my hand as tactfully as I can. "Schwartz says you're the
best in your business. That's what we need."

"Oh. That's very ... very nice, thank you, yes. But ... But ... *yes!*"

With his spasmodic, explosive speech and awkward physical gestures Dassidario looks like a man trapped in a rubber
suit filled with yellow jackets. Schwartz plunges into the verbal breach. "You bet, Doc. He's an absolute electronics wiz;
nobody even comes close to him. Whatever you need with
bugs and such he can do. Guaranteed."

At the mention of bugs, Dassidario's mouth twists in apparent distaste. Or is it just another mannerism? "Schwartz
says you're from Akron," I say, looking around the brilliantly-
lit apartment.

"Yes ... but ... *yes.* Akron. That's where I live. I keep this
apartment for when I come to New York ... on business. Like
now. Schwartz called me, so I came—"

This could go on all day but I don't have all day. "I understand," I say. "Why don't you let me tell you our plan. Then
you can decide whether you'd like to be on the bus."

Instantly I know I said something wrong. Distaste is
smeared thick as peanut butter all over Dassidario's face. "Well,
no ... no, I ... I *never* take buses," he stammers. "All those
people, crowds ... Oh, no. I can't. I don't care for cabs, either,
but they're ... they're better, no one else in them, at least right

then. I walk whenever I can; that's best of all. It's good exercise, too ... isn't it, Doctor?"

"Yes," I say, very gently. "*Very* good exercise. But why don't you call me Thomas."

"Oh ... Yes—yes, certainly." A tiny nervous chuckle wriggles to freedom past Dassidario's teeth. "Most doctors I've met ... well ... they ... they *want* to be called Doctor."

"Doc Purdue ain't like any other doctor you ever met," Schwartz chirps.

"Yes ... yes ..." Dassidario wrings his gloved hands before his face. His body writhes. He looks as if at any minute he might keel over, convulsing. "It's all right, Mr. Dassidario," I say. "Call me anything you like. Whatever makes you comfortable. About the bus, though: that's just an expression. Remember Ken Kesey?"

Dassidario's eyes bulge with the effort of thought. I envision first one eyeball, then the other, being blown from their sockets, fired like missiles, splat against the spotless white wall. "Being on the bus is just a way of saying you're in the game," I say. "That you're signing on with us."

Dassidario's relaxed posture tells me I've relieved him of a great burden. "Oh, yes ... yes, of course. But ... *yes.* Ha-ha, on the bus; I see, Dr. ... *Thomas.* Yes, why don't you ... tell me ... your plan."

"For starters ... or better, for the bottom line ..." I begin, then stop. Christ Almighty, I'm talking like him. "Maybe for a half-million dollars you'd be willing to take a little bus ride? On a *figurative* bus?"

A smile struggles manfully across Dassidario's face. "Yes ... oh, but yes, **yes**! For a half-million dollars I *might* very well ride on your bus ... *Thomas.*"

A large man in a dark three-piece herringbone suit and

bowler hat lumbers through the passageway into the British Airways terminal at Kennedy Airport. He shakes hands cordially with Schwartz, who shouts, "Great to see you, Al. Didn't think we'd be gettin' together again this quick—it ain't even a year since those music box murders last Christmastime."

Big Al Resford regards me with mischief-loaded eyes. "Nor I, Broadway. P'aps our friend Thomas here has become bored with the humdrum existence of a healer and has ... shall we say, taken to looking for trouble?"

"Fairer to say the shoe's on the other foot, Al."

"Well, life is a funny proposition, isn't it?" Big Al smiles warmly as he pumps my hand. "A pleasure to see you again, Thomas. Actually, I confess, I do look forward to the next few days. Judging from our phone conversation, it sounds very ... interesting."

We make our way to the exit, Schwartz scrambling to keep up with his two longer legged companions. "'Twasn't necess'ry for you to come all the way out here," Al says. "Particularly at this hour, what? Twenty after midnight already, my goodness. I could have simply taken a cab to a hotel and met you in the morning."

"No trouble," I say.

"Besides, Trudy woulda killed me," Schwartz pipes in, "if we ever let you go to a hotel. She's got the guest room all fixed up and she spent the whole afternoon in the kitchen."

"Ah. Marvelous. Cinnamon rolls for brekkers, then, is it? I shall not even try to conceal my enthusiasm." Al catches me staring at the black leather bag dangling from his right hand. "Yes, Thomas," he says. "I have the bait, as you so aptly put it. I'll warrant your poor fish will be unable to resist."

11

Hail, hail, the gang's ...

We sit in a rough circle in my workshop, islands in a sea of restoration tools and half-repaired music boxes. At my feet is a small leather suitcase. Impressive things do come in little packages: this one holds the two thousand hundred-dollar bills Hugh Curtis freed up for operating expenses.

Sarah's on the couch next to me. Ask her why she's here, she'll say to keep an eye on me. Ask me, it was the customary triumph of curiosity over indignation. Take your pick. Just remember, if one's true the other's not necessarily false.

Fenton Dassidario perches on the outermost edge of his chair, eyes bulging, digesting my speech, word by word. Schwartz, Al Resford, Espinoza, Sammy Shapiro, and Hugh Curtis occupy a semicircle of workchairs to the right of Dassidario. To Dassidario's left are Edna Reynolds, Frank the Crank, Soapy Sandy, Mick the Dick, and Cleveland Gackle. They're all listening hard, with the possible exception of Gackle, whose eyes shine more brightly than I'm happy to see. But Schwartz looks unconcerned. Since it was his hand LoPriore stomped, I guess I'm comfortable if he is.

When I finish my recap of the plan, Sammy Shapiro leans forward in his chair. "Sounds good, my man—except for maybe one thing. We grab LoPriore's birds, your English pal there dumps 'em overseas, and you figure we clear five mill. But you've never seen LoPriore's stuff, right? So what if you're wrong about what's there? And what it's worth."

Before I can open my mouth Sarah is on her feet. "Mr. Shapiro, 'what if' is you'll get your fair share of what the 'stuff' *is* worth. *That's* 'what if.' But I know Thomas pretty well, and if I were you I'd bet he'll be right on the money."

A married couple is a pair of scissors, forever slashing against each other, destroying anything that comes between them. Sarah's face is blazing. In a poker game Sammy Shapiro would wipe up the floor with my wife, but open warfare's a different story. I give Sammy my ultimate suffering-fools look, the one I count upon to send unprepared medical students dashing to their rooms for a quick change of underwear. "First part of this game's very low risk, Sammy; by half-time I'll have a solid estimate of the payout. Anyone who's unhappy then can walk with fifty thousand dollars in his pocket. Fifty-K sound all right to you for one day's light duty?"

"Suits me." Sammy's brassy sneer conveys agreement if not acquiescence. He leers at Sarah. "Must be nice to have a woman have so much faith in you, Thomas. Sometime you gotta tell me your secret."

"You'd never understand it," says the Ice Matron.

Time to move along. "Let's have a look at the lure," I say. "If Sammy's our fisherman, Al owns the bait shop."

"Well not precisely *owns*," Al says, smiling. "More like a rental arrangement, you might say." He bends to pick up a small cardboard box on the floor between his feet.

Sammy Shapiro, pushing forward, scores a direct hit on Hugh Curtis's shoe. "Sorry, my man," Sammy mumbles, barely turning around.

Hugh grunts, rubs his foot. "Asshole," he mutters.

Schwartz and I exchange glances and shrugs. Maybe I should have gotten another fisherman, but who? In any case, too late now.

With infinite care Al lifts an object swathed in plastic bubble-wrap, then unwinds the bubble-wrap slowly and gently. As the plastic falls free there's a mass insuck of breath, and well there might be. More than a hundred years of high-powered collecting and dealing is assembled in this workshop, but Big Al might as well be making a demonstration to greenhorns.

He's holding a gorgeous little Greek temple, seven or eight inches high, all gold and enamel, the enameling being a lustrous turquoise with highlights of greens and yellows. The octagonal base rests upon six elegantly turned round gold feet, and each base façade is decorated with a lovely floral painting. Atop the base, up three golden steps, is an engine-turned pedestal with an enamel-faced gold watch mounted vertically at the top. Four garlanded colonnades rise from the left and right extremities of the platform to support an extravagantly-worked round golden roof. Gold-and-enamel finials are set at points corresponding to the colonnades below, and from the center of the ceiling is suspended a faux-chandelier of sparkling cut glass, as if it were illuminating the watch. From the inner aspect of each rooftop finial rise four S-shaped supports; these come together above the center of the roof to support a gold-and-enamel diadem with a tiny, graceful surmount resembling an urn.

Silence. Not even Sammy has anything to say.

Big Al smiles. "Watch closely." Everyone leans toward him as he reaches behind the structure to turn first a key in the base, then a tiny knob behind the watch. The hands of the watch move slowly toward three o'clock.

When the hands hit the hour the piece comes alive. The watch chimes three times, water appears to flow down the colonnades, and from somewhere inside the base comes the sound of a rare, very early musical movement, a delicate, ethereal arrangement of an early French folk song, full of trills. At the first note a tiny bird pops up from the top of the temple. No more than three-quarters of an inch long, with a beak of ivory, the bird is precisely feathered in iridescent blue, green, yellow, and red. It moves about under the diadem, turning side to side, flapping its wings and tail, cocking its head, and opening and closing its beak as it sings a note-perfect accompaniment to the tune. Finally, as the music ends, the bird pops back inside the temple, disappearing as suddenly as it had appeared.

Al's chuckle breaks the silence. "Impressive, what? Do you imagine this will interest our friend, Thomas?"

I'm lightheaded, breathing at twice-normal rate. "I'm sure," I finally manage to get out. "You say you ... rented that piece?"

"You might call it a rental, yes. We'll chat later about the fee. Not to worry; it's actually quite reasonable. What's important is that the piece be returned in the same condition it was lent. Otherwise I'm afraid there will be considerable unpleasantness."

Understatement runs strong in Al Resford's speech. I don't want to even imagine the nature of that unpleasantness. "When it's not being shown it'll be in your personal care, Al," I say. "And we'll definitely limit its exposure."

"Hey, my man. One minute."

Sammy's on his feet again, pointing at the temple which is now resting under Al's large, protective hand. A headache takes root behind my left eye, begins to grow luxuriantly.

"What would you say that bait of yours is worth?" Sammy asks. "Ballpark, say."

Al's nod in my direction is almost imperceptible but it's definitely there. "'Tis a rare item," he says, "quite as elegant as they come. Difficult to set a precise value but I should think between one and one and a quarter-million of your dollars would be close."

Sammy whistles. "That's expensive bait, my man."

"Oh, Mr. Shapiro ..."

Every eye turns to Big Al.

"I suggest you not think too terribly hard about it. It could be ... well, don't you know—distracting. P'aps you should keep in mind the little saying about curiosity and the cat."

All said very lightly, but Sammy Shapiroes learn early to keep an eye sharply focused between lines. "Uh, yeah," Sammy says, then swallows hard. "Tell the truth, I don't know if I want to be responsible for a thing like that."

"You won't be," I say. "Your job is just to get our mark salivating. I'm the one who's got to make sure he doesn't drool on it."

Frank the Crank laughs out loud. "Hey, Doc, I think you missed your call. You coulda been a great second story man, a legend in your own mind. But you sure better not screw up. Something blows, ain't no way you're not gonna land in a pretty spicy stewpot."

"Don't worry, Frank." Sarah's smiling, but there's sadness in her eyes. "Thomas doesn't just tell his stories, he lives them. He takes the truth, twists it and bends it, then turns it back on itself until no one, himself included, has the slightest chance of recognizing it. Make-believe is real; real's make-believe. If something goes wrong, Thomas will just decide that wrong is right and we'll all go home happy."

Nervous chuckles snake their way through the little crowd. Poor Dassidario writhes in his chair, trying frantically to decide whether he ought to show amusement or remain silent. "Hey, Mrs. P, know what?" Frank shouts. "I've been sayin' for years now, your husband's the biggest liar I ever met but at the same time he's the most honest guy I know. I never could figure."

"Don't waste time trying now, Frank," I say. "Just keep your mind on LoPriore. He's not like most people. Most people don't expect to win every game, probably wouldn't even like to. But if LoPriore could figure how to win without playing at all, he'd do it. Also, far as he's concerned, hitting below the belt isn't a foul; it's double points. Getting Hugh's wife to help grab Hugh's snuffboxes and then turn up conveniently dead in Central Park was probably the biggest parlay in his career."

I pause long enough to let the murmurs rise and fade out. Schwartz leans over to pat Hugh on the back.

"So: we know LoPriore's game; we play by his own rules. Just a few basic cautions. Number One: No booze." I sniff in Hugh's direction. "I let Johnnie Walker and Old Granddad sit in at this meeting but that's it. Now they stay in the bleachers 'til the game's over. Clear?"

Hugh colors, seems about to say something. But then he just lowers his head and nods.

"And no drugs." I stare at Cleveland Gackle. "Nothing that could screw up a person's thinking or time perception. Sammy, no nasty mouthwork. For a half-million dollars, give or take, you can manage to stay zipped for three days. And everyone: definitely no talking to anyone outside this room; also the less to each other, the better. New York's one big ear."

"I think we understand, Thomas," Edna Reynolds says drily.

"I sure do," chirps Frank the Crank. "For a clean half-mill I'll put my nose onto any treadmill you want."

I suppress a smile. When it comes to processing homilies, proverbs or metaphors through Mixmasters, Frank's in his own special league.

Twin images battle for front-row space in my mind: Washington at the Delaware, Custer at Little Big Horn. I draw in a chestful of air, blow it out.

"Let's go."

12

Fenton Dassidario licks his lips nervously as we cross East 57th, heading north on Eighth Avenue. In his right hand Dassidario's got a thick leather case, old and well-used; with his left hand he pulls a small wheeled suitcase designed to fit beneath an airplane seat.

"Such crowds!" he murmurs, whether to himself or me, I'm not sure. But as hard as he works at staying clear, bending this way, angling that, people still keep brushing against him. I'll bet the minute he checks into the hotel he goes straight to the shower. Won't use that white perfumy stuff hotels call soap, though. Dassidarios usually carry their own soap with them, good strong green bars with pumice. I smile at him; he forces a return grin. "This job sounds good, Dr ... *Thomas*," he says.

He'll be all right, I tell myself. Yes. But ... *yes*.

"It looks to me like you've got a good group, and that's the most important thing. Mr. Shapiro's a little unpleasant, but I suspect he'll do his job. And Broadway Schwartz—such a nice man, I've known him for years—but oh, what he has to do for a living! Rooting in filthy attics and contaminated basements, picking through piles of old, dirty things that once were owned by people who're dead now. And of course, before they were dead most of those people were terribly sick ... I do hope nothing ever happens to Schwartz. I worry about him."

"Something *will* happen to Schwartz," I say. "Just like some day something will happen to you and me and everyone else."

Dassidario lets go of the suitcase, pulls a handkerchief from his pocket, carefully mops his face, moving always away from nose, eyes, mouth. Then he stuffs the handkerchief away, takes hold of the suitcase handle, and as he starts back into motion begins to speak slowly. "Yes ... I know. But ... but—did you see that brown spot on Mr. Gackle's shirt? Probably some sort of gravy, I'd say; you could practically see bacteria swarming on it. There's so much sickness in the world, such terrible diseases. Why can't people be more careful?"

We dodge through the Columbus Circle crowd, turn east on 58th. As Dassidario scoots across Sixth Avenue toward the Regency Tower Hotel, a young blonde woman smiles at him. She's slim, wearing a tank top that shows a butterfly tattoo on her left breast, and shorts cut so high she can't possibly be wearing panties. Dassidario shudders, walks faster. "Better to swim in a sewage tank than let a creature like that come within a foot of you. Like that Sandy woman; I know that type, yes. Women like her should be kept under strict quarantine."

By the time we get to the door of the hotel Dassidario is practically running. The blue-uniformed doorman says good evening, swings the door open; Dassidario goes through into the lobby. I follow a few steps to the back. Dassidario's shoes click double-time on the marble as he walks up to the registration desk. Help you, Sir?" chirps one of the hops, a small man who could have played Johnny in the old Philip Morris ads.

"Thank you, I'm fine," Dassidario squeaks. He tightens his hold on his bags.

Behind the green marble counter a young blond man in a navy-blue blazer watches Dassidario approach. "Good evening, Sir," he says. "May I help you?"

Dassidario nods. "I'd ... like a room, please. For four nights."

The clerk studies him. I know what he's thinking, and I'll bet so does Dassidario. Not quite the usual Regency Tower client, this little man with a bald head shaped like an inverted pear. Just a tad scruffy, with his wrinkled, open-necked white shirt and gray cotton pants, and by this hour of night beginning to need a shave. Those big eyes, that constant blinking. And white cotton gloves—in August?

But the clerk says mildly, "Yes, Sir ... four nights. For one person?"

Dassidario blinks furiously. He studies the clerk's bland face. CHARLES, says the engraved brass name plaque on his left lapel. "Yes," says Dassidario, just a bit sharply. "Isn't it quite clear I'm alone?"

Charles nods. "Certainly, Sir. Smoking or Non?"

"Non-smoking. And I'll be able to tell immediately if there has been any smoking in my room."

"No need to worry, Sir." The clerk's smile is reassuring. "We are quite strict about that. Now." He punches a few keys on the computer to his left. "I have a nice single room on the Twenty-third floor, a double-bed—"

"I don't like to feel crowded," Dassidario says. "Do you have a suite?"

"I believe we do, Sir." The clerk takes a moment to commune with his computer, scratching lightly at his left eyebrow as if that might help him make sense of this odd little man. "We *do* have a lovely suite, on the thirty-second floor, Sir. With a magnificent park view. But ..." His voice trails off as he looks Dassidario up and down.

"But ... what?" asks Dassidario.

"Well, Sir ... the daily rate would be five hundred and

forty-five dollars. That's actually our summer rate. In season, it's eight-fifteen."

"That will be fine," Dassidario says primly. "I'll take it." He pulls his wallet from his pocket, takes out an American Express Gold Card, and hands it to the clerk, who holds it up to the light. The clerk squints. "Mr. Dass-idario ... First National Bank of Akron. You're visiting us from Ohio. On a little vacation to the Big City?"

"Yes." Dassidario's thin lips curve into a hint of a smile. He's being underestimated and patronized, but I suspect the woods are full of the bloody corpses of foolish people who snickered behind their hands at Fenton Dassidario, that ridiculous little man. I'm feeling better about our game all the time.

As the clerk returns Dassidario's credit card, he brings his palm down on a bell on the counter. Johnny the bellhop leaps forward; Dassidario snatches up his carrying case and suitcase. "You can show me to the room if you want," he says. "But I'll carry my own bags."

Stiff little bow from the bellhop. "As you wish, Sir."

"Room Thirty-two-oh-one," says the clerk, his voice as guarded as the expression on his face. He passes a key across to the bellhop. Then he stands and watches Dassidario and the bellhop walk away toward the elevator. Christ-what-a-fruit-cake is written clearly on the young man's face. Thank you, Charles. That's exactly what we want you to think.

Charles now turns his attention to me. "Help you, Sir?"

"I'm looking for a friend," I say. "Ms. Coveyduck—Maude Lynne Coveyduck. I'm not sure which room she's in."

Charles taps a few keys on his computer, then wrinkles his forehead. "Coveyduck, Sir ... could you spell that, please?"

"Just like it sounds," I say. "C-O-V-E-Y-D-U-C-K."

"Hm. Way I had it." Sad shake of Charles's head. "I'm

sorry, Sir; I have no record of any Coveyducks here. Are you certain—"

"I was pretty sure she'd have checked in this afternoon," I say. "Maybe she was delayed; I'll go have a drink, check back later."

Charles smiles. "Thank you, Sir."

"Thank *you*," I say, then hoof in the direction of the hotel bar. Once around the corner, out of sight of the front desk, I scoot into an open elevator and push the button for the 32nd floor.

Dassidario and I, locked door behind us, scan the large living room of the suite. On the far wall, floor-to-ceiling windows look out on Central Park. The furnishings and decorations are all swoopy, swirly pale pink, delicate blue and beige.

Dassidario strolls through a doorway to our right, eyeballs the bedroom, then smiles his tight little smile and nods to me. "Yes, Thomas, it's ... perfect. But ... *yes*. With the door closed, any number of people can hide in here."

On the coffee table in front of the sofa is a big basket of fruit, token of appreciation from management to a schmuck willing to pay more than five-hundred dollars a night out of season for a place to lay his head. But Dr. Purdue's fancy little shell game simply would not go over in a cheap hotel. Sometimes you do have to spend money to make money. I pick up an apple, shine it against my sleeve; might as well get my money's worth. As I take a big, crunchy bite out of the apple, Dassidario jumps a foot, nervous disapproval all over his face. I didn't wash the apple, preferably in Lysol.

"Little nervous, are we?" I ask.

"That blonde woman ... outside the hotel ..." Dassidario jabs a condemnatory finger toward the window, in the direction of Columbus Circle. Guilty as charged; punishment, death.

"It's just unfair, Doctor, *so* unreasonable, that men should be burdened with a compulsion to immerse themselves in deadly contamination. Syphilis and gonorrhea, all those centuries of debilitation and degradation, and finally when penicillin came along, what happened? You're a doctor; you must know. The germs mutated. They became resistant to antibiotics. And that wasn't nearly the worst of it. There's no cure at all for herpes, is there? And viral genital warts—those nauseating heaped-up masses oozing white discharge? Burn them off and practically before you're out of the doctor's office, they're back again. And now of course AIDS—that's supposed to be the ultimate sexual deterrent. But next year, next month, maybe next week, mark my words: a new sex-related disease will appear and make HIV look like a picnic. We may see genitally-transmitted Ebola virus: peoples' faces sloughing off at the moment of orgasm, brains turning to oatmeal, vaginas becoming bowls of red oozy mush, penises and testicles liquefying and dripping away. It's not beyond the scope of imagination, is it, Doctor ... *Thomas?*"

Obviously not, I think, but I'm not here to try to cure poor Dassidario's phobias. In fact, the less I mess with his mind, the better. I hold out my hand; he looks curiously at me.

"The key," I say.

"Oh yes ... yes. Of course, sorry." The little man reaches into his pocket with his white-gloved hand, comes out with the room key, and being careful to avoid actual contact between himself and me, drops it into my hand.

"I'll take it right up to Schwartz; he'll get the copies made and you can have it back tomorrow," I say. "Just don't get yourself locked out of here between now and then."

"Oh, no, no." Dassidario's face asks whether such a thing is even possible. To my mind it seems considerably more likely than the appearance of a Genital Ebolalike Virus Syndrome, but who am I to tell fortunes? "I'll be staying in the rest of tonight," Dassidario continues. "Then tomorrow I have a lot to do in the other place ... the Regina. I'm sure I'll be there all day, 'til the meeting."

"Good." Foregoing my customary farewell handshake I head toward the door. Dassidario bends over his old brown leather case, opens it gently, rests a hand lightly on his electronic surveillance materials. The tender touch of a grateful supplicant. So clean. Safe. No waste products. I can see Fenton Dassidario in his jammies, kneeling at his bedside to offer up prayers to an icon on a computer screen large as the universe. His heaven will be one hundred percent electronic, populated by virtual angels playing digital music on their harps.

13

Two o'clock next afternoon, temperature and humidity running neck and neck in the high nineties. Edna Reynolds, encumbered only by her purse, strides up Madison Avenue like a Salvation Army general leading her Christian soldiers onward. Captain Purdue and Lt. Schwartz, each lugging a brace of heavy traveling bags, struggle along behind her. Perspiration sluices down their foreheads, across their cheeks.

At the corner of 60th I call time, set down my two bags. Edna looks at me with undisguised contempt. I swipe my forearm across my face. "Weather like this isn't going to be good for wearing makeup."

Schwartz looks concerned, but Edna gives my remark an unceremonious brush. "While you're made up the only *schlepping* you'll be doing will be at night, when it's cooler. *And* darker. Just leave it to me. I'll be using top-quality theatrical makeup, the stuff they wear under those scorching stage lights. It won't run."

"It better not," I mutter.

"You can goddamn well take whatever I say to the bank," Edna snaps. "I thought you knew that, Thomas."

"I do. Sorry, I apologize. Just getting a little cranky—this stuff is heavy for Christ's sake. Fabric. Sewing equipment. Makeup kits."

Edna reaches for the suitcases. "Thomas, you diddle-damn wuss—here. *I'll* carry it."

I elbow her aside, then bend down and heft my load. "Okay ... Mother. Let's go get you set up. Espinoza ought to have your room ready by now."

Three hours later, back in my workshop. Last walk-through for Purdue's Merry Band of Pigeon-Pluckers. Schwartz distributes keys all around, takes care to give the original to Dassidario. "Number's not on them in case they get lost," I say. "Room Three-two-oh-one, Regency Tower Hotel. That's thirty-two-oh-one; remember it. Also remember this is a play we're putting on; we've got to be perfect with our entrances and exits. Anyone who's not supposed to appear in any particular scene stays off-stage—*far* off-stage. No dropping in for a little visit, not at the Regency Tower, not at the Regina. Sammy, how'd it go with LoPriore? Tonight's all set up?"

Sammy sniggers. There's broad common ground under his feet and LoPriore's, the major difference between them being that Sammy sublimates his killer instinct. "Piece o'cake, my man," Sammy sings. "He answered the phone, I told him my name was Saul Schifrin and I could get him something for his collection like he hadn't seen even in his dreams. Right off he tries to put me onto one of his flunkeys, but I say to him, 'Hey, my man, I don't sell musical bird-temples by Jacob Frisard to servants. Now you want to hear about it or don't you?'"

Frank the Crank chuckles. "I sure woulda liked to see his face right then."

"Yeah? Well, I'm not so sure *I* would've." A momentary pause, then Sammy's off to the races. "LoPriore wants to know how I know about him and where I got his phone number, and I tell him I got my ways just like he's got his, and it just happens I know this couple—American, but they live in France—

they've got a collection that just won't quit and a pocketbook to match. They're over here to do some antiqueing, and they brought this musical bird-temple to take to the Decorators' Show this weekend at the Armory. So he better make his pitch before then, and it's a ten percenter for me. He says I get my cut when he gets the temple, and what's their phone number? No *way*, I tell him. If he's interested he meets me on Central Park South, in the Ritz Carlton Lobby, eight o'clock sharp, and I'll take him over. He should look for a guy in his thirties, seersucker suit, white carnation in the lapel. AMF."

Count on Sammy to leave me at sea. "AMF?"

Edna's glance is pitying. "Adios, motherfucker," she says with exaggerated gentleness. She hands Sammy an artificial flower.

Sammy double-takes, claps his hands. "Hey, that's *it*, my lady, white carnation. Bet you got the suit too."

"Safest bet you'll ever make." Edna pats the black tote bag on the floor at her feet. Your disguise's in here too. Mustache, bifocals with clear glass, a mole for your cheekbone. If he ever sees you again he'll never recognize you." She looks at me, then laughs wickedly. "He'll never recognize you, either, Thomas," she says.

"I sure hope not." I check my watch. "All right, less than three hours 'til eight o'clock. Let's get some food; then it's Sandy, Gackle, Edna ... and me, Regency Tower, Room Thirty-Two-oh-One. In place by a quarter to eight."

14

Regency Tower, Room 3201, seven minutes after eight. Shave-and-a-haircut, loud and clear.

Edna and Gackle side by side on the sofa look at each other. Edna leans over, adjusts Gackle's tie, then wiggles herself spine-straight.

Quick peek in the wall mirror. Edna's a genius; what a piece of work I am! It's as if I'd put my head on upside down. My mop of wiry black hair is gone, shaved into the wastebasket at the Regina, and there's a natty Van Dyke beard glued around my mouth. This Earl de Pinza is one quaint dude. He winks at Soapy Sandy through the thick glass in his heavy, black-rimmed specs. Sandy grins and walks off through the door to the right, into the bedroom.

Time.

I saunter across the room, go through the motions of looking through the peephole, then crack the door and peer through the narrow opening. "Yeah, *what?*" I say, nasty-nasty.

"Hey, my *man*," Sammy croons. "It's Schifrin. Come on, open up. I got a man here wants to meet you."

Edna scores again. I've known Mr. Hustle for more than ten years, and if I'd passed him on the street I wouldn't have given him a thought.

I open the door slowly, step back to let the visitors in,

then narrow my eyes and reach past Sammy and LoPriore to close the door. My heart's driving an impressive Krupa riff up into my throat. I ... am ... in ... charge, I tell myself silently as I position myself between my visitors and Edna and Gackle.

LoPriore is right up there at the top of any Most To Be Avoided In A Dark Alley List. Dressed in a pair of severely cut white trousers and a white turtleneck with a left breast pocket, his face is a map only Rand and McNally could love. Blue eyes—odd in an Italian—the color and consistency of a Minnesota lake in January. Thick scar tissue over his eyebrows. Big hawk's nose, obviously rearranged and not by a plastic surgeon. The left corner of his mouth seems permanently twisted into a unilateral sneer, showing a primo set of teeth, all the better, my dear, to chew you up and spit you out. Hair shiny black but the neatly-trimmed mustache is just beginning to streak white. He matches me glare for glare. I work hard at not blinking.

"I thought I told you not to bring anybody up here," I growl at Sammy.

"Hey, my man!" Sammy gestures grandly toward his companion. "I heard you; I ain't deaf. But I ain't dumb, either. This guy here isn't just *anybody*. This's Vincent LoPriore."

I give LoPriore a slow once-over. "That's supposed to impress me?"

"It oughta. Mr. LoPriore's got a killer mechanical bird collection. I can't believe you never heard of him."

"Huh! American collections aren't worth thinking about. Compared to what's in Europe, *any* U. S. collection is trash."

Trash is the cue word. Edna comes rushing from the sofa as Sandy materializes at the bedroom door. "Earl de Pinza, you watch your language," Edna barks. "And while you're at it, mind your manners, too. That's not the way I brought you up." The expression on her face would wilt watercress. "Mr. LoPriore, is it?" she says. "And Mr ..."

"Schifrin," Sammy says. "Saul Schifrin."

"Mr. Schifrin. I'm Evelyn de Pinza, Earl's mother. That's his father over there."

Gackle steps forward, hand out. "Pete de Pinza, pleased to meet you."

"And ... oh, Sally, dear." Edna makes come-here motions at Sandy. "This is Sally, gentlemen, my son's wife. For which I sometimes think she deserves a medal."

From the moment Sandy appeared in the doorway LoPriore's eyes have been only for her, and why not? Her low-cut white summer frock puts a generous amount of tanned cleavage on display, and she knows exactly how to display it. She walks over slowly and shakes hands, first with Sammy, then with LoPriore, who doesn't seem in a hurry to let go.

"I'm pleased to meet you," Sandy says, favoring LoPriore with a coy smile.

LoPriore looks like a wolf on the prowl who's just sighted a plump, juicy lamb. "Vincent LoPriore." A rumble. Just saying his name, the man is scary.

"And I know Mr. Schifrin," Sandy goes on. "This has to be the gentleman you told us about. The one who has such a marvelous collection."

"This's him, all right," Sammy chirps. "I know he's going to want that piece you brought over, the bird-temple. No way you're going to have to take it to the Armory."

"Pfaw!" I damn near spit on the fluffy beige carpet. "An *American* collector is going to walk into my room and go away with my Jacob Frisard bird-temple? Don't make me laugh. What do you have in your collection, Mr. LoPriore? A couple of circa nineteen twenty Griesebaum birds in clunky silver cases? Over here that's what they call a collection."

The Griesebaums, Karl and his son Mathias, are Germans who've been making good quality singing bird boxes since

1905. But Griesebaums are Fords and Chevvies in a singing bird world where Rochats are Cadillacs; Bruguiers, Ferraris; and Frisards, Rollses.

Only the possibility of making off with an incomparable mechanical musical treasure—and maybe along with it the gorgeous hunk of womanflesh at my side—is stopping LoPriore from wiping up the room with me and slinging me through the window like an oddly-shaped discus. Sandy fetches me a limp-wristed slap on the arm, says in a pout, "Earl, stop that! You ought to be ashamed." Then she rests that warm white hand on Lo Priore's forearm, in the process giving the thick, black hair a little fondle. "Earl is *such* a snob," she says. "As far as he's concerned, nothing in America is any good. He'd like to have his birth certificate re-written to say he was born in Paris instead of Great Falls, Montana."

Edna laughs, a good sour chuckle. "*We* still live there, my husband and I. Montana Mining School was fine for his dad, but not for Earl. He had to go to Harvard."

"You went to Harvard?" LoPriore actually sounds impressed.

"Class of 'seventy," I say. "BA, Fine Arts."

"So he's never had to work for a living." Gackle, resplendent in his jeans, cowboy shirt and boots.

"I wouldn't call running one of the most important art galleries in Paris not working, Dad."

"Huh! Important to *who*? Those so-called paintings in your so-called gallery look like they came out of a kindergarten class. I might say you're a pimp but a pimp at least sells something useful."

Edna turns on him, hands on hips, chin out. "Pete, I swear! The two of you could embarrass a woman to death. I—"

"Mr. LoPriore ..."

All the time Gackle, Edna and I were performing, Sandy

was fluttering her lashes at our patsy. "Mr. LoPriore, I'll bet you'd like to see the Frisard, wouldn't you?"

"Sally!" I spit out her name as if it tasted like curdled milk. "I'm not going to sell the piece before the show. I've got people coming to look at it."

Delicate shrug. "Well, you did let Mr. Schifrin bring Mr. LoPriore here, so you ought to at least let him *see* it. Tell you what." She takes me by the shoulders, points me in the direction of the bedroom. "Go get the bird-temple. Mr. LoPriore, Mr. Schifrin, Mom and Dad—come over and sit down. I'll get us something to drink."

She moves toward the honor bar in the far corner of the room. LoPriore shoots me a look out of the corners of his eyes, an insolent challenge that both frightens and exhilarates me. I'm out onto the tightrope now, no safety net underneath. I watch LoPriore and Sammy follow Edna over to the sofa. Sammy winks as he turns to go. Crazy bastard, I could slug him.

The six of us sit around the coffee table. LoPriore stares at the wrapped bird-temple; the rest of us try not to stare at LoPriore. As I take away the bubble-wrap our pigeon's eyes bulge; he actually gasps. All pretense of nonchalance, out the window. Slowly his hand comes forward; he jerks it back, then extends it to gently touch the crown of the temple. He slides off his chair onto the floor on his knees, examines each side, then tilts his head to peer beneath the base. I turn the clock hands to four; the tiny bird pops up and moves in its lifelike way, tweeting accompaniment to the delicate music.

As the song ends and the bird drops back into its recess, LoPriore looks up at me. His eyes are haunted, the skin on his cheeks slack. When he asks, "Where is the mark?" it's no more than a hoarse croak.

Thomas Purdue would say, Down on his knees, begging to be taken. But right now I'm Earl de Pinza, and damned well better stay him. I open the door on the back of the temple, pull a penlight from my pocket, direct the beam against a small brass plate on which is inscribed in elegant script the name of the maker. LoPriore peers in.

"Satisfied?" I say.

"It's lovely," LoPriore breathes. "Wonderful."

The change in his manner is astonishing. Collector's passion has pushed to the fore, camouflaging all those nasty personality traits, and presenting a side of the man with which I have no trouble sympathizing.

But sympathy's not what I need to be feeling right now. "Have you ever seen a Frisard?" I ask LoPriore, taking care to frost each word with as much condescension as I can manage. Then, I add, very quickly, "In a picture, I mean—say in Wallinger's book. Do you know the Wallinger book?"

Wallinger is the now-elderly Englishman who years ago put together the definitive book on musical miniatures, a magnificent work with exhaustive text and endless color illustrations of the finest examples in the world. Any serious collector owns two copies of the book: one to use for almost-daily reference, the other to keep in pristine condition on the shelf. Asking LoPriore whether he knows the Wallinger book is like asking the Archbishop of Canterbury whether he might be familiar with the Bible.

My question brings back the fundamental LoPriore. "Do I know Wallinger's *book*? I know *Wallinger*—personally. I've been to his home, seen his collection. And I've seen more Frisard pieces than I suspect *you've* seen pictures of. In fact, I own two."

Both statements are undoubtedly true, but LoPriore and I are playing two different games. LoPriore figures he's winning his match, but in mine he's just placed himself into check.

"Really?" I say. "Two Frisards?"

Smug smile, little nod. "That's right."

I glance at the bird-temple on the coffee table. "But I'll bet they're just singing bird-boxes—you don't own a super-Frisard piece like my temple here, do you?"

Give LoPriore this: he doesn't weasel. He doesn't even hesitate. "No," he says. "Not until now." He points at the temple. "What's your price, Mr. de Pinza?"

I blow out a breath, then turn away and walk to the window, where I stand, hands behind my back, rocking on my heels and pretending to stare out at the park.

Finally, LoPriore says, "Listen, de Pinza: you have something I want and I'm going to leave with it. I'm not here to Jew you down. What's your price?"

I turn around, very slowly. "Mr. LoPriore, you're doing a fine job of reminding me why I live in Europe. Europeans have class. Even in a straight business deal there's a nice lunch and a glass of wine. For something like this, a Frisard—"

LoPriore cuts me off. "I don't need any airy-fairy lectures about how much class Europeans have. My time is valuable. You want to sell; I want to buy. Now, what's ... your ... goddamn ... *price?*"

I look calmly at Sandy, say, "Get the refreshments ready."

As she shimmies toward the little bar-kitchenette I turn back to LoPriore. "We're going to have some excellent wine and fine cheese. You're welcome to join us, both you and your broker there. But if your time's too valuable, you know where the door is."

For the next hour we sit and gab. The cheese is good, but the wine tastes like white grape juice because that's what it is. LoPriore gets real stuff, a nice French Vouvray, but the scammers are swigging down nonalcoholic crap straight from upstate New York. All the while LoPriore can't keep his eyes off the Frisard temple or the conversation away from it. I refuse to even come near talking about a sale, just keep putting LoPriore down as a crass, uncultured American.

Soapy Sandy's performance could land her an Oscar. Every time I push LoPriore to the breaking point, Sandy fetches him back with a smile or a glance that would melt December ice in Barrow. She goes on about my collection in Paris, how it fills the entire third and fourth floors of our good-sized house. How it includes automata by Jaquet-Droz; birds by Leschot and Bruguier; a case full of watches by Breguet and Henri Capt; not one but two organs by Davrainville; music boxes by Francois Nicole and Henri Raymond Nicole. She remembers every line, drops every name I taught her. "You *must* come and see the collection when you're in Paris, Mr. LoPriore," she gushes. "You'd *love* it."

"Talk about casting pearls before swine," I snort.

Before LoPriore can open his mouth Sandy is up on her feet, shouting. "Oh, Earl—you are *such* a snob. *I'm* sure Mr. LoPriore has a beautiful collection. Otherwise, why would he even be interested in our— Oh. *I* know what!"

Everybody looks at her and waits, everybody but LoPriore knowing what's coming.

"Mr. LoPriore!" Sandy says. "Let's go *see* your collection. Earl, I'll bet it's super. Bet you money."

"Horsefeathers!" I shout. "Applesauce! A couple of clunky Griesebaums. *Late* clunky Griesebaums, at that."

She turns to LoPriore. "What do you say?"

"Oh, well ..." Lo Priore makes an ocean-roll gesture with the flat of his hand. "You mean, all of us go over to my place? Right *now?*"

I laugh my nastiest sneer.

Sandy grabs her purse off the table, opens it, pulls out a roll of hundred-dollar bills. She counts off ten, flings them onto the table in front of me. "*I* say Mr. LoPriore has a great collection," she snaps. "Are you going to put your money where your mouth is?"

I yawn, get up from the table, stretch, and give Sandy a supercilious smile. Then I stroll off through the bedroom into the bathroom and close the door behind myself.

Sandy will need about three minutes to rest her hand on LoPriore's hairy forearm, give him that red-lipped smile, tell him how I really had no right to talk to him that way and why doesn't he call my bluff and invite us over to see his things. Which would win her a thousand bucks and besides—she thinks when I see he's for real I'll be more inclined to sell him the Frisard.

Three minutes. I count them off.

As I come back to the table LoPriore stands up. "Tell you what, de Pinza," he rumbles. "Why *don't* we all go over to my place and I'll show you my collection."

His efforts to force out the hated words are so funny it's difficult not to smile; I manage by concentrating on what he'll do to me if he ever tumbles. "Nah." I brush away his invitation. "At this hour? For a couple of clunky—"

"Earl, it's only nine-thirty," Sandy says. "And I swear: you make one more crack about clunky Griesebaums and I'm going to ... *hit* you." She sticks her face into mine, shouts, "*I'm* going. Mom, Dad—you're coming, too, aren't you? Wouldn't *you* like to see Mr. LoPriore's collection?"

Gackle and Edna do a masterful job of looking back and forth at each other, then at me, then at Sandy. Finally, Gackle shrugs. "Well, yes." Edna smiles tentatively. "Seeing that Mr. LoPriore was nice enough to invite us I think we all ought to go. Including you, Earl."

Sandy gives me an I-win-you-lose toss of her head. "Come on, then," she says. "Let's go get a couple of cabs."

"No need for that." LoPriore flashes those wolfy teeth. "I live only a few minutes' walk from here."

"Oh," Edna says. "Is it ... safe, though?"

LoPriore laughs. "Eh, Mrs. de Pinza, when you're with Vincent LoPriore you don't have a thing to worry about."

Like his mother didn't.

His smile as we move toward the door says he's going to win as big as I'm going to lose, and the one pleases him as much as the other. But he still doesn't know what game he's really playing, and in that contest it's now double-check.

Very carefully—I'm not acting now—I pick up the beautiful little bird-temple, walk into the bedroom with it and make a point of shutting the door tightly. Then I walk to the closet, open the door. Big Al Resford blinks into the light of the room, steps out and stretches. "I trust all went according to plan," he says *sotto voce* as he takes the temple out of my hands.

All of a sudden I feel a thousand pounds lighter. "Went perfectly, Al. We're on our way."

"Very good." Big Al gently places the temple into its padded carrying case. "Then you'll not be needing me further at the moment. We're to meet at your place about midnight?"

"As close to as possible."

15

Balmy August night, a lovely short walk from the Regency Tower to the Carroll Parkside. As the doorman says, "Good evening, Mr. LoPriore" he puts his nose in grave danger of concrete burns. LoPriore barely gives him notice. I take care to give him even less.

We crowd into the elevator, get off on the third floor. Outside LoPriore's apartment our white-clad host turns a key in one lock; then as he inserts the second key he says gruffly, "Just a minute ... have to disable the alarm."

He pushes the door open; a steady beep sounds from inside. We all stand in place—all of us, that is, except Cleveland Gackle, that idiot, who starts forward as if he hadn't heard a word LoPriore said. I grab at Gackle's jacket; he stumbles, goes down at LoPriore's feet. "Sorry"—Gackle mutters up at LoPriore—"I slipped." He points at his feet. "New boots."

LoPriore, clearly disgusted, punches in four numbers on a keypad next to the door.

I bend to give Gackle a lift but he shoves me away. "Move, off, Earl, goddamn it. I'm okay. Don't need any help gettin' up."

LoPriore pushes a light switch. To this point, the only illumination was from a little lamp on a table under the keypad, but now the chandelier reveals the living room of a man who thinks big. Furniture antique and heavy, German-Austrian stuff that sells in fancy shops by both pound-weight and amount of carving. A massive sideboard on the far wall must have been taken completely to pieces to get it through the door. The beige, blue, and gold rug looks very much like one I saw a couple of months earlier at a Sotheby auction, a Bokhara that sold for $55,000—plus the usual 15% buyer's premium.

"Mr. de Pinza ..."

I turn to look at LoPriore, then realize he's addressing Gackle, not me. Gackle acknowledges him with a nod.

"You're from Montana, right? Lived there all your life?"

Gackle nods again.

"And you're in mining?"

"A third nod. "Mining engineering. Why?"

All of a sudden the room is too quiet.

"Why?" LoPriore's lips are like razor blades. "Because I'm thinkin' a man your age, a mining engineer from Montana, is about the least likely chunk of Adam's flesh I can think of to be falling-down stoned and stinking of marijuana. So I'm wondering what's going on here."

I'm wondering how soon I can kill Cleveland Gackle. LoPriore's hand moves ever so slightly toward the drawer of a small table, and I wonder whether I'll ever get that opportunity.

Edna steps forward—better, charges forward, snorting flames and smoke. "Mr. LoPriore, it just so happens my husband has cancer," she barks. "*Lung* cancer, gone into his bones. He never smoked a cigarette in his life; it was all that radioactive stuff down in the mines." She cuts loose a honker of a sob, pulls a handkerchief out of her purse, wipes at her eyes. "In France you can get marijuana from a doctor if you need it; Earl's been getting it for his daddy. It's the only thing that helps his pain and suffering. *That's* what's 'going on here,' Mr. LoPriore." She glares at him, then takes a step toward the door. I think it's time we left."

With every angry word from Edna, LoPriore's face gets redder, his mouth more twisted. Goddamn, I can see him think: She's going to have them all out the door in nothing flat, and there goes my Frisard bird temple. He puts a hand on Edna's shoulder. "Mrs. de Pinza, I *am* sorry. I never thought ... well, it just never occurred to me. I'm sorry for your husband's trouble and I apologize." He looks at Gackle. "You *are* okay, aren't you?"

Gackle waves off his concern. "Don't worry, Sonny; I ain't about to sue you. Anyway, it was my new boots. I just slipped, that's all. Forget about it. No harm done."

Edna's face says she'll accept the apology but not because she really wants to.

"Thank you." LoPriore gushes honey and molasses. He pats Gackle's arm, man-to-man, then gestures toward the rear of the room. "Right through that doorway to the collection. Mr. de Pinza, if you get tired I'll find you a comfortable chair."

Gackle nods thanks.

We walk down a hall, past several doors opening to the right, into the collection room. As LoPriore flips the light switch there comes a sound from my gang like that of a crowd at a Fourth of July fireworks display. Ooooooh, aaaaah.

The room is huge, about twenty by fifty, and it makes the Palace of Versailles look tawdry. A massive crystal chandelier glitters at the center of the ceiling; all around it are adjustable ceiling spotlights set to strategically illuminate the contents of the room.

And what contents! The far wall is taken up by bookshelves, and even from where we're standing it's obvious there are no

Modern Popular Library volumes. The whitewashed walls are hung with artwork having to do with birds: sketches, paintings in every imaginable medium, drawings, lithos both color and black-and-white. Scattered on pedestals through the room are bird sculptures, here one of a kingfisher in bronze, there one in inked *papier-mâché* of a heron. But all this is window dressing for the bird-related mechanical and musical items. Some of the larger pieces stand by themselves on custom-designed pedestals or wall shelves; others are within locked glass cases. But everything is strategically placed so as to draw the eye back to the far wall, where a large bird, magnificently set out in iridescent feathers, sits on a stand atop a giant painted urn. From either side of this bazooka hummingbird, garlands of artificial flowers twine their way up the wall to surround an enormous portrait of Mamma LoPriore, glaring down from her heights with an expression that could turn the entire contents of the kitchen refrigerator rancid. This whole room, then, this entire stupefying display of gorgeous birds, is LoPriore's shrine to his mother. Hail Birdie, full of piss and vinegar.

Gackle pulls out his handkerchief, mops at his forehead. I don't dare look at Edna. "Artwork from Leonardo to Kothenbeutel," LoPriore intones. "Audubon to Picasso. Over there is my library: I've got every important work on birds since Gutenberg, mostly first editions." He's looking at me directly now, eyelids drooping slightly, just the tiniest hint of a smile on his thin lips. "But you didn't come here to see books, eh? This"—he rests his hand against a large, two-bird cage hanging from an ornate wall bracket—"isn't worth your time. Sentimental value, that's all. I keep it because it was my first bird machine."

LoPriore smiles smugly, takes a tiny key from his pocket. "Ready to get your socks knocked off?" He unlocks the case in front of us, slides the glass door open. "Anyone gets past the door alarm and starts breaking cases, it sets off a three-way horn: loud siren here, beepers downstairs at the concierge's and at the closest cop shop."

"You don't take chances, do you?" Sandy chucks him an invitation if I ever heard one.

LoPriore turns his wolfy grin on her. "You bet I do, Honey, all the time. I take every chance I can get—except dumb ones. Them I leave for other people."

Wonder whom he might be talking about.

LoPriore carefully selects one of his thirty-two (I count them) bird boxes, an exquisite little oval creation of tortoiseshell, ivory, gold and silver with nicely-set pearls and a fine enamel painting on the lid. He pushes a button; up pops a tiny bird, all iridescent blue, green, and red. The little fellow moves its beak, head, wings, and tail in the most realistic fashion while it chirps an intricate birdsong.

Finally, performance finished, the bird drops abruptly back into the box. "Bruguier," LoPriore says smugly, replacing the miniature tweeter into the glass case. "All my bird boxes are by Bruguier, Jaquet-Droz, Maillardet, Frisard, Leschot, or Rochat." LoPriore sounds like a high priest at his altar. "Look as hard as you want, Mr. de Pinza. You won't find a single Griesebaum here, clunky or otherwise."

I nod politely.

LoPriore leads us to the next cabinet from which he takes two elegantly-worked wooden boxes. He opens them one at a time. Each is filled with gorgeous gold and mother-of-pearl needleworking tools constructed during the earliest days of the nineteenth century in the Palais Royal workshops of Paris. Centered in each box is an enameled medallion, one featuring floral garlands, the other a courtly scene. Small brilliantly feathered birds pop up from beneath the medallions, move about as they sing their songs, then disappear back into the recesses.

I'm on the cusp of flipping LoPriore a little compliment from the back of my hand, but instead I jump a foot as a gravelly voice, practically in my ear, shouts, "I say, Buddy, *nice* singing! *Very* good, what-what?" This odd statement is followed by a terrific squawk.

Sandy screams, then, embarrassed, covers her mouth with her hand. A colorful parrot, a riot of red, green, and yellow, is sitting on a low circular brass perch next to LoPriore. The parrot slowly raises one foot and tilts his head to the side, coming to regard me with one unblinking eye.

"I didn't know you had live birds," I say to LoPriore.

"I don't."

He probably wouldn't appreciate the observation but LoPriore looks as if he'd just swallowed a very tasty canary. "Look a bit closer, eh, Mr. de Pinza."

The bird is still moving on its perch; it raises a wing to pick underneath with its beak, and as it does I notice a small hole in its side with a winding arbor within. From behind me Edna stage-whispers, "Phalibois. How marvelous!"

Go depend on amateurs. Edna Reynolds, The Doll Lady of NYMBCA, long-time collector and restorer of automata, knows a mechanical animal of that quality and with that sort of humor built into its performance would likely be the work of Henry Phalibois, a late 19th-century French automaton maker. But how does Evelyn de Pinza, my gray-haired mother from Great Falls, Montana, come to spout this kind of arcane information? I hold my breath. Maybe it'll go past LoPriore.

I should live so long. Mein host is onto my mum like gangbusters. "Well, Mrs. de Pinza!" He leans forward from the waist, all the better, my dear, to leer at you. "Phalibois, eh? I didn't know you were a collector."

I get busy checking exit gates, but Edna doesn't miss a beat. "Oh, no," she says sweetly. "No, Mr. LoPriore, I'm afraid not. It's just that some of my son's activities ... well, rub off on me a bit. Earl, you remember, don't you? Last year, when we came to visit you in Paris, you took us to that man's store ... what was his name? Victor, yes, that's right. Victor D'Arcy. Such a nice fellow, with that shop full of old musical instruments and moving dolls and animals. Remember, we saw one of these parrots there, exactly like this one?"

Amateur though she may be, Edna Reynolds is one tough cookie. Victor D'Arcy is a dealer in antique musical instruments, mechanical and otherwise, with a beautiful shop right in the middle of Paris. Any serious mechanical music collector would instantly recognize the name Victor D'Arcy.

LoPriore obviously does. The corners of his mouth twitch hilariously as Edna says to him, "Mr. D'Arcy told us how it works—with one of those old-time recording cylinders inside. You can push a lever to set it on time-delay, so it seems to go off by itself. I'll bet that's what you just did, isn't it? Pushed the time-delay lever while you were walking past it to the showcase a couple of minutes ago?"

Advantage back to the good guys. With a few casual words my gray-haired mother from Great Falls both takes us out of immediate danger and cuts LoPriore's legs right out from under him, making his rare and amazing automaton seem practically commonplace. But Edna's not finished. "Is this the same one?" she asks LoPriore. "Did *you* buy Mr. D'Arcy's parrot?"

"No," LoPriore mutters as he replaces the workboxes into their case. "I've had Oscar for a long time." He gives Oscar's lever a petulant push. That's the last we'll hear from *that* bird tonight.

LoPriore closes the little lock on the glass showcase. All through his dog-and-birdie show his smile was almost genial, but now it's anything but. In the twin mirrors of his soul I see a promise that I'm going to pay for not only my own sins, but those of my mother as well.

"Look in these cases over here," LoPriore snarls as he leads us to two fair-sized glass enclosures along the west wall of the room, "You don't want to miss what's in *them*."

That was a you-Mister, not a you-all, directed to Earl de Pinza, telling him he'd better make damn sure to pick up loud and clear.

The cases are filled with small boxes, set neatly onto seven full-length risers arranged like bleachers. In the center of the left case a round pedestal interrupts the middle riser to display a magnificent box, rectangular with cut corners, and ornamented lavishly with enamel and diamonds. Two round medallions are set into the top at equal distances from the ends, the left bearing an enamel miniature of Napoleon; the right, Josephine. Not that I'd ordinarily recognize Josephine, but I've seen this particular representation of her more times than I can count—in Hugh Curtis's living room. As LoPriore takes the box out of the case I want to cut off his fingers.

LoPriore pushes the start lever; an elegant comb and cylinder mechanism begins to play a delightful French tune. Two miniature birds pop up from beneath the medallions, face each other, and sing accompaniment, at times as alternating solos, at other times as a duet. When the music stops and the birdsong ceases, the little singers turn to face their human audience for an instant, then disappear. An altogether wonderful performance except for the sneering, insulting face hanging over the stage like an malevolent god.

"See?" LoPriore opens a little hinged door at the rear of the case. "This is a snuffbox; the snuff went into the compartment here. A musical snuffbox with double singing birds. Guy owned it didn't want to sell ... but I can be persuasive. In the end I got his whole collection. He could've sold me just the double-bird

snuffbox but he didn't want to do that. Sooooo ..." LoPriore
makes a show of returning his treasure to its pedestal. "You
want to hear any of the others?"

"No." I wave my hand in imperious dismissal. "I didn't
come here to be bored to death by stuff I've seen a million
times already. Your double bird there's nice but not really
special. A Leschot, isn't it? Marked on the underside of the
base, just to the left of the spring assembly."

I could flick a quarter, ping! off my finger, right into
LoPriore's mouth. "How ... how the hell did you know *that?*"
he growls. "The maker, okay. But the site of the mark? The
exact site?"

"Easy. I have one myself. Could have had another last year,
but what did I need two for? I let a friend buy it." I look slowly
around the room. "I guess I don't understand what's such a big
deal. You've got other Leschot pieces."

"Sure I do. But I didn't have a Leschot double-bird snuffbox."

"Oh." I shrug indifferently, hoping the chill I feel isn't
showing. But worse is on the way. LoPriore leans over to come
face to face with me. "I *wanted* it." His voice is soft but hoarse
with passion. "And *he* didn't want to sell. I don't take no for
an answer, de Pinza. I hope you don't have to find that out
for yourself."

Cleveland Gackle clears his throat, then raises his hand
like a third-grader. "Sorry, Mr. LoPry-oree but I got to use,
you know. The facilities."

LoPriore points absently toward the living room. "Go back
the way we came in; then go out the other doorway into the
hall. Third room on your left."

"Much obliged," Gackle drawls. He makes a hat-tipping
motion, hustles out the door.

LoPriore watches Gackle shuffle away, then turns his attention back to us. Against the dark skin of his face, his den-

tal arsenal stands out white and sharp. "Okay, now we're warmed up," he says. "Time for the good stuff."

Those teeth, perfectly spotted in a beam from one of the overhead track lights, shine like shivs. LoPriore is the most dangerous kind of predatory animal: calculating, clever—and thoroughly unpredictable. No rhinoceros, he: lower head and charge. You may know he's coming, but never from which direction.

So here comes LoPriore, showing his good stuff. A singing bird in a hanging cage of gold, with a fine enamel-faced clock on the underside. Jaquet-Droz, circa 1795. Another cage with a mother bird inside, feeding her open-beaked, chirping babies to the tune of a lovely little *sur plateau* musical movement. A caged duet by Leschot—stylized birdcage eighteen inches high, gold inlaid with pearls and turquoises, with a watch on the front of the base. The watch strikes the hour, then plays music on a fine comb-and-cylinder movement while two golden automaton figures strum a harp and a guitar, and two birds sing accompaniment. Another trinket by Leschot: an automaton clock with an hourly display featuring a bird that hops on the ground, cocks its head, and sings a duet with a herdsman's flute. As the tiny fingers of the herdsman move over his instrument, his eyes dart back and forth, watching a cat pounce repeatedly but unproductively at his feathered musical partner.

LoPriore seems to take special delight in an automaton of a young woman sitting on a sofa, turning the curved brass crank of a tiny, high-pitched organ. A bird tries to repeat the tune but incorrectly; its mistress shakes her head sadly. Then she plays the organ a second time; now the little bird gets the tune right. The young woman's face shows joy; she appears to toss the bird a bit of seed from a dish; this sends the little fellow into joyous song, all trills and embellishments, a French folk melody called "*Malbrouck se'en va t'en Guerre.*" You know it as "The Bear Went Over the Mountain." Or if you're British, "We Won't Be Home Until Morning." Or if you're a Rotarian, "For He's a Jolly Good Fellow." Or if you dig classical music, the theme for the French Army in Beethoven's tone poem, "Wellington's Victory."

As the exquisite performance ends, LoPriore flashes teeth. "Like that, eh? Well, better hold on. That was just the *good* stuff. Now for the *very* good stuff."

We follow him across the room to a table on which sits a small (that's to say about twenty inches high) earthenware vase with an elegantly-feathered bird perched atop it. If the song and movements of this bird are primitive by comparison to the previous examples, it's understandable because the automaton was made by Agostino Ramelli in the sixteenth century. Water and air circulate inside the vase, simultaneously producing the song and the movements of wings and tail; then the water cascades down in the form of fountains and waterfalls to recirculate to the interior.

At this point Gackle finally returns from his journey, tiptoeing through the room to join us in front of a mechanism by the seventeenth-century Huegenot Salomon deCaus, who—according to LoPriore—is said to have invented the steam engine. The deCaus automaton features an owl-teacher and four songbird-pupils. The owl turns to face each songbird, which performs as if on command, then becomes silent as the owl addresses the next pupil. The birdsongs are the product of an organ hidden in the wooden case beneath the tableau; the entire mechanism is powered by hydraulics.

While LoPriore demonstrates this amazing trinket, Gackle and Edna stand behind me whispering. I shush them but it's useless. Finally I turn around. "Mother, Dad, if you're not interested in these, would you at least be quiet while *I'm* hearing them?"

"I'm sorry, Son." Edna rests her hand on my arm. "All that water, it makes me have to go. I was asking Dad where's the ladies' room."

Gackle takes Edna by the elbow. "Come on, Evelyn, I'll just take you. Be easier that way."

I watch with relief as they leave, then turn back to the show. Sandy's eyes are glued to LoPriore. Sammy, on the other hand, looks here, there, all around the room. Probably trying to figure the selling price of the collection individually and in aggregate.

LoPriore's losing his battle to stay cool. "Now here ..." He clears his throat, moves his hand toward a piece I've been trying not to stare at since we came into the room. It's an automaton clock on an oval ormolu table, the gold-leafed wooden clockbase carved in a graceful floral pattern. A large oval-headed key protruding from the far end of the base tells me there's wonderful music inside. On the right portion of the base stands the trapezoidal clock with its dial of intricately arced ormolu and colorful enamelwork, twelve Roman numerals set in gold, and filigreed golden hands. Atop the clock is a gold-framed mirror; a saucy bird, beautifully feathered in red and black, perches on the inside post. Looking up at him from the left side of the base is a golden figure of a young woman in a flowing robe. Her face shows tenderness and concern; her right hand is raised toward the bird, index finger outstretched.

LoPriore sniggers. "Not exactly a Griesebaum, eh, Mr. de Pinza? Martineau, circa eighteen forty, with a first-class, four-tune David Lecoultre comb and cylinder. Works on the hour if you want, but also goes at will. Watch close."

He reaches behind the clock, pulls a round-headed brass pin. The air instantly fills with a clear, sweet arrangement of the overture to Rossini's "Thieving Magpie." First-class music

indeed, basically a mandoline arrangement but with interspersed simultaneous runs up and down the comb teeth that
whip every hair on my body to attention. The young woman
slowly extends her golden arm toward the bird, who responds
by cocking its head, fluttering its wings, and gliding down a
nearly invisible wire to light on her finger. Now the music
shifts from the single-note reiterations of mandoline arrangement to rapid, bird-like trills, and the little red-and-black bird
sings along, delivering its melody directly into the delighted
face of the woman. With the final chords of the music the
bird turns suddenly, flutters back up the wire to its perch
above the mirror, and the young woman lowers her hand.
Musically, visually, a performance no less than extraordinary.

Sandy gawks without reserve; even Sammy looks genu-
inely impressed. Since LoPriore pulled the start pin I've been
fighting to keep my sneer of untouched superiority intact. It
hasn't been easy.

"Nice, eh?" LoPriore nods an answer to his own question.
"When the clock sets if off on the hour, it also chimes. But,
hey—there's more."

Not so fast, I think, and say, "David Lecoultre musicworks,
you said. Comb has all soldered dampers then, doesn't it?"

Bingo. If LoPriore's not careful he's going to dislocate his
jaw. For just an instant his face asks how the *hell* did I know
that? Simple. LoPriore's collecting interest is birds; for him the
music is incidental. But I collect fine cylinder music boxes, so
I know that although damper wires are usually fixed with tiny
brass pins into tiny round holes beneath the tips of the comb
teeth, David Lecoultre, a maker of outstanding Swiss cylinder
boxes during the early nineteenth century, often soldered his
dampers directly to the undersides of the teeth. And if you've
ever had to replace a set of those dampers—as I have—you've
probably cursed Lecoultre to the hottest regions of hell—as I

have—for his hideous idiosyncrasy as you hacked your exasperated way through a jungle of inexact wire attachements, melted lead tuning weights, and sizzling fingers.

LoPriore dismisses my zinger with a casual wave and a muttered, "Sure, soldered dampers. What else?" He moves quickly to the next table, shows us three amazing birdcages from the mid-eighteenth century, one by Leschot, the others by Eppinger and Defrance. The caged birds are life-sized and amazingly lifelike in song and movement. They even jump from limb to limb inside their cages. LoPriore tells us Defrance's was displayed in the Tuileries Palace in 1746. And no, they're not real birds, restored by some genius taxidermist. Only the feathers can claim prior existence. These are scratch-made chirp-and-twitter machines with metal bodies and beaks of bone or ivory, each a work of daunting originality and competence.

A moist cough from Gackle announces the return of my parents. Mother looks tired; Dad, solicitous. "I'm sorry, Earl, but I think we need to go back," Edna says. "I'm worn out ... jet lag, I suppose."

"But we haven't seen half of Mr. LoPriore's collection!"

The look on Edna's face brings me back to reality. Fortunate that some of my crew can stay tone-deaf to the Sirens of mechanical music. "All right, Mother—you did have a long trip, didn't you?" I look sideways at LoPriore. "Well, thanks. Enjoyed the visit. I've got to admit, you do have a nice little collection."

He looks as if he might split his gut.

"Yes, thank you, Mr. LoPriore," Edna says. "It was *very* interesting."

Gackle sticks his hand forward. "Much obliged, LoPryoree." He pumps the hand of our host as if trying to bring forth water from LoPriore's mouth.

LoPriore brushes off Edna and Gackle like a pair of pesky gnats. "What do you say, Mr. de Pinza?" he rumbles at me.

"Wouldn't your bird-temple fit right in here? Come on, now—what's your price?" Again the teeth.

I take aim at the Achilles heel, pray my shot is on target. This guy has not an ounce of tolerance for frustration. I think about the cage he showed us with Mamma Bird and the babies: Little Vincent must have had only to squawk and Mamma filled his open beak with a juicy worm. I need to get him really pissed *and* afraid he might lose out on something he wants. Shift him into rhino mode.

I set my feet. John Wayne. Skewer LoPriore with my eyes. "I don't like your attitude," I say slowly. "Back off. I've been talking trade with someone who's got a music box I'm interested in, and—"

"Just tell me who." LoPriore is practically vibrating, hopping from one foot to the other. "Like I said—I don't take no. Tell me who and I'll get you that music box. Then—"

"I don't need your help," I snap. "In case you haven't figured, *I* get what *I* want, too. If I want to sell you the bird-temple, *I'll* call *you*, not the other way around. Kapeesh, Goombar?"

Mission accomplished. LoPriore's face could bring a grizzly bear to cardiac standstill.

I turn like a soldier on dismissal, march back into the living room, Edna, Gackle, and Sammy on my heels. Sandy, however, lingers in the Collection Room. That's so she can sidle up to LoPriore, whisper to him to cool it. Just give her a little working space and he'll end up with the bird-temple, she'll end up with his payment, I'll end up totally screwed, and how would he like that?

Just how much he'd like that is obvious from his smile as he comes out of the room with Sandy.

16

Half-past midnight. The gang is in my workshop, chatting in pairs and threes, chowing down on cake and coffee Sarah had ready for us when we came in. God forbid a hardworking gang of con artists should go hungry.

"Time to roll," I call out.

They look at me, full-mouthed—everyone but Hugh Curtis at my left. "You see my things?" Hugh asks tersely.

"All there, don't worry. We'll have 'em packed in ten minutes, tops."

"I had one hundred thirty-four snuffboxes."

"I got one thirty-three," I say, "plus the Leschot, star of the show, sitting on a little round pedestal right in the middle. One-three-four. Okay?"

"Wiseass." Hugh turns away, drains his cup of coffee.

"Now"—I hold up a pad of yellow pages—"Al and I added up what LoPriore's things ought to be worth. My estimate wasn't even close."

All of a sudden no one's eating.

"We were hoping for five million—a half-mill for each of us. But it looks like we might get twice that."

"Jesus, Doc!" Frank the Crank rocks back in his chair. Next to him, Schwartz takes off his fedora, runs a handkerchief across his forehead, then clamps the omnipresent hat back on.

"Put it this way," I say. "The Breguets, Bruguiers; the Jaquet-Droz and Rochats—we know they're big bucks. But trying to put prices on LoPriore's very early pieces is like trying to appraise a unicorn. Twenty million all together if we weren't in a hurry? Fifty? It's blue sky territory. But we have to move the things fast and all at once; we can't be too greedy. A million apiece ought to hold us for a while."

Big Al Resford breaks the murmur. "There's a point we should p'aps consider, Thomas."

"What's that?"

"About those ancient pieces: it's quite clear how badly Mr. LoPriore needs to own things. Now just suppose he decided he must have a deCaus—or a Ramelli or an Eppinger or a deFrance—but none were known to exist, let alone be available for purchase. Might he not—very quietly, to be sure—have commissioned those pieces? There are some very fine constructive artists on the Continent."

I never thought of that. The articles in question appeared so finely made and so appropriately old I never gave a thought to the possibility of forgery. But there was no denying the possibility of Al's hypothesis, distasteful as it was. "Fair point," I say. "Is there some way we could authenticate them?"

I know the answer before it comes. Big Al shakes his head slowly. "Not 'til they're across the pond, I'm afraid. Given the talents who'd have been involved, dismantling would likely be necess'ry, p'aps even a bit of chemical analysis."

"All right, next question. If every one of those rarities is a dud can we still clear five million?"

"Oh yes. With that number of top-quality bird boxes and miniature automata? I should be disappointed if we get less."

Poor Espinoza looks like a starving man suddenly force-fed too rich a diet. A couple of days ago he was staring at the wrong end of coercion and eviction; now it looks as if he'll be able to keep his home and business in any style to which he'd like to become accustomed.

"Sounds good to me," says Frank the Crank. "Half a million apiece."

"More than I usually get for a couple nights' work." Soapy Sandy bats her long eyelashes at Mick the Dick.

"Okay, then. We're going to need a big roll of plastic bubblewrap. Also, Lyons Rent-A-Truck sells heavy-sided cardboard boxes, all different sizes. Hugh, Gackle, how about you pick them up in the morning? Six big ones ought to do it. We'll leave them broken down flat, carry them out the window at the Regina, down the fire escape, up through the service entrance to LoPriore's, set them up there. Knife and a roll of clear plastic tape. Now, who's going up to pack up and haul out?" I scan the room. "Me, Hugh, Sammy. Gackle and Dassidario will be there, but they'll have their own work to do. And Schwartz and Sarah're going to be keeping track of Sandy while she's with LoPriore—"

"Schwartz and *who?*"

Sarah is on her feet, furious. "I thought just Schwartz was going to be doing that. When did I come in?"

Casual shrug. "I said both of you, last night. You must have missed it."

Sarah Heartburn addresses her audience. "Did *any* of you hear him say that? *Anybody* in this room?"

"Whoa, wait," I shout. "Sarah, I think I said it but if I didn't I apologize. In a fancy restaurant a couple's less obvious than a single man. Besides—a nice dinner in a good restaurant: piece of cake. What's the problem?"

I usually don't ask a question when *I* know I won't like the answer. If we were alone Sarah would tell me loud and clear that an evening on the town with Broadway Schwartz in no way resembles her idea of a piece of cake, and by the way when was the last time *I* took her out for such an evening? But in company I'm safe. Sarah doesn't say a word, just drums fingers on the table next to her.

"Better than just sitting here, biting your nails, waiting and wondering." I say.

Her little smile tells me I've won the skirmish but I'll pay.

"Okay, settled. Mick—you're going to get the truck, have it there on time. And we want Frank ready and waiting at his store when we get there with the goodies. "Al ..."

Big Al watches patiently as I give my new idea a quick mental once-over. Sure, why not? "Al, you were going to wait with Frank at the shop—but why don't you help pack. You can go to Frank's in the truck with the boxes."

"Yes, of course." Al approves the change. "No reason for me to be idle all that time."

"Good. Then we'll have four of us. Plus maybe Gackle or Dassidario, if they have any spare time."

"Thomas, are you ignoring me purposely or are you simply being stupid?"

Edna the Doll Lady. Never minces words, only opponents. "Neither," I say. "Edna, it's just that at your—"

"At my age and in my condition? Is that what you mean?"

"Well, yes. That *was* what I was going to say."

"Don't bother," she snaps. "Maybe I *am* seventy and maybe I've had a couple of small strokes. But I am still perfectly capable of going down one level of a fire escape and up three flights of stairs. And it just so happens I've packed and shipped more fragile and valuable dolls and automata than I suspect you've ever seen."

I work hard at not smiling.

"Wipe that shit-eating grin off your face or I'll do it for you." Edna's dudgeon is at an all-time high. "I'll tell you this much: I'm not about to sit around here wondering whether you puppies are getting it right. Maybe I can't go down the stairs afterward with a full box—but you just figure on five packers."

"Five it is," I say, my face still unwiped. "Broadway: you've got that driver's license?"

"Hey, Doc, what do you think?" Schwartz pulls a small card from his shirt pocket. I look at it and laugh. "Beautiful. Axel Moncrief, huh?" I hand the card to Mick the Dick. "Here you are, Axel. Take good care of it. And drive carefully."

Soapy Sandy leans over, looks hard, makes a terrible face. "Oh, gross! Mick ... that's you?"

"With a little help from Edna," I say. "Don't worry; it washes right off. We don't want anyone recognizing your handsome husband and sending him up for twelve to twenty, do we?"

"No." Sandy pretends to pout. "I'd get lonely."

I'll bet, I think, but I don't say it. "What about you?" I ask Edna. "Did you get what you need to know about LoPriore?"

"Every bit. I've seen his face plenty long and close enough. Got a good handle on his clothes, too. When your father"—she rolls her eyes in Gackle's direction—"was supposed to be taking me to the john he was actually walking me through our friend's bedroom. I checked his closet and bureau drawers. Pants: white linen or light worsted; I'll pick up a couple of pairs in the morning and alter them. Eight possibilities for the shirt: white cotton or silk, sport shirt or turtleneck, long sleeves or short. I'll get one of each. When he leaves his place to go pick up Sandy, someone needs to be watching and let me know what he's wearing."

"Somebody LoPriore hasn't seen and never will see during the whole operation." I run eye tape over Big Al, bulging comfortably in his customary three-piece suit, bowler hat on the floor next to his chair. "Al, do you think you could, well ... step out of character a little for the occasion? Be a little less obvious?"

Edna chuckles. "I'll pick him up a shirt and a pair of summer slacks off the rack at Macy's. No one'll give him a second look."

"Great." I take a deep breath before plunging into the unpredictable currents at the far end of the pool. "Gackle, how about you? Get all the information you need?"

"Far as I can tell," comes the not-unexpected answer.

"Tell us."

Gackle leans back in his chair, lifts his cowboy-booted feet, rests them on the low coffee table. Sarah's whole body goes rigid. "Man's got a good arrangement," Gackle drawls. "Like he told us himself. That's a Rumley Guardian Angel alarm system, fine as they come. Try walkin' in there without pushin' the right buttons on the keypad and off it goes: A person couldn't hear himself think. Inside of thirty seconds you're toast. Here comes the apartment super up the stairs, with a battalion a cops right behind him. Yep." Gackle smiles, nods vigorously. "They don't come better than a Rumley."

"I'm glad you have such admiration for the opposition," I say. "Do you also have some idea how to get around it?"

"No problem," Gackle says laconically. "The keypad numbers're one-eight-nine-two. Just push 'em, same as he did. It'll shut right off."

"But how do you know ..." Then the penny drops. "*That's* why you took that fall."

"Sure. Person starts punching numbers into his keypad, ninety-nine times out of a hundred he ain't gonna stop 'til he finishes, no matter what. You could shoot him, he wouldn't drop over dead 'til after he hit the two. Soon's I saw LoPriore's finger move I went down. I was just hopin' you weren't gonna get in my way ... trying to help me."

"Sorry," I say over Sammy Shapiro's snicker. "Okay, Cleveland ... is that really what people call you? Cleveland?"

"Uh-uh." Gackle shakes his head. "Pete, usually. Or sometimes Alex. My old man was a big baseball fan, and happened I was born the day Grover Cleveland Alexander—they used to call him Alex or Pete; don't know why Pete, but anyway—I was born the day back in 'twenty-six when he come outa the bullpen hung over like a son of a bitch and struck out Tony Lazzeri to lock up the World Series. I woulda been Grover Cleveland Alexander Gackle but there was only three spaces on the birth certificate so here I am, Cleveland Alexander Gackle. Pete."

Old Pete, hung over on booze, throws three strikes past one of the most dangerous batters in the American League. His namesake, flying on grass, casually disposes of a slugger at least as scary. Who am I to argue? For all I suddenly care Gackle can claim the cost of his pot on this job as a business expense. "That's why you introduced yourself as Pete de Pinza," I say.

Gackle shrugs.

"Fine. Back to the locks. What about the ones on the display cases?"

"Those dinky things?" Gackle's scorn is withering. "They won't be no more problem than one on an airline suitcase." He fumbles in a pocket, finds a little chain of tools which he swings in front of his face like a clock pendulum. "I got a pick here'll open any one of them, bingo! Don't even have to think about it."

"How about the door locks?"

"Now there's something else altogether." Gackle swings his legs off the coffee table, sits up. "The regular door-lock, that's nothing. I could pick it, loid it, whatever; have it open faster'n LoPriore could with the key. Problem's the deadbolt; it's a Winchester SuperSec ... that means supersecurity."

"I'd have never thought of that," I say.

My sarcasm bounces off Gackle's hide. "Oh, it's a honey, all right. They call it their pickproof deadbolt and it damn near is just that. Got all sorts of extry features—captive double deadbolt arrangement, saw-resistant steel, heavy-duty reinforced strike, full of collars and shields ... whew!" He scratches behind his left ear. "Even if we didn't care about not leaving any signs of a breakin it'd still be one hell of a job."

"Pete. The question is, can you get past it?"

For answer, the maddening Gackle shrug. "I might ... but more likely I might not."

I look at him; he looks at me. "Well, not without leaving some mark or other on the door or the lock," he adds quickly. "Especially on the inside of the lock."

"So what're we going to do?"

"Only one thing *to* do. Use the key."

"Oh, thank you, Pete. Right, great idea. We'll use the key! I'll go right now, give LoPriore a call, ask him to lend me the key to his apartment for tomorrow night so we can rip him off. Why didn't I think of that earlier?"

If I could bottle Gackle's immunity to sarcasm I'd win the Nobel. "No needa that, Doctor," he says pleasantly, then reaches into his pocket. "Got it right here." He smiles, dangles the key in front of my nose. "We'll walk right in and out again, easy as pie."

Somehow I manage keep my voice even. "All right. Tell us."

"Warn't no trouble," says Gackle, and now, no mistake, there's mischief in his eyes. "Just a matter of knowing what people do. There's *always* extry keys in a house, and ninety-nine times out of a hundred they're in one place outa three: in with the socks and underwear, at the back of a top middle desk drawer, or inside some kitchen container or other. When I was supposed to be in the head I checked the bureau drawers, but no dice. So I went into the den and sure enough—

right at the back of the top middle desk drawer. Other keys there, too, maybe ten or so, but I left the rest. Take 'em all, there's more chance of him noticin'. Now, a person can't have these keys copied, at least not legally. Company's got an arrangement with the locksmiths. But I 'spect Broadway knows somebody who could help us, ain't I right?"

Gackle flips the key to Schwartz, who reaches out to make a neat catch, then grins and pockets the key.

"We'll leave the original back in the drawer tomorrow," Gackle says. "Then we can lock the deadbolt from outside with the copy—after we reset the alarm."

"Told you he was the best, Doc." Schwartz's two-penny contribution.

"I never doubted you, Broadway," I say, coming as close as I ever do to crossing out of Storyland into Lietown. "Okay, Pete, now the service door—you checked that out on your own this afternoon?"

"Yep. No trouble there. Just a Sarti single deadbolt with a pushbar on the inside, it's got to be at least twenty, twenty-five years old. I'll have that sucker open inside of a minute."

"And the safe?"

"In the bedroom, inside the wall of his clothes closet. Martinsdale, three-number combination, with a hundred-number dial."

"Well? And spare me the maybe you can and maybe you can't."

"A person never can be sure." Cleveland Gackle *will* make his point. "But I've opened my share of Martinsdales and then some. I s'pect it'll be yawnin' before you get the first carton packed up."

"Great. Now, Sandy—"

"Or at least by the second carton," Gackle drawls.

I give him a weary look—not difficult at that hour of morning, after the day I've put in. "Okay, Sandy. How'd you do?"

Soapy Sandy holds up a passport-size photograph. "I was getting a little worried," she says. "He's not an easy guy to get close to. But when you went out of the room there at the end I nailed it." Little nervous giggle. "I was just hoping the old lady wasn't going to yell down from the wall there, 'Hey Vinnie, she's got her hand in your pocket.'"

I squint at the picture, a miniature version of the central icon in The Shrine of Our Lady of Perpetual Intimidation. No question, I blink first. Birdie LoPriore was obviously nobody's pushover, a battleax with a bun of gray hair pulled severely to the back of her head. The way she'd glared into the camera suggested the photographer had said cheese and she was severely lactose-intolerant. "Bet life was no fun for Vinnie when he got a B in school or threw an interception," I say, as I slip the photo into my pocket. "One more thing: Sammy."

"Yo, my man."

"Go straight home from here. Call LoPriore; really turn the screws. Tell him you damn well don't intend to let a weasel like him pull a whizzer on you, and if he doesn't have whatever it takes to get that bird-temple, then you—Saul Schifrin—have other clients who do. Get him as sore as you can, I mean *really* pissed. Get him reckless."

Sammy grins. This idea appeals to him in a big way. He claps his hands, dances a little jig in place, then waves his hand as though he were hailing a bus. "Got a question, my man." He snaps fingers in my face. "All that other stuff in the apartment: that library ... the *art work*. We're leaving a damn fortune there, dig?"

The room fills with murmur. This has to be stopped fast. "The birds are LoPriore's heart and soul," I say. "Let's not go grabby. Never mind it'd be tough lugging all that stuff out of there; never mind artwork and books would be harder to make disappear in a hurry than rare mechanical birds. The real problem is if we strip the place we won't be able to play the last act according to script—which means none of us'd ever feel safe again."

"Thomas is quite right," murmurs Big Al. "A clean shot through the heart is terribly efficient, don't you know. Stop the heart beating, the liver and kidneys will die as well."

Al has a way with words. He also has a way with Sammy, not at all surprising. A fast-talking, sharp-dressing grifter like My Man has a short career if he doesn't own a good sense of when the con's not working. Sammy's hands, waving in front of his face, look like a pair of hysterical little white birds. "Okay, okay," he says. "Figure I didn't say word one. Just thinkin' a little, that's all."

"We need to be thinking," I say. "There's always the possibility something might go wrong and we'd need to make a quick adjustment."

"But we don't want to do anything to make it more likely something will go wrong—do we, Mr. Shapiro?" Big Al, smiling as always.

Sammy reads. He isn't smiling. "Oh, no," he says. "Definitely not."

I tell everyone to get a good night's rest, sleep late. Sandy, practically twitching on her chair, pokes Mick's ribs. "Hey, I'm wired, couldn't fall asleep right now if you paid me," she says. "Let's go take a walk down Broadway, sneak preview, you know. Like we're going to do when the game's done and we're living over here."

Mick looks from his wife to me; the left corner of his mouth twists upward into a sheepish little smile. This guy is no slouch, but it must a full-time job trying to keep up with Sandy, whether on the street or between the sheets. Does he ever wonder what's going to happen when he's forty, say, or fifty, and his lungs, heart and dick just can't cut it at that pace anymore?

He turns back to Sandy, grins. "Sure, baby. You want to walk on Broadway, we'll hop a bus, go walk on Broadway. Come on."

Maybe he doesn't wonder. He's a detective, and maybe he's learned from his work—just as I have—that a lot of people never make it to forty or fifty. Seize the night, Mick.

"Five tomorrow afternoon," I say. "Everyone back here. Game time."

Chairs scrape the floor as everyone gets up to leave. Hugh Curtis, suddenly deathly pale, grabs my arm. I reach out to support him, lower him slowly back into his chair. "Hugh, what's wrong?"

"Don't know," he mutters. "Dizzy."

The gang gathers to watch as I push Hugh's head down between his legs; after a moment he groans, "No ... no good." Schwartz and Sammy make room as he slides onto the floor, rolls to his side. Big beads of sweat form at his hairline.

I reach for his wrist. "Pulse's kind of fast, little weak. Do you have any pain, Hugh? In your chest?"

"Uh-uh." He shakes his head ever so slightly, then abandons that as a bad move. "I ... was fine ... but when I got up, all of a sudden ... I was dizzy as hell." He takes in a deep breath, blows it out, repeats the sequence. "I think ... I'm getting better."

I check his pulse again. "Slowing down. Sarah?"

I'm about to tell her to go into my bedroom, get my medical bag but I should have known. She's already making her way past Al, holding the little black satchel out to me. I grab my stethoscope, pull Hugh's shirt up toward his face, listen to his chest. "Heart sounds fine. Still feeling better, Hugh?"

"Long as I don't raise my head."

I get to my feet. "Hugh, this's never happened to you before, has it?"

"I've never passed out in my life," he calls up from the floor. "Never even came close."

"Okay. Maybe just a little viertigo—maybe from a middle ear virus, who knows? You'll probably feel fine in the morning. Stay over here tonight, sleep on the sofa like you did last week."

17

Next morning Hugh feels great. "Can't imagine what happened to me," he says as he scarfs down pancakes as fast as I flip them from the skillet onto his plate. "When I stood up, the whole world started spinning."

I'm going to check you over," I say. "Soon as we're done eating. I called my nurse, told her to set me up a room."

"Thomas, I don't need a goddamn—"

"*I* don't need a packer and hauler on split-second timing tonight who might go down right at the scene of the crime. Listen, Hugh: there're thirteen people on your team in this game. Maybe you were just tired, maybe it was your emotions—but I need to make sure. I'm going to give you a complete physical and a couple of tests, and ... I'm going to run a urine screen. Check for alcohol metabolites."

"You bastard!" Hugh slams down his fork. "You don't trust me?"

"Relax." I lean over the table into his face, holding the empty skillet as if I might just use it to induce anesthesia. "The first thing they teach you in med school is never trust anyone, and fact is it's a damn good rule. You wouldn't believe some of the stuff that's come out in my office over the past twenty years. Think about it: On whose account have we got thirteen people playing a high-stakes game?"

Hugh goes red, then picks up his fork. "All right, all right—but you'll see. There's nothing the matter with me. It'll be a waste of time for both of us."

"Not really," I say. "Making me feel better has to count for something."

"Well, what did you find?"

Hugh, wearing only his undershorts, sits on the edge of my office examining table. Most patients in that position and condition have an air of vulnerability but Hugh looks formidable, hulking and hairy. His shorts with their broad red and white stripes look like the sort of garment a man might wear as he climbs into the ring to fight for the heavyweight championship of the world.

I shake my head. "You're healthy as a horse. Heart, lungs check out fine; normal neurological. EKG, EEG: both okay. Blood and urine're still out; they'll have the results by two this afternoon. I'll call in to check."

"Huh!" Hugh lowers himself to the floor. "Feel better, Doctor? May I get dressed now?"

I sit down at the little worktable, begin to write on the chart. "Yeah, go ahead, get dressed. We're done. I'll just finish up here, then I'm supposed to meet Sarah for lunch."

"That's something new." Hugh chuckles. "I don't remember you ever running over to meet Sarah for lunch on a workday."

I check the office door; it's shut. "She's never been involved in a multimillion dollar kickover," I say softly.

"Problems?"

"Just Sarah being Sarah. No, I don't really think any problems. Sometimes it's hard to get her to say yes, but when she does she's in with both feet." I smile. "I just think the feet are a little cold. Better if I can warm them up."

Hugh laughs. "You can do that."

18

Sarah's waiting outside Planned Parenthood. I look at my watch: quarter to twelve. "No, you're not late," she says. "I'm early. For some reason I was having trouble concentrating."

"I wonder why." I take her hand; we start down the sidewalk.

"Is Hugh all right?" she asks.

"He's fine. Just a bit of nerves, I think."

That earns me her wait-a-minute look. "Thomas, I absolutely can't understand how you can be so calm."

"I'm a little on edge."

"A little?" She stops walking, stares at me. People brush past us, not looking, not noticing. New York in August. "You do realize what it is you're doing?"

"Sure," I say lightly. "But let's don't discuss it out here."

There's a DELI sign a couple of doors down the block. I take Sarah by the elbow, steer her along the sidewalk, into the deli, all the way back to a corner table. "Here." I pull out the chair for her. "Sit down, talk. But quietly, get it?"

"Thomas, you're beginning to sound like a gangster. You're even behaving like one."

I start to laugh, then slide into the chair opposite her, lean across the table. "What can I say?" I whisper. "I do something, I do it right."

"But that's just the point," she hisses. "If this ... *job* of yours isn't done right, people are going to get hurt. You get crazy ideas—and I end up getting involved in them." She holds up a hand. "I'm not finished. I'm worried you may have gone overboard with this one. Last Christmas when you were determined to play detective and solve those music box murders—"

"If I hadn't, the case wouldn't have been solved. Ever."

A pickle-faced waiter saunters over, slings two menus onto the table between us, walks away. Sarah seems not to notice. "But you came pretty close to getting yourself killed then, didn't you? And what you're up to this time is actually illegal. Breaking and entering, Thomas? Grand larceny? Can't you see that?"

"Sure." I take her hand between mine. "But it's the only way to set matters straight. My good friend has been robbed and swindled. His wife's been killed. If I do nothing, that killing goes down as an accident and Hugh has zero chance of getting his collection back."

"Who gives you authority, Thomas?"

"Who died and left me boss? How about Madeleine Curtis?" Point, Purdue.

Sarah taps a finger on the table, tries to regroup. "All right," she says. "Then why can't you just take back Hugh's collection of snuff boxes? That's what was stolen. That's what he'd get back if he could go to court."

"Sarah, please. Think about it for a minute. If all we do is grab Hugh's things LoPriore will know Hugh was involved, and he'll only start by making hamburger out of him. But our game makes sure LoPriore won't be able to do anything to anyone. He gets a punishment to fit his crime; we fulfill our responsibility to society."

"Thomas, I swear—you can talk anything away. Consorting with these criminals your friend Schwartz dug up. That

Cleveland Gackle character. Fenton Dassidario. Soapy Sandy Stickyfingers and Mick the Dick. My God, Thomas—"

"Sarah, I like them. I'll admit, Gackle could drive me crazy—"

Score! Sarah's hand flies to her mouth but too late to catch the giggle. "Well, now, maybe he could," she says. "And then again maybe he couldn't ... Oh, Thomas, *damn* you!" Her eyes shimmer. "And Dassidario—what ever is the matter with him? The way he keeps off to the side, away from everyone? And those white gloves?"

"Mysophobia—excessive fear of germs. I had a mysophobic patient a few years back who used to say the world was just one big cesspool. Can you imagine going through life like that?"

Nurse Sarah shakes her head sadly. "No, I can't. But one person *does* bother me, Thomas—Sammy Shapiro. There's no way I'd *ever* trust him. And nothing you say can change that."

"What do you think—*I* trust him? I'd have to be crazy. Last night after the meeting Big Al took Sammy out for a drink; you know why? So Gackle and Dassidario could get into his apartment, bug his phone."

"You think of everything, don't you?"

Accusation or compliment? I can't tell. I'm not sure Sarah can either. "I hope so," I say quietly.

"You want to order?" The waiter, skinny and sourpussed, stands with his pencil poised. "Or are you just gonna sit here yakking and tie up my table for the whole lunch hour?"

Before I can come out with something rude, Sarah says, "Bring him a big plate of bologna. A dish of applesauce for me."

"You want some rye bread with that?" asks the waiter.

"Sure, rye bread," I say. "Who do you know takes bologna straight?"

As the waiter leaves, Sarah and I burst out laughing. "But seriously," I say. "This is the right thing to do; this is the right way to do it. Why Gackle's in, or Dassidario, or Sammy, or anyone else, I don't care. Doesn't matter."

"They're in it because they're going to walk away with something between a half million and a million dollars," Sarah says sharply. "And for that matter so are you."

"Nothing wrong with that. But it's us who're going to walk away with a pile of money, not just me. Unless you want to drop out.

Sarah colors. "No. I said I'd help, and I will. But I'm betting there's something else in this for you."

"Something like what? Get real, Sarah. It's just going to feel good to sock it to that slimeball LoPriore. This plan's the only way he's going to get what's coming to him. His lawyers know every loophole, every way to turn a case right back on a poor sucker who tries to play it straight."

"You're doing it again, Thomas. Conjuring a world out of whole cloth—and why? Because the real world's just not interesting enough to keep you entertained." Wide brown eyes turn full heat on me. "I know you, Thomas. I haven't heard this whole story yet."

"Well, of course not. It isn't over."

Without a word the waiter slams the bologna and applesauce onto the table between us. Plates clatter. I spread mustard on a slice of rye bread, spear a couple of slices of bologna, lay them onto the bread. "I'd offer you some," I say to Sarah. "But with you being a vegetarian—"

She waves me off. "Never mind. I ordered it for you. For me, applesauce." She spoons a mouthful through a wicked grin. "Go on. Keep talking."

We're drinking coffee when buzz, there goes my beeper. Sarah freezes. "But you're on vacati—" she begins. Then she remembers.

I peer at the red numbers—not a combination I recognize. As I scramble to my feet Sarah looks at me, shakes her head. "I can't understand why you don't carry a cell phone."

"Just another damn thing to run off in the morning without," I mutter more to myself than her. Then I hotfoot to the pay phone on the back wall of the restaurant.

When I get back she doesn't say a word. Her look is sufficient, more than. "Al," I tell her. "Calling from a pay phone. He needs to talk to me."

"Trouble?"

"Hope just a wrinkle. I'm going to meet him at the workshop."

"Go ahead." Sarah opens her pocketbook, starts rummaging through it. I fumble in my pocket for money.

Sarah glances up. "You look like a greyhound at a stuck starting gate." She smiles, if sadly. "I said go; now beat it. I'll pay."

I leave a light kiss on the top of her head. "See you later."

Big Al did not come alone; he brought Dassidario with him. Eyes bulging, mouth agape, the little man with the round fetal head sits so far forward on his chair I want to strap him in for his own safety. Al, as always, is composed, reclining against the back of the sofa, his bowler on the seat beside him. "Not that I doubted you, Thomas," he says. "But you were certainly right about keeping watch on Mr. Shapiro. When I saw our friend go into the building I thought we might have trouble; when he came out less than five minutes later I'd have wagered a tidy sum. Unfortunately for Mr. Shapiro I was spot-on. A bit of celluloid in the proper place and I was into his flat. He was not a pleasant sight. As if four direct shots in the chest weren't sufficient, he got one through the mouth as well. I'd say our killer has a wry sense of humor." Touch of rueful smile. "Beastly mess—blood all over the carpet and the wall behind him. I doubt the landlord will return his damage deposit."

Wry senses of humor seem to be popping up everywhere. "So Sammy *did* get greedy. Damn!"

Al turns slowly to face Dassidario, who responds by looking as if he might go into cardiopulmonary arrest. "Give Thomas the tape," Al says.

Slowly, Dassidario pulls a cassette from his pocket. Slowly, the trembling white cotton glove extends it in my direction. I take it, being careful to make contact only with the cassette. The little man rewards me with a look of gratitude.

Al nods at my stereo system. "Mr. Dassidario recorded this conversation over Mr. Shapiro's phone less than an hour before his unfortunate demise. I think you'll find it enlightening."

The conversation is less than two minutes long, but it is, as Al thought it would be, enlightening. I feel disgusted. "Half a million at least—and that wasn't enough for him. The son of a bitch just had to go for a little side deal."

"Oh yes." Al seems to take it in stride. "Some people are never satisfied; unfortunate, that. Of the Seven Deadly Sins, I've always found greed the deadliest. But of course *we* become the beneficiaries, don't we? Ironic, what?"

Sammy was a congenial fellow, entertaining in his sociopathic way. But any sympathy I might feel for him, or sadness at his brutal death, washes away on a wave of irritation. He might have ruined a brilliant payday for twelve other people because he thought he saw a way to put a few more bucks into his own pocket. "Sounds from the tape as if we're okay, though," I say to Al. "Sammy didn't say enough to louse up the operation."

Al nods gravely. "My impression, exactly. And I think the full story should remain severely among the three of us."

Just a glance from Al sends poor Dassidario twisting into spasms. Al's voice turns softer; he even smiles at Dassidario who looks back at him with hope-tinged dubiety. "Everyone knows Mr. Shapiro's ... proclivities, Thomas. When the group next meets, just tell them he fell victim to his own greed but fortunately did not compromise our plan."

"Way I was thinking. But we need to be awfully careful— this guy's killed two people now." A thought occurs to me. "You did get the bug back, didn't you, Al? Out of Sammy's phone?"

"Of course." For punctuation to Al's mild dismissal Dassidario jabs a rigid finger three times at his leather briefcase.

"One more thing. Dassidario ..."

"Yes? Yes?"

Oh, for a syringe of Valium. "Make me a copy of that tape, would you please? Give it to me, along with the original, tonight at the meeting. Can you do that?"

"Yes ... of course ... *yes.*" Dassidario's jaw twitches, convulses. "But ... *yes.*"

19

Twenty minutes later the three of us chug into the Regina lobby. Espinoza, resplendent in a shiny electric-blue shirt and canary slacks, gives me the glad hand. His face looks better. "Lot less swollen today," I tell him. "Color's fading, too."

"Jes." Espinoza's smile is that of a man incubating a major case of the happies. "Will feel even better tomorrow, Doaktore."

Our suite is the garment district after a direct hit by Tornado Edna. Piles of fabric, scraps of cloth everywhere. At the eye of the storm its creator looks up from behind her sewing machine. "Everything on schedule?" I ask.

Edna gathers gray hair between her fingers, pushes it back away from her eyes. She's exhausted but she's not about to tell *me* that. "Everything but Mick and Sandy."

Another wrinkle? "What do you mean?"

"I mean they haven't come, either of them. They were supposed to be here at twelve o'clock"—she glances at her watch—"and it's after one. I'd have called them up but I don't have their number. Or an address."

"I do."

I charge to the phone, grab it and dial, but there's only the machine at the other end, Sandy's voice telling me how sorry Mick and she are to have missed me, but my call *is* important to them and if I'll leave my name and phone number at the beep she promises they'll get right back to me. "This is Thomas," I say. "It's a quarter past one. Your appointment was at noon. Where the hell are you?" I slam down the phone—getting a bit irritable, are we?—and start unbuttoning my shirt.

Dassidario backs a step away.

"*I'm* here," I say to Edna. "Do me. If Mick and Sandy don't come by the time we're finished we'll send out reconnaissance troops."

Al smiles a silent understanding.

I open my belt, drop my pants, point at the doorway off the far end of the living room. "That's surveillance headquarters," I say to Dassidario. "Make sure the maid won't find any evidence of your equipment."

"Oh, no ... no ... I mean yes ... but ... but *yes*. What I mean is, there's not a chance, Dr. Purdue. You don't have to worry."

Dassidario's tone suggests I might be the Chief of the Spanish Inquisition, standing before him in my undershirt and jockey shorts. "You see ... these days, there's no need for ... well, *wires*, or anything like that. It's all tiny transmitters and receivers. The one on the phone'll go inside, out of sight. And the general receiving system"—he pats his beloved leather briefcase—"will be locked whenever it's not in use. It looks like any old briefcase; I can't imagine the maid will even notice it." He holds his treasure toward me like an offering, making certain to keep it and himself beyond the farthest reach of my hands.

"Cool, Dassidario. I'm just checking. Relax."

Dassidario grins nervously—what doesn't he do nervously?

I take my costume from Edna, pull on the shirt, step into the trousers. She studies me critically, cocking her head to check one angle, then another. "Shirt's fine, but the pants are a little baggy in the hips and over the bottom. Come here." Edna grabs the waist of my pants, pulls it tight between her fingers. "Ow!" I yell as she sticks a pin cleanly into my left buttock. "Jesus, Edna, be careful."

"Sorry."

I look over my shoulder; she's laughing. Al chuckles; even Dassidario contributes a tentative titter to the general merriment. "There," Edna says. "It's pinned. Step out of it and try on the others. I'll have them all ready by the time you'll need them; don't worry."

Everyone tells me don't worry. Thank you one and all, but I just don't like the way this afternoon is going, not a bit.

We're close to finishing fitting my eighth and last potential costume. Dassidario and Al are in the back room, setting up and checking electronic equipment. All of a sudden a key turns in the door lock, then bodies rush into the room. Edna lets out a little scream.

Espinoza, Mick, and Sandy freeze. "Oh, sorry." Espinoza is contriteness itself. "I no mean to scare you. But they say they got to see you right away."

Mick looks like the wrath of God. Unshaven, dark rings under bloodshot eyes. If we needed him to play a cornered raccoon, Edna wouldn't have to make him up at all. By comparison to Sandy, though, he's a daisy. The Soapy One is haggard, skin white going yellow. Left eye swollen shut, upper lip cracked, white summer dress decorated with a maplike array of brownish bloodstains.

She looks at me staring and bursts into tears.

Mick drapes a protective arm around her. "She got busted last night after we left here. I finally got a shyster this morning; he got her sprung less than an hour ago. But I don't

know how the hell she's gonna do her bit, way she looks. Plus,
she was up all night, didn't get a minute's sleep. Six other
women in that cell with her, drunks, hopheads, whores, all of
'em yelling, screaming, fighting ..."

Sandy's gone now, sobbing, honking, blubbering out of control, a scratched record of remorse. "Sorry ... sorry ... sorry ..."

Espinoza goes back to the desk. The rest of us sit around
Edna's cluttered sewing machine and listen to Mick's story.
He holds out his hands helplessly. "Sandy said let's go up to
the Carnegie Deli, get a piece of cheesecake and some coffee,
so we're on our way up Seventh Av, crossing 50th, when I
damn near go down on my face. Shoelace. I stop and tie it;
Sandy just keeps goin'. Next thing, I hear somebody yell 'Pickpocket! Pickpocket bitch!' and I think, Oh, shit, and take off.
Half a block up there's Sandy, two big guys got her between
them. Her left eye's already closed and blood's runnin' from
her nose all over the front of her dress. I'm set to go into our
Emergency Plan: run over, say I'm Lt. Clemons, Undercover
Vice Patrol, I saw the whole thing, here's your wallet back, I'll
take the young lady downtown, no need for you to be bothered—but then one of the guys spins Sandy around, the other
slams a pair of cuffs on her, and they hustle her into a squad
car just pulled up at the curb. She walked into a sting—dipped
a *real* undercover cop."

Sandy snuffles, wipes at her eyes with a dirty, bloody handkerchief. "I didn't even think—just saw the wallet in his back
pocket, and did an automatic grab."

Goddamn it to hell: she didn't even think. With a million-dollar payoff right around the corner she went for a penny-
ante wallet snatch. "Doesn't seem unreasonable to expect just
a *little* thinking where five million dollars are involved." The
bitterness I hear in my own voice surprises me.

"Thomas!" One word is all Edna needs.

I sigh, look back to to Sandy and Mick. "Sorry," I mutter.

Mick nods acceptance. Sandy wipes at her eyes again, blows her nose. "I don't blame you," she says, trying to fix her one working eye on me. "I've loused the whole ... thing up." This starts her crying again.

Edna looks at me. "Now what?"

Who's the mastermind of this operation? Time for Master to kick his mind into overdrive. "Let's get everybody over here, fast." I tick on my fingers, "Schwartz. Gackle. Hugh. Frank. Sarah."

"How about the motormouth?" says Mick. "Shapiro."

"We'll talk about that—later." I grab up the telephone, start punching numbers.

By two-thirty everyone's in place around Edna's sewing machine, trying—largely without success—not to look at Sandy. Schwartz gnaws on a fingernail. Frank the Crank clears his throat. "Must be something big, Doc—I mean, for you to tell me to lock up the shop and get right over here."

"I've got bad news and worse news," I say. "Bad news first. Sammy Shapiro's dead—shot."

"This is the bad news?" Schwartz is aghast. "I ain't so sure I want to hear the worse."

"I ain't so sure you do either," I say. "But you're going to, in just a minute. Sammy tried a hustle that blew up in his face—typical Sammy, trying to play both ends against the middle. Doesn't look like he spilled the beans, though; the plan's still all right."

"A smart mouth and a stupid head." Edna is furious. "That's as bad a combination as there is."

Murmur of assent, finally broken by, "Hey, Doc. I'm waitin' to hear the heavy shoe."

Leave it to Schwartz.

"The heavy shoe," I say, "is Sandy got busted last night. Cops messed up her face, she hasn't had any sleep for going on thirty-six hours. Looks like she's out of our game"—I glance at Mick and Sandy, try not to look as disgusted as I feel—"probably out of her soaps for a while, too."

"No, no, Doc; soaps'll be okay." Mick corrects me. "They'll just rewrite the scripts, say her boyfriend beat her up, something like that. Like they do when one of the women gets pregnant. "Hell, the producer'll probably love it."

"Good, Mick. I'm glad no one in Television Land is going to be disappointed. But we've still got a problem: a one-performance contract, curtain goes up in less than five hours. And physically or mentally, Sandy's not in shape to go on."

Louder murmur this time, insistent, unhappy. Again, Sandy bursts into crying. Sarah pats her hand, whispers a few words into her ear. Sandy actually smiles at Sarah; Sarah smiles back. The miracle nurse-counselor of Planned Parenthood strikes again. I can't begin to imagine what she said to Sandy.

Frank the Crank cranes his neck to scan the room. "Looks to me like we're SOL without her. I mean Edna, excuse me, but you're not exactly enough of a spring chicken to take over for Sandy. And—"

"And I'm chopped liver."

Sarah, the only other woman in the room, is on her feet, hands on hips. She glares at Frank, who suddenly takes on the appearance of a man with eight ounces of minced fiberglass down the back of his shirt. "Well, no, Mrs. Purdue; that ain't what I meant. It's just that, well ..."

Time to put him out of his misery. "He means it's hard to picture you playing the Whore of Babylon," I say. "Sandy was going to keep LoPriore interested and out of our way—"

"While you clean out his apartment." Sarah is steaming. "And you think *I* can't do that?"

"Feed LoPriore a story that'll keep him staring into your eyes for three hours? You, Sarah? Of all people? Come on."

Sarah looks around the circle. "*Somebody* has to—and I don't see anyone else here who can. There's not much choice, Thomas. Either I do it or no one gets the money they came here for. And Hugh doesn't get back his collection."

This woman will be the death of me. Mrs. Simon-Pure, all wool and a yard wide, volunteering to play Scheherezade to a caliph who'll have her head off the instant she drops a word that doesn't ring true. "Sarah ..." I try to sound much more patient than I feel. "I think we need to figure some other way to get LoPriore out of his apartment and keep him there for a while. What you're offering to do is dangerous."

"Oh, thank you. I hadn't realized that. Was it going to be less dangerous for Sandy?"

I'm three words into reminding her she needs to give Sandy points for being both a professional actress and heavy on street smarts when Schwartz butts in. "Hey, Doc, you know what? When your missus tells me something, I believe her."

Edna is sizing Sarah up. A crafty smile spreads over her face. "He's right, Thomas. Sarah'll have a man like LoPriore eating out of her hand ... when I'm done with her."

"What do you mean, 'when you're done with her'?"

"It's too late to change the whole plan," Sarah says. "Or to recruit someone else. I said I'd be a part of this group and that's what I am. Now let's stop wasting time and get moving."

Leave it to Sarah to develop the ultimate definition of honor among thieves. "But you're not Sandy," I say. "And as good as Edna is, she's not going to make you look—or sound—enough like Sandy to fool LoPriore."

Sarah folds her arms across her chest, glowers at me. Oh, *stupid* husband. "Well, of course not. That's not what I have in mind."

I know I'm going to regret this but there's no way around it. "What do you have in mind?" I ask.

When Sarah finishes there's silence. Finally, Espinoza says, "Oh, Doaktore, I tell you, you got one smart wife there. Like my poor wife was. I get in a jam, she always the one get me out."

"Sounds to me like she's got the hole plugged." Frank the Crank is convinced. So is Schwartz. "I gotta admit, Mrs. Purdue, you fixed it up maybe better'n it was in the first place."

Applause fills the air. Sarah takes a small bow.

I wave my white handkerchief. "Okay, Sarah—looks like you're on. Just remember: when the going gets tough, the tough tell stories. But now we've got other holes. Schwartz, you'll have to do a solo tail on Sarah. No other woman to go with you."

"Easy, Doc. I'll call Trudy, tell her to get her hair fixed up, buy herself a new dress and maybe a hat. I mean, how often does she get to go to dinner in some five-star restaurant?"

Why didn't I think of that? "All right, Broadway, sold. But if Al plays doctor at the Regency Tower at five-thirty, we don't dare have him wait outside The Carroll Parkside at seven to see what LoPriore is wearing. LoPriore spots him, game's over."

Up goes Frank the Crank's hand. "I've got nothing to do right about then. I'll watch for Big Vin and call Edna. Easy."

Schwartz: easy. Frank: easy. Everything's easy. Fine. Who am I to argue. "Now, Dassidario ..."

Every muscle in the little man's body goes into sustained contraction.

Doctor Sympathy flashes his tenderest smile. "I assume you've tested out the bugs for LoPriore's apartment, and Sandy's ... uh, Sarah's hair."

"Well ... but ... but of *course*." Dassidario looks as close to offended as he dares. He opens his briefcase, pulls out a small round object, hands it to Sarah. "There's a hairpin on it," he tells her. "Roll your hair up and pin it in."

Sarah looks from Dassidario to the bug in her hand, then back to the pop-eyed little man.

"Go ahead," I tell her. "He says put it in your hair, put it in your hair."

Still looking a bit suspicious, Sarah gathers her hair in one hand, works it into a roll at the nape of her neck, pins the little device inside. Dassidario stands on tiptoes to peer from a safe distance. "See," he says. "It doesn't show at all." He fiddles with a dial inside his briefcase. "Say something, Mrs. Purdue."

Little self-conscious laugh. "I've never been on *Candid Camera* before."

But she is on Candid Microphone. Her words come to my ears simultaneously from her mouth and from a speaker in Dassidario's briefcase.

"There's another receiver inside the phone." Dassidario points toward his surveillance headquarters in the back. The little man is in his glory. Talking about electronic doodahs he's perfectly articulate: no pauses or stammers, no facial convulsions. "It operates on a different frequency, over a second channel. Anything that comes through is recorded, whether I'm listening or not. And for backup I have it set so when Mr. LoPriore's phone rings, ours rings, too. If he picks up the receiver to make a call, our phone will beep. We're ready, Doctor."

"Very good, Dassidario. Now—" I check my watch: 3:10. "Edna, I guess you'd better get going with Sarah. You can be done by five?"

Not a word in reply from Edna. Her face says it all, clearly and in spades.

"Okay," I say. "Everyone back here at ten minutes to five. From then we're on a tight schedule; everything's got to go just so. No more curve balls."

Do I hear someone snickering?

Madison Av is teeming: late summer afternoon in full bloom. Buses, trucks, cabs, cars honking, blowing exhaust. People on the sidewalk, faces tight, ties loose, go-go-go. Do *I* look like that? Better not.

I stroll into a luncheonette, sit at a back table, order a corned beef sandwich and coffee. I look out past the counter into the street. From this distance the people moving along the sidewalk look like fish swimming upstream, gliding, flowing, all sleek and smooth. I eat slowly, sip the coffee, go over the revised plan. Once, twice, three times. No loose ends. The Hebrew National clock on the wall says 4:35. I stand up, throw money on the table and start back to the Regina.

Where I'm in for a new surprise. There's a woman with Edna, and this babe is the Whore of Babylon set down in modern-day New York. Peroxide-hair waved across the left side of her forehead, love curl in front of her right ear. Creamy makeup thick and luscious over her cheeks, a ton of eye shadow, six pounds of lipstick, and a blue minifrock nicely draped to display cleavage and thighs galore. All this balanced on a pair of stiletto heels half a foot high. I stare, then step closer. "Sarah?"

"Shirley McCoy," she says in the randiest voice I've ever heard. I take her extended hand, then drop it as if it were a plate of culture medium in an H.I.V. lab. "I'm Sally's sister— you know, Sally *McCoy* de Pinza. Pleezmeetcha."

Edna and Mick can't hold it back. It's me they're laughing at. "What the hell did you do to her?" I bawl.

That really sets them off. Sarah swings up to me, runs a finger lightly across my cheek. "Whatsamatter, Baby?" she croons, flashing a pout out of a '40s detective flick. "Don't you *like* little Shirley?"

"I'm just wondering where little Shirley learned to talk and move like this."

"From her clients." She shimmies her chest equipment under my nose. "I'm not blind, Baby, not deaf, either. How long've I been counseling single mothers? And how do you think they got to *be* mothers?"

"Sarah ..." It's a rare occasion when Thomas Purdue is lost for words, but it does happen. Not for long, though. "You're going to walk through New York ... and take on a character like LoPriore? Looking like that?"

"Chill, Thomas." Edna snaps. "What do you want: I should dress her up in a Salvation Army cape? She'll be fine—terrific, in fact. Christ Almighty, she's bailing this whole operation out. What the hell's the matter with you?"

There are any number of answers I could give her, but what comes out is, "I didn't think she had it in her to do something like this."

Edna snorts. "Thomas, you're a very bright man but in some ways you're an infant."

While all this is going on, the troops are reassembling, one by one and in pairs. Edna's crack brings snickers from Gackle and Frank, a chuckle from Schwartz, a mild smile from Al and a tentative one from Dassidario. Only Mick and Sandy have straight faces.

"Great," I say. "I'm glad everyone's in such good humor." I pull a small piece of paper out of my pocket, extend it to Sandy. "Time to move. Here's LoPriore's work phone number. Get him!"

Sandy sweeps the crowd with her one open eye. Clouds move in over her face. "I'm sorry, guys," she says. "I just don't know how I could've screwed up like that."

This is a dime she's got to move off, fast. "It's done, Sandy, forget it. We're still in business. Besides, nobody but you could've got that picture out of LoPriore's pocket." I pat my own shirt pocket and grin. "And that's what's going to cook our pigeon once and for all. Now stop apologizing, and get him on the goddamn phone before he leaves work for the day."

Even with her face decorated as it is, Sandy's gorgeous when she smiles. "I'll make sure he knows if he doesn't jump he's gonna lose that bird-temple forever. That he's not the only fish in my stew."

"Sea, Sandy."

She looks at me, uncertain. "See what?"

"Sea, S-E-A. The only fish in the *sea*. Not stew."

"Oh, I don't know." I look around. Sarah's grin is elfish. "I kind of like stew. It's got a certain ring."

"Fine! Stew, sea ... Christ, what am I arguing about? Go, Sandy!" I grab the phone off the hook, slap it into her hand.

She punches in the numbers. "Hello ... yes, hel*lo*, Mr. LoPriore. This is Sally de Pinza. Lis-sen, about that bird temple. If you're interested ... like I mean *really* interested, you've got to get over here right away. Yeah, that's what I said. Regency Tower. My sister Shirley'll meet you in the lobby ... Yes, yes. We'll explain when you get here."

Sandy's smiling as she hangs up the phone. So is Sarah, who's flouncing toward the door. "Now if you'll excuse me, I've got to get myself over to the Regency Tower. Got a heavy date, a rich guy, real class. Don't want to be late."

"Sarah!"

She stands, one leg bent forward at the knee, regarding me coolly.

"I'm going with you."

The wind drops; her sails fall flat. "What are you talking about, Thomas?" The old Sarah-voice is back. "Sandy's going with me ... and Al. You're supposed to be staying here, getting Edna suited up and keeping a general eye on things."

"I'm going to keep a general eye on you," I say. "From the closet—with the door shut."

She stamps her foot, actually throws a mini-tantrum. "Thomas! I don't need—"

I move past her, open the door. "You can consider this part your final audition: pull it off well and we go ahead. But if things don't go right"—I motion Sandy and Al forward—"I'm going to be Al's reinforcement. Now, come on; we've got to get there and set up before LoPriore makes it from Union Square."

Big Al is smiling as he goes past me into the hall. "No offense, Al," I say.

"None taken."

20

A block from the Regency Tower we split up. Al, Sandy and I go ahead, through the lobby, into the elevator, to Room 3201. Sarah will follow in a minute and wait in the lobby for LoPriore.

Amazing how much you can see through a keyhole. Try it sometime. Down on my knees in the bedroom closet I have a clear view of Sandy stretched out on the bed, Dr. Resford standing solicitously over her. I stare at this touching little tableau for seven or eight minutes that feel like seven or eight hours.

Finally a key turns in the lock of the outside door. Then the fishwife music of Shirley McCoy's voice: "... got a lit-tle problem. Earl beat Sally up."

"He what?" LoPriore's rumble stiffens Sandy on the bed.

"Beat her up, the son of a bitch, and it's not the first time, either. I got a doctor, he's inside taking a look at her. But we can still make this deal go down."

"Yeah?"

"How much'll you give for that bird-temple?"

"Uh ..."

"Listen, Mister, no screwing around. Either you want it or you don't. If you do, it's got to be tonight. Now what'll you give?"

"How's a hundred thousand sound?"

"You know what? I think maybe you didn't hear me." I imagine Sarah looking at LoPriore as if he were a cockroach, just slithered out from under the toilet. "I said no screwing around, there's no time. Get real—now—fast. Or else turn yourself around, get back on that elevator, and go on back home and jerk off."

Who talks to Vincent LoPriore like that? I swear I can hear him swallow air. "*You're* gonna sell me the bird-temple?"

"At the right price—which is a hell of a lot more than a hundred K." Her voice lowers a notch. "We better go on inside; I want to see how Sally is. Come on."

Now radio becomes television as first Sarah, then LoPriore come into my field of view. Ladies first, LoPriore must have figured, let her be between him and whoever or whatever is inside that bedroom. His right hand is in his pants pocket, probably wrapped around a pistol small enough to carry in weather too hot for a jacket, big enough to do whatever it might be called upon for.

Sarah runs over, grabs both of Sandy's hands. LoPriore rocks back and forth on his heels, next to Sarah. "Doin' okay, Sis?" Sarah croons.

Sandy, dying swan, nods, sad little smile on her face. What a pair these two women are. If they ever decide to get together after this game is done, I'm going to keep my eyes wide open, my back to the wall.

The large man standing at the far side of the bed, holding a stethoscope and a reflex hammer—*my* stethoscope and reflex hammer—blinks mildly.

"You don't mind me saying, your husband did some number on you," LoPriore says.

Sandy starts crying. Sarah pats her hand. The big man across the bed nods emphatically. "Indeed he did. I'm quite concerned about her, actually. Possibility of internal bleeding, p'aps a serious head injury. I've arranged transport to the hospital."

"'Indeed he did!' 'P'aps a serious head injury!'" LoPriore turns to Sarah. "Hey, Lady, this's the best you can do for a doctor? Bloomin' limey quack, probably doesn't have an independent license, works for a shitpot city hospital? I can call *my* doctor, if you want."

From the bed, Sandy shakes off the idea. "Thanks, but I like Dr. Alberts."

LoPriore shrugs. "Sootcher self."

"But I won't ... be able to do what I said ..." Sandy starts crying again.

Sarah hushes her, pats her hand again. Then she looks at Al. "Could you excuse us for a few minutes? We need to talk ... some business."

Al makes a show out of consulting his watch, then peers into Sandy's one open eye. "I really do think she needs to go—"

"Just for a minute, Doctor. Please. It's important."

"Very well." Al gathers himself up, starts to the door. "But we can't wait much longer. If the Aid Unit does not arrive very shortly I shall take her myself, in a cab."

As the door closes behind Al, Sarah turns to LoPriore; the look on her face sets me back on my heels. This is one mean Jane. Vincent, I think you're about to dance on a very not griddle.

"Okay, Mr. LoPriore—here's the deal. My prick brother-in-law's coming back here in about an hour, hour and a half. Then he's going out with a collector, dinner, and to see the guy's collection. He'll be away 'til about midnight. Sally was going to meet you here while he was gone and sell you the bird-temple, so Earl'd think the maid probably took it. But this way's even better. By the time Earl gets back, Sally'll be outa here and f'sure she's gonna be at the hospital all night. Before

Earl goes out, he'll check and make sure the bird-temple's okay. But"—she pulls a key from her shiny little purse, dangles it in LoPriore's face—"I got Sally's room key. You go get the money, then you can take me out for a nice dinner ... and then we come back. You get the bird-temple, Sally gets enough dough so she can live halfway decent 'til she can *really* nail Earl in the divorce. And Earl gets screwed over double. How's that?"

"'Enough dough.'" LoPriore is grinning all over his face. What a ballsy broad. "Okay, lady ... so how much is 'enough dough'?"

"Half a mill, not a penny less."

Half a mill, holy shit, says the expression on LoPriore's face. Less than half what the goddamn thing's worth. I'm in like Flynn, and what a great fuck-you for that asshole de Pinza.

I hear the bedroom door open. Dr. Alberts leans around the edge. "I say—"

"Hold it a minute, Doctor." Sarah runs over, tries to close the door, but Al keeps coming. "I'm sorry, but I shan't risk this woman's well-being a moment longer." He strides to the bed, pulls down the covers, looks at LoPriore. "I say, give me a hand helping her up."

LoPriore swings Sandy's legs off the bed and down to the floor. "Easy now." He looks back to Sarah. "Okay, Sis. You got a deal."

Sarah nods. "You *can* get the ... uh, payment tonight? I mean before ... delivery."

"One phone call, my personal banker brings me whatever 'payment' I want, where I want it, when I want it. Okay? Now, where do you want to go eat?"

"Mindy Roberts."

LoPriore's face is hilarious. Christ, it says, what a twat! Mindy Roberts, fanciest place in town ... But he recovers himself quickly. Five hundred dollars on top of five hundred thousand? Peanuts. Sales tax. "Mindy Roberts you say," LoPriore rumbles. "Mindy Roberts it is. Now"—he extends his arm—"maybe we oughta get on the road? Not hold up the doctor here any more? And," he lowers his voice, "not be here when your brother-in-law makes his stop-off."

Sarah gives him a big, open-mouthed smile as they all move toward the door. "While you're talking to your banker I'll go to the hospital with Sally and make sure she's set up comfortable. Meet you at Mindy Roberts at—what time's it now?"

They're in the living room, out of sight. "Ten t'six," I hear LoPriore growl.

"Meet you at a quarter past seven," Sarah says.

"You got a date, Lady." The outside door slams.

I sink—slowly—to a sitting position. Do my knees and ankles ever hurt, and everything in between. No pain until it was over, good old adrenaline. I sit there, counting off minutes, ten of them. Then I work myself to my feet, stretch, and go catch the elevator to the lobby. Quick peek, clear coast, out the door, hit the sidewalk running.

Back at the Regina suite, high-fives all around. One guy I don't recognize; I've never seen anyone so hard on the eyes, and keep in mind what I do for a living. Then it hits me: Mick. "Looking good," I say. "That patch over your eye, the scar across your cheek—your mother would scream if she saw you."

Mick grins, then shuffles a few steps across the floor, swinging his left leg outward so as to keep his right hip elevated. "Don't think the gimp'd do much for her state of mind, either."

Edna gives me the fish eye. "I gather Little Shirley passed her final audition."

"With bells on. You should've heard her, Edna. Earl de Pinza? All she wanted was to screw him to the wall—hated his smelly guts, the bastard."

"Well, of course," Sarah says. "What a nasty man; who wouldn't hate him?"

"But Sarah: who *is* Earl de Pinza?"

It takes a couple of seconds to sink in. "Oh, Thomas," she finally says. "I could slug you, I really could."

Soapy Sandy laughs out loud.

"Thomas! Come here."

The mastermind turns a blank look on Edna.

"Come *here*," Edna repeats, *con brio, sforzando, fortissimo.* "You're the only one not made up and our game's going to be down the tubes if I don't get you ready damned fast." She picks up her box of theatrical makeup. "Get your ass *over* here."

At a quarter to seven the LoPriore hairpiece is in place on my shaved dome. Edna's gluing on the mustache, wide, thick, and black, when the door opens and Hugh Curtis walks in, arms full of collapsed cardboard cartons. He looks at me, shakes his head, and chuckles. "Jeez, Thomas—I wouldn't have believed it."

Up go Edna's quills. "What do you mean you wouldn't have believed it? Am I goddamn good or not?"

Hugh smiles wryly. "You better be."

"Well, I am and you know it. Now, can it, Hugh. Sit down and shut up. I've still got a little work to do."

She's smoothing and working my lip brush when Gackle and Al stroll in, carrying a giant roll of bubble wrap. "Courtesy of Frank the Crank," Gackle says, setting his burden on the floor.

I look at my watch. "If you're close, Edna, let me take two minutes, get them on their way."

"Go." She stands up, stretches.

I open the drawer of the dresser behind Edna's sewing machine, take out eight pairs of rubber surgical gloves. "Dassidario!" I yell into the back room.

The fetal head peers anxiously around the corner from Bug Central. "Come on in here," I tell him. The glued-on mustache makes my smile feel funny. Maybe just as well. "We're ready to roll."

"But ... yes ... *yes*." Dassidario scoots into the room, looks me up and down. "I ... I haven't seen Mr. LoPriore ... yet. But you sure don't look like ... like ... well, like *you*, Doctor."

"He's got the walk down just right." Hugh is clearly impressed. "Look at him swagger, huh?"

I hand two pairs of gloves to Al, Hugh, Gackle and Dassidario. "One to wear, one for a spare. But careful with the spare. Drop a glove, figure you've left one of your balls in that apartment."

Dassidario holds up his white cotton-gloved hands, palms out. He looks like Jolson crying for his Mammy.

"All right, all right! If you can work in them, *I* don't have any problem." I take back his two pairs of surgeon's gloves.

Eight minutes to seven. The phone rings.

We look like seven mannequins set into a backdrop of chaos. Edna breaks the freeze, picks up the receiver. "Frank? Goddamn it, of course I'm ready. Shoot."

As she listens her eyes narrow in concentration. "Okay," she finally says. "White cotton turtleneck, leather loafers, white linen bellbottoms. White oxford shoes. Got it."

She hangs up the phone and with an air of triumph strides to the closet. "LoPriore's out of there," she says. "On his way to Mindy Roberts."

I've known all along there would be a point when we could no longer back out. This is that time.

To my surprise everyone looks calm. *I* don't feel calm. I'd figured Dassidario would be needing diapers by now but the little man is all business, walking with Al, Hugh and Gackle into the bedroom toward the fire escape.

Mick and Sandy are sitting together on the sofa; Sandy's eyes roll up. How long has it been since she's had sleep? "Go on back home, Sandy, sack out. Better if you don't crash here, right in the middle of everything. Mick, walk her to the subway. Then grab the truck."

Edna shoves me roughly into the chair, goes back to work.

Ten minutes later she steps back to size me up. She smiles. "Beautiful! Mamma Birdie wouldn't know the difference. You've got extra shoulders sewn into the turtleneck, elevators in your shoes—they'll give you an inch. And you've got LoPriore's extra twenty pounds sewn into the shirtfront and trousers. You're set."

Mirror, mirror on the wall ... Vincent LoPriore stares back at slick me. Pull-on black wig with receding hairline; subtle makeup for dark, Italian skin; mustache; just a trace of five-clock shadow. Only one thing missing: I turn on the full-power sneer. Perfect.

Edna picks up the picture of Mrs. LoPriore from her work-table. "What do you say, Birdie?" She chuckles, holds the photo up to face me. "How do you like your son?"

I take the picture, slip it into my breast pocket.

The phone rings a second time.

This is not in the script.

Edna grabs the receiver, slams it to her ear. Her face says in no way does she like what she's hearing. Finally, she croons into the phone, "Certainly, Mr. Espinoza—you'll just have to give me a minute to get decent ... dressed, I mean. Yes ... yes, I understand."

She hangs up the phone, regards me furiously. "Get out of here. Go! Espinoza's bringing two cops back—no idea why. Pretty obvious they wouldn't let him say."

Go where? How? "What if they've got a guy watching the door? I walk out, I'm dead meat. And so are you."

Edna looks around. "Fire escape?"

"Same problem. Better hope they weren't watching when the Four Musketeers went out and down. Besides, I'd get my nice white suit all dirty, which I suspect LoPriore never does."

Edna's as close to frantic as I've ever seen her. "Murphy," she croaks.

"Yeah, whole goddamn day's been one big Murphy's Law. But what the hell—"

"No, the Murphy bed." Edna points toward the far wall. "We could hide you in there."

"No space. I'd suffocate in five minutes."

Edna blows out a chestful of exasperation. "It's always something," she grumbles. "Just one goddamn thing after another." Then she smiles—grimly but nevertheless. "We're going to have to wing it ... Son."

"I'm going to be late for my appointment, Mother."

"Can't be helped ... Dassidario's briefcase! Go in the back, close it up, put it in the closet. Quick!"

As I tear ass into the back room, I hear the knock at the door. "Yes, just a moment," Edna calls out in her best little old lady voice.

I shut the door behind me, flip Dassidario's briefcase shut, carry it to the closet, and stand it beside the four suitcases Schwartz and I lugged through the heat. Looks like just another leather case; pray they don't open it.

Now, what? Stay in here, go out there? I'm not even a cop and it would look suspicious as hell to me to open a closed door and find a nasty-looking guy in a white outfit sitting there twiddling his thumbs. Edna's right: it's always something. I open the door, stride into the living room.

Where Edna is facing Espinoza and two blue uniforms. The cop on the left is a tall hulk with dark skin, a scar at the corner of his eye, and an expression nastier than Monday morning. The kind of man you're glad is a cop, because if he weren't he'd be someone the cops would spend a lot of time pursuing. As I come into the room he gives me a look that would fry an egg. His partner is a young guy in his twenties with blond hair that hangs down over his forehead and a pair of eyes the color of the Caribbean Sea. Such a nice, gentle-looking fellow–and that's what he trades on, I tell myself. Don't trust him for a second.

"Mr. Espinoza, what is going on here?" Edna storms. "You led me to understand this is a nice, quiet hotel."

"Yes, yes, it is. But—"

"Where's the fire escape, please, Ma'am?" This from the blond cop.

The-jig-is-up, says Espinoza's pan. His arms wave wildly. "I am sorry, Miz de Pinza. Is not my fault. Somebody call—"

"Through that room." Edna points into the bedroom.

As the cops disappear into the back, Edna turns to Nozey. "Mr. Espinoza, I demand an explanation," she says loudly. "I insist you tell me what's going on here." All the while she encourages him with her hands. Talk, goddammit, *talk. Say* something.

Espinoza almost smiles. Almost but not quite. "Oh, Miz de Pinza, I try to tell you. Somebody call nine-one-one, they say they see mens come out of here on the fire escape, go down in the alley. So nine-one-one send the cops—"

"Men? Coming out of here?" Edna packs every possible ounce of indignation into her voice. "That's ridiculous! My son and I are the only persons who've been in this room since—"

"I am sure of that," says Guillermo Sincerity Espinoza. "But is not me who call the p'lice. I am very sorry, Miz de Pinza."

The two patrolmen come back into the room. "You and your son are here by yourselves, then, Mrs. de Pinza," says the blond, untrustworthy cop. "Little visit to the city?"

"Yes. I've been out sight-seeing most of the day." Edna points toward the sewing machine, surrounded by scraps of cloth and lengths of thread. "Then I spent a little time sewing: they don't have fabric stores like this in Montana, you know. And now I'm ... I should say, I *was* ... just trying to get a little rest before I go out to supper."

"I'm sorry," the nice cop says, smiling in a way many people would consider disarming, but which puts me on all-systems-ready. "Can I ask you to show us some ID, please?"

"Well, I never! What do you think, I'm some sort of crook? I've never in my *life* been so insulted—"

The dark cop rolls his eyes. "I'll go check the alley," he says, and disappears into the bedroom. I hear him clanging down the fire escape.

"It's nothing like that, Ma'am," says the blond cop, ever so soothingly. "Just routine. See, we have to fill out papers. Someone called in an apparent burglary. If I don't say I've checked out the persons on the scene I'd get into serious trouble with my sergeant. You wouldn't want me to get into trouble, would you?"

What I'd like is to put your balls in a vise and turn the handle hard as I can, says Edna's face. But she works herself up to look charmed. "No, of course not, young man. I'm sorry to be such a bother. Just that this is terribly upsetting, you understand."

"Of course, Ma'am. I appreciate your co-operation, really I do."

Edna takes a plastic card from her purse, hands it to the cop. He looks from the picture on it to Edna and back again. "Evelyn de Pinza, from Great Falls, Montana. You're a long way from home, Ma'am." He glances at me. "You're from Montana, too, Mr. de Pinza?"

I'm living in France, now," I say, squeezing hauteur into

my speech as if I were emptying toothpaste from a tube. I take out my wallet, extract a Visa card, hold it up in front of the cop's face. He nods; I replace it in my wallet, put the wallet safely back into my pocket. He gives Edna's driver's license back to her.

As she slips the license back into her purse, Edna shoots me a glance. After Schwartz's hand got introduced to LoPriore's foot I told Broadway to get us all phony driver's licenses and credit cards—just in case our mark needed a bit of convincing here or there. Edna gave me a bit of a rough time about being overly anal. But a doctor has to be compulsive; miss a symptom, a physical sign, or a piece of a patient's history and you may well end up with a dead patient. Amazing, the number of similarities between good doctors and good con men.

"Hear any noises out there, Mrs. de Pinza?" Nice cop, back on pursuit. "Like my partner just made going down the fire escape?"

Edna shakes her head slowly. "No ... no. Nothing like that. Just the usual New York street noises."

The cop points toward the closed door left of the bedroom entry. "Does that room have access to a fire escape?"

"No!" Edna and Espinoza say together. "Second bedroom," Espinoza adds.

"Mind if I take a look?"

Edna tells him to suit himself.

The cop opens the door, goes inside. Edna, Espinoza and I exchange uneasy stares. A moment later the dark cop walks back in from the hallway. His partner returns from the second bedroom. They shrug at each other. "Alley's empty," the dark cop says. "Nobody anywhere in any direction."

I think I hear Espinoza sigh.

"Nothing in there, either," says the blond cop.

"All right." Dark cop nods. They both head for the door.

"Sorry to bother you, Mrs. de Pinza, Mr. de Pinza," says the blond cop. "Maybe it was a mistake, maybe a false alarm—somebody's idea of a joke."

"It's not very funny to me," Edna says.

"Or us. 'Night, Ma'am." The dark cop leads his partner out the door, closing it behind them. Espinoza follows them into the hallway. Edna plops into a chair. "Whew! Guess the guys got inside at LoPriore's before Darth Vader there hit the alley."

"Murphy took a coffee break. Thank God."

"Also thank God those cops never met Vincent LoPriore."

Five minutes later Espinoza is back, knocking softly at the door. "They gone," he whispers as Edna lets him in. "I watch, make sure the car leaves before I come back."

Edna smiles at him. "You did good. Gave us enough time to get ourselves together. Not to mention hiding Dassidario's electronic crap."

Espinoza's eyes take on a poleaxed glaze. "I forgot—where you hide all that? The 'lectronics, all that stuff, the li'l man's briefcase ..." That was as far as poor Espinoza could get.

Edna snorts.

"I closed up the briefcase, put it into the closet with Edna's big travel bags," I say. "Only thing I had time to do. Sometimes you get lucky: I guess they didn't open anything."

Espinoza looks stricken. "*Vay iz mir,*" he murmurs, very softly.

"It's all right," Edna says. "I'll get the briefcase out now and put it back. Dassidario won't even know anything happened." She turns to me. "You'd better get on your way, Thomas. You're already, what? Twenty minutes behind schedule?"

"Just about. I don't think we can take the time to get you upstairs to help pack—"

"It's all right, Thomas. A little time off right now won't do me any harm. Maybe Nozey here can get us a couple of milkshakes."

Espinoza smiles. "Any flavor you want, Miz de Pinza. Compliments of the management, for your trouble."

Outside the Regina I turn downtown and walk to 62nd, then over to Fifth where I head uptown. No patrol cars, no policemen, at least not that I can see. Unmarked cars, though? Plainclothes cops?

Relax, Purdue. Reported possible burglary, indignant old lady and her son, false alarm. By now the cops've already forgotten about it. Be a smart guy and do the same. Keep your mind on the business at hand.

There's the Carroll Parkside, doorman out front, sweating bullets in his maroon wool coat. Can he hear my drumming, dancing heart?

21

On my way past the alley I cop a peek. Nothing but a pile of garbage cans—good. My gang is upstairs, waiting on the stairwell outside the third-floor service door. Waiting for Thomas Purdue, now close to twenty-five minutes late.

They *are* there, aren't they? Waiting for me? They didn't get nervous about my being so late, get confused, get into an argument, get cold feet, get the hell out of there? They didn't get noticed, get busted? Did they?

It goes against my nature but I need to believe. I can doubt the existence of God, doubt Sarah's fidelity, doubt I'll ever find another music box to buy—but what I *can't* doubt, not for a moment, is the reliability of my new business associates. That I have to believe with all my heart. With the reward for a good performance of at least a half-million dollars, and the reward for a bad one something I prefer to not even consider, I can't take a misstep because I stopped to think, what if ...

Stepping smartly in beat with my jazzy heart, I turn under the sidewalk canopy, then zip through the front door into the Carroll Parkside. "Hey— Oh, good evening, Mr. LoPriore," I hear behind me. "Sorry, you were goin' so fast ..." The rest of the doorman's speech is lost, plowed under my wake.

Now comes Test Number Two. Keeping my head partially

averted from the concierge at his little wooden desk, I scoot up to the elevators, push the button. Chance favors the prepared. The doors to the left elevator part like the waters of the Red Sea.

"Forget something, Mr. LoPriore?" the concierge calls.

"M'rahzeh," I grumble, hoping it'll pass for "my" something-or-other. And that my surliness will be well remembered. I swoop into the elevator, jab the CLOSE button.

I get off into an empty third-floor hallway, walk quickly around the corner to the service door, edge it open. Instantly, Gackle is at my side.

"Everything okay?" I whisper.

"Huh!" Cleveland Gackle at his most patronizing. "Lousy little Sarti? I have trouble with a piece of shit like that, you can forget about your whole operation."

He clearly did not give Mary Jane the night off; his clothes and breath reek of her perfume. But all right. Grover Cleveland Alexander, booze; Cleveland Alexander Gackle, grass. He'll open every damn lock in the place. Believe, Purdue.

We hustle down the hall to LoPriore's apartment. I take a pair of surgical gloves out of my pocket, slip them on. Gackle, already gloved, sets to work at the door.

I have to admire the crazy bastard. Credit card out of his pocket, zip! Through the main door lock like a clerk at a convenience store clearing a purchase. Then a key into the Winchester pickproof deadbolt, one turn and it's open sesame. The regular beep-beep of the alarm sets my teeth on edge but Gackle just closes the door, turns to the control panel, pushes four times. The beeping stops.

Gackle smiles smugly. I breathe.

"I'll start gettin' into the cases," he says.

I push the hall door open, take a half-step into the hall. Did another door just close? I stop, listen hard, hear nothing.

Out I go, taking care to leave the door barely ajar. I stride arrogantly toward the elevators: if any of the neighbors do come out, nothing would make them smell a rat faster than the sight of Vincent LoPriore skulking cravenly down his own hallway.

Wearing rubber gloves.

I stuff my hands into my pockets, don't take them out until I'm at the service entrance. I ease the door open. Hello, Hugh Curtis; hello, Dassidario; hello, Big Al.

Which suddenly gives me an idea.

A few quick whispers. Al smiles, nods agreement, then vanishes back through the service door.

Hugh, Dassidario and I trip the light fantastic down the hall to LoPriore's. If a neighbor happens to come out of his apartment or off the elevator, great. *Let* him see Vincent LoPriore escorting three suspicious characters loaded down with cardboard cartons and bubble wrap into his apartment just about a quarter to eight in the evening.

But no neighbors appear. As I close the door behind us I'm actually a little disappointed. Dassidario makes straight for the telephone on the little table just inside the door. Hugh and I hurry back to the collection room.

Once again I have to pay homage, if privately, to the impressive skills of Cleveland Gackle. Fully half the glass cases are open, and while Hugh and I stand admiring his workmanship he pops off another two locks. "Sorry I'm late," I say. "We had a little trouble—couple of cops ..." I stop, ask myself why the hell I'm wasting more time now? "But everything's okay." Which comes across as probably the lamest string of words I've ever uttered.

Gackle stops just long enough to turn his red-rimmed eyes on us. "Hey, you guys," he says sweetly. "You gonna stand there all night with your finger up your ass or are you gonna start packin'?"

22

Count on Cleveland Gackle to say what needs saying. Yes indeed, it's time to pack. "Big things into cartons first," I say to Hugh. "Then we can fill spaces with the little bird boxes and your snuffs."

"Cocksucker," Hugh mutters. "I wish he could be here to see this."

"Chill," I tell him—then a terrible thought hits me. "Hugh ... You didn't just happen to invite LoPriore to this party, did you? So we'd have no choice but to ice him?"

Hugh stares at me for a moment, then laughs harshly. "You do know me, don't you? Sure, I'd have loved to do that—but this is your party so I'm minding my manners. At least as long as everything works."

Believe, Purdue. "It's working just fine," I say as confidently as I can. "And it's going to keep working. Let's go—Moving Day."

Gackle is like a house afire. By the time Hugh and I have the first carton only half full he's down at the far end of the room, nearly every showcase lock dangling loose or on the floor. While I'm thinking how much easier it would be if we had our full complement of packers, the downstairs buzzer goes off.

All three of us slam on the brakes. Gackle looks stricken. That's right: he was in here when I got my brainstorm out by the service door. "It's okay," I call across the room to him. "We're just giving LoPriore another three feet of rope."

The buzzer rings again.

I walk slowly to the far wall, push the buzzer. "Yeah?"

"Mr. LoPriore?" The concierge.

Say as little as possible, say it nastily as possible. "Yeah?"

"There's a doctor down here, says you called him. Dr. Alberts? English guy."

"Yeah, great. Send 'im up."

"You okay, Mr. LoPriore?"

"Yeah. Little indigestion."

I sprint into the living room, crack the door to the hall. Less than a minute later I hear the elevator door rattle. I open the hall door; Big Al strolls in. He takes a moment to scan the living room, sizes up the massive furniture. "My, my," he murmurs. "'*Tristan und Isolde*' in carved mahogany." He drapes an avuncular arm around my shoulder, starts walking me back to LoPriore's collection room. "Now we'd best get packing, what?"

We've got the Jaquet-Droz golden birdcage and the Leschot cage-duet boxed, and Al and I are lifting the Ramelli fountain off its table when Dassidario materializes at my elbow. "I've got all the phones tapped," he says. "And a transmitter hidden and checked out in every room but this one. As soon as we bug the birdcage I'm done."

Big Al takes the fountain from me without missing a motion. "Hold the carton ... ah, there we are." He lowers the fountain gently into its resting spot, then straightens up and smiles. "Go along now and help Mr. Dassidario."

Al and Hugh go on cleaning out showcases as Dassidario and I walk over to LoPriore's first bird machine, a large brass cage suspended at eye level from a wall bracket. Inside the cage are two birds, one on a perch, the other on the floor, both ready to burst into song and dance at a flick of the on-lever. Dassidario watches closely as I lift the cage off its hook and set it on the walnut table which until a few minutes ago held the Leschot duet. The little man wrinkles his nose. "They ... look like real birds."

"They are," I say. "Most of these birds in cages had metal bodies but some of the makers—Rochat in particular—preferred to use real bird carcasses. More realistic. The Victorians were less squeamish than we are about hurting and killing animals."

"I won't have to touch those birds, will I?" Dassidario is clearly no Victorian.

I shake my head. While I was talking I was also loosening four screws on the bottom of the cage. As the plate comes away in my hand I turn the cage sideways, point inside. "Look."

Dassidario's expression of disgust turns to astonishment. "Oh my," he breathes. "I never dreamed they were so complicated."

"They're not really. The bellows and that little piston-whistle provide the sound; the cam-wheels control the song and movements, one cam for each function. The rest is just wire linkage. Your stuff is what's complicated. A little black ball sends out waves in the air, which are picked up by another little black ball miles away. *That's* complicated."

Dassidario, the giant fetus who can see the invisible, shrugs off the compliment. "Oh, well, Doctor, not really. It's not—"

"Look here." I point inside the cage. "Do you want to stick your bug on the inside of the cage wall, or on the bottom?"

He jabs a spastic finger at the bottom plate. "There," he says. "On a vertical wall, the adhesive might give way ... much safer on the bottom."

I slide the plate loosely into position, which appears to confuse Dassidario. "What are you doing?"

"Checking clearance. If somebody turns the birds on, we

don't want the mechanism to go clunk, right into your little snooper-box, do we?"

"Oh, no, no ... Of course not. But ... right ... *right*." His face glows with understanding. "Good thinking, Doctor!"

"Thanks." I point at a spot toward the edge of the circular base. "Right here ... go ahead, put it on. Then I'll get the cage back together and hang it up."

The next hour and a half passes in a blur, not only because we're moving so fast. If you're a collector you understand; if you're not, don't worry about it. An assortment of mechanical musical wonders like this comes along less often than blue moons or hens' teeth, and watching it literally pass through my hands is dizzying. A Solomon deCaus owl-and-birds; an Eppinger jumping canary; a Leschot bird-cum-music-cum-automaton chime ringer. Five incredible pieces by Jaquet-Droz. Oscar the Parrot, that marvelously realistic joke by Phalibois. Endless numbers of singing bird boxes. Hugh's elegantly-crafted holders of snuff. If I could, I'd linger over each piece, examine it carefully, run my fingers over the beautiful inlays—and of course, put each one through its paces.

As I take Hugh's Leschot double-bird snuffbox from its pedestal in the showcase I nearly give in to temptation. My finger is on the start lever when I glance at Big Al, working at my side. Maybe it's my imagination; maybe he really is giving me a wordless warning. Whatever, I draw back my offending finger, cut a generous length of bubble wrap, wind it around the snuff box, lower it into the yawning carton.

I understand now what makes a thief tick. A real thief, that is, not the twitching, drooling punk who breaks into your house to snatch the price of a day or two's relief from withdrawal, nor the no-brain slob who shoots up a bank branch office, leaving someone dead or worse in the process. I'm talking about the truly grand larcenist who'll spend a month, a year—however long is required—to make off safely with Whistler's Mother or the Leonardo Codex. The prize itself is only a trophy, no more the real object of a great thief's activity than a finished painting was to Rembrandt or a symphony down on paper to Mozart. Once a painting is completed or a symphony written there's a letdown, and the artist is compelled to begin again. While I pack the last bird box away I'm dismayed to find myself wondering whether there might be other rotten apples in The City who deserve to be relieved of their collections.

Al and I are taping the final carton shut when it occurs to me that for some time Gackle has been helping us pack. "The safe!" I shout.

Everyone looks at me curiously.

"Gackle, goddamn it. Did you get into the safe?"

For answer, he holds out a bulging envelope with an address window. The addressee is Vincent LoPriore at this location, the return address that of the Tall Oaks Insurance Company. Stapled to the outside of the envelope is a business card. David Mulgrew, Mulgrew Agency, downtown address, phone and fax numbers. I reach for the pen in my shirt pocket.

"No need of that, Doc," Gackle drawls. "I got all the information. Name, address, phone number, policy number, amount of policy—"

"Which is?"

Gackle pulls a small notebook out of his pocket, flips it open, reads, "Eighteen million dollars, plus. I'd say he's payin' big for this one."

"P'aps not," says Big Al. "Under ord'n'ry conditions I doubt any company would insure a private collection to anywhere near such an extent. But I suspect Mr. LoPriore is in a position to control a great deal of insurance business. I'd wager the availability of his insurance and likely a great deal of his premium is the price Tall Oaks considers fair exchange for the accounts he sends them."

Gackle tears the page out of his notebook and hands it to me; I fold it in half, put it carefully into my wallet. Then I pull the papers out of the envelope. "Ah—good. Number one on the list is that double-bird cage, with ... yes, real birds. It was bought on the twentieth of May, nineteen eighty-two, and"—I run my finger down the page—"he was telling the truth; great. That *was* his first machine."

Carefully, I refold the insurance papers, stuff them back into the envelope, hand it back to Gackle. "Time to start locking up the barn. Put this back in the safe, Pete, exactly the way it was."

He heads off toward the bedroom. "Don't forget," I call after him. "Put the original door key back into the desk drawer. And leave that little piece of paper I gave you underneath it."

"I already done that," Gackle says over his shoulder. "You think I can't remember nothing?"

"Just checking. Don't take it personally."

I look around. The room is naked but not disheveled. Grab, but no toss. Snatch, but no smash. Perfect.

"Hey!" Hugh barks. "Where the hell's the little fruitcake? Mr. Wizard with the white cotton gloves."

"Remember the plan?" I say. "Dassidario went out the service entry as soon as he got the bug into the birdcage. Right now he's in the back room at the Regina, checking out reception, listening to every word we say."

Hugh's face travels through red to crimson to a rich maroon. "You can apologize later," I tell him. "Let's get this stuff out of here."

23

Al and Hugh start lugging cartons out the door; I take a moment to call Dassidario. "Yes," he tells me, "but ... but *yes.*" All the equipment's functioning fine. The phone at the Regina is recording our conversation; he can also hear my voice through the birdcage-bug. On the second channel Sarah and LoPriore are coming through loud and clear from Mindy Roberts.

By the time I hang up the phone Gackle's got the safe and its contents back to pre-robbery condition. Without a word we grab a carton between us and head off, out the door, down the hallway, down three flights of stairs to the service entrance, into the alley behind the garbage cans. Three trips for each of the two teams and all six cartons of goodies are liberated.

On our final run Gackle resets the alarm. Outside in the hall, he leans his end of the carton against the jamb while he locks the deadbolt with the copied key. If a neighbor comes out, no sweat. I'm Vincent LoPriore, carrying large cardboard cartons out of my apartment, down the back stairs.

In the alley, tight smiles all around. We're doing great but we're not home yet. Gackle, Al, and Hugh peel off their gloves; Hugh stretches one glove around all the others, stuffs the elastic mass into his back pocket. Gackle salutes, then strides off on his way to the Regency Tower.

Al, Hugh and I ferry the cartons up the alley, pile them against the edge of the building, right at the front corner. People are walking by, of course, but we get no more than the briefest curious glance. Nearly nine-fifteen now, dark enough. I'll have no trouble passing for LoPriore, even to the doorman.

At the curb in the loading zone, engine running, is a dark panel truck, brown or deep maroon. My stomach starts doing barrel rolls? Screw up here, there'll be no chance to regroup.

Hugh walks out of the alley, across the sidewalk to the truck. He taps on the driver's side window, then turns around and takes off toward the Carroll Parkside entrance.

The door to the truck eases open. A big man gets out, limps a couple of steps toward Al and me. He glances in the direction of the Carroll Parkside and nods. Which means Hugh has stopped on the far side of the doorman, asked him for a light, and is chatting him up, making sure to keep his face away from us.

With surprising speed Mick flat-wheels to the back of the truck, opens the doors, looks around to check the doorman. Another nod. Big Al picks up the lightest of the cartons, moves deliberately toward the panel truck, pushes the box inside, climbs in after it. No rushing, no rude shoving through the pedestrian traffic, no furtive glances backward. He's a man loading cartons rightfully his into a truck. Only one person—the doorman—might wonder why Big Al Resford is loading cartons into a truck from the service alley of the Carroll Parkside. But Hugh Curtis is keeping the doorman occupied.

Five cartons left. Mick scuttles over, flashes a thumb-up. We grab the nearest box. In his eagerness to limp convincingly Mick trips over one of the remaining cartons, nearly goes down in a sprawl. I manage a brief, impromptu juggle; finally we get our load to the panel truck. Al, right there, shoves it forward.

Mick and I start back to the alley. Down the sidewalk, in the light beneath the Carroll Parkside entry canopy, Hugh's flying hands send bizarre shadows every which way as he spins his yarn to the spellbound doorman. Now I understand how Hugh built his footwear empire: he's not much for idle chatter, but when it comes time to make a sale Hugh Curtis can talk the ears off a field of corn. Were Hugh on board ship with Ulysses the Sirens would've been dead meat. Long after the sailors were safely through the channel those nasty little nymphs would've still been gawking at their feet, admiring their new Curtis shoes.

Just as Mick and I reach the alley, another kind of siren goes off. "I say, Buddy. *Nice* singing! *Very* good, what-what?" This followed by an ear-splitting squawk.

"A freakin' parrot!" Mick ducks into the alley, I right behind him. "Jeez, man—you put a live bird in there?"

"Not quite." I try to keep from laughing. "Mechanical. When you tripped on the carton you must have jostled him enough to move his switch to the delay setting ..." Mick's face is smeared with silent confusion. "Forget it—I'll explain some other time. Let's get the other three boxes into the truck before he performs again."

And when he does he'll perform for our benefit, I say to myself as we head back across the sidewalk with the third box of treasure.

We dance through the pedestrians with our million-dollar payloads, up to the panel truck for a gentle heave-ho. Hugh, bless his confabulatory little heart, is still jabbering away, the lit cigarette in his hand making fireworks patterns in the darkening night.

As Mick bends over the last remaining carton I nudge him. "Take the other side."

"What difference does it make?" he says, then shrugs. "You want this side, take it." He shuffles around to the far end of the carton.

"Listen close, Mick. We'll pick the carton up but just stand here. When the parrot starts talking, move."

We bend down, straighten up with our load. I balance the carton on one bent knee, pull what I'm looking for out of my shirt pocket, clutch it against the side of the carton.

Then we stand there.

And stand there. Mick shifts uneasily from one foot to the other. Maybe watched parrots never talk. Or Oscar's lever shifted back to off. Maybe his spring ran down.

A couple of pedestrians give us a study; I get uneasy. If someone decides to get a cop, he'll probably check thoroughly enough to blow my LoPriore impersonation all the way up the river to Sing Sing. "Hey, Doc," Mick stage-whispers over the box top. "How the hell much longer—"

"Shhh ... soon. Very soon. With or without the parrot." Come on, Oscar, you little bastard, I plead silently. Talk.

A pretty girl in a minimal tank-top strides smartly past the alley, her blond ponytail and lactation gear bouncing in impressive syncopation. Oscar picks up on her. "I *say*, buddy ..." cuts sharply through the cardboard.

The girl stops in her tracks, gawks at Mick and me.

She grabs with both hands at the little purse on her left shoulder.

"Now!" I snap. A loud, snarled, "Outa the way, bitch," and we're rushing across the sidewalk. "*Nice* singing!" Oscar shouts. "*Very* good, what-what?" Then the big squawk.

The girl answers Oscar with a shriek. She's riveted to the sidewalk, jaw slack, goggling. Some day she'll tell her grandkids an amazing little story. I turn around to look over my shoulder.

Timing is everything. No way the doorman could've avoided hearing our performance; now he's staring right at us. As my eyes meet his I see his body stiffen. Out shoots his right arm. "Hey!" he yells. "Mr. Lo— Hey, wait a minute!" He starts running toward us.

I drop the small piece of paper. "Go!" I holler across the carton to Mick. A fast dodge-step around an elderly couple walking a little brown wiener-dog, and we're in the street at the back of the panel truck.

"Hey, stop. Hold on—"

The doorman's voice cuts off in mid-command as he bends to pick up the paper I dropped on the sidewalk. With a grunt, Mick and I shove the heavy carton into the truck; I jump in after it. "Don't forget to limp," I growl at Mick as he slams the doors behind me.

"Over here, Thomas." Big Al takes my arm, guides me toward the front of the truck, against the back of the bench seat. "Hold on now, else you'll be tossed about considerably."

No sooner said than the truck lurches into traffic. Were I not gripping the back of the seat I'd be sailing ass over tea kettle past the cartons to the rear of the truck. "Hey, Mick! Take it easy," I yell. "Don't get stopped by a cop."

"I'd not worry, Thomas." The calm voice of experience. "Back here almost any change of direction or speed makes it appear the driver is behaving recklessly. I suggest you just relax and enjoy the ride."

24

As the panel truck riproodles its way downtown, Al and I clutch the bench seat, scrunch to the floor. When motion finally stops and the motor cuts out we clamber past the cartons to the back of the truck. An instant later the doors swing outward; there's Mick's ugly, scarred face. Mick jumps in. Al and I hop down to the street, slam the doors, hustle down the six concrete steps to stand underneath the Wind Me Up sign.

I knock on the door.

Practically before I'm finished, the door opens on Frank the Crank's grinning kisser. "Oho—I see the good Mr. LoPriore has come to dump his cheap little trinkets in my shop."

"Cut the crap," I say. "I'm just here as the schlepper, remember?"

Al moves past me into the shop.

"But of course, Mr. LoPriore."

Frank's a little high for my taste but better that than a visit from his Black Angel. He taps his dome, gleaming in the light from the signboard above us. "It's all up here, Mr. L-P, the whole routine. Not to worry about Frank, no sir, not for a minute. I was actually expecting to see Mr. Moncrief."

"Mr. Moncrief is waiting in the truck," I say. "I'm going back now, help him load in the goodies while you and Mr. Resford keep yourselves highly inconspicuous."

"Not to worry, Mr. LoPriore. You know me. Reliable as the night is long. Soul of discretion." He chortles as I roll my eyes and walk away.

Three quick trips, the six cartons are on the floor in front of the counter. The four of us set to work undoing part of what we'd done at LoPriore's. "Smart move, Doc," Frank says. "Having me rope off the loading zone in front of the shop."

"Seemed like the only way to make sure we'd get the space," I say. "Where'd you get the No Parking signs?"

Frank wags a finger roughly southeastward. "With all the construction they're doin' in this city? Little after five-thirty I put on a hard hat, went over to West Tenth, picked up the signs like it was my job, got 'em set up here, before six. After we're done, I'll get 'em all back to West Tenth. Nobody'll even know they got borrowed."

"You do nice work, Frank."

I stand back to admire the lineup on the counter. There are some twenty-five pieces: singing bird boxes, a necessaire, a singing bird-jardiniere, the Leschot cage-duet, a singing-bird pistol, the deCaus owl/bird automaton. Sotheby's would kill to be able to print that display on the cover of one of their catalogs. "That should do it," I say softly.

"Quite." Wholehearted agreement from Al Resford. "Time to take positions, I should say."

Mick and I pull off our surgeon's gloves, toss them to the side, stand in front of the counter opposite Frank. I pick up the necessaire, extend it toward Mick.

"Hold it ... right there." Frank the Crank, angling for Director of the Year. "Doc, turn your head a little bit more ... now try to look nervous. Mick, turn toward me ... just a little ... good! Now, move, but slowly ... great! One more now."

I replace the necessaire, then Mick and I bend over an open carton, come up slowly with a Maillardet bird-in-cage.

"Turn a little," Frank coaches. "That's it ... I want Mick face-on, and Doc, let's get your profile in this one. Right, perfect. Cheese."

We lower the Maillardet back into the carton. Frank claps his hands. "Okay. That's it, right? No, wait a minute. Mick." Frank snaps his fingers, holds them out to Mick like a claw. "Driver's license, please, Sir."

"Oh."

I have an uneasy moment as Mick fumbles in his pocket. He *does* have it with him, doesn't he? Yes, he does. Frank takes the little card back to the messy pile of books and papers by the wall in back of his desk, pulls open the copy machine lid, lays the card on the glass. A moment later he's back at the counter, copy in hand. "Thank you, Mr. Moncrief," he says mockingly. "Mr. Resford and I can take things from here. I trust you're satisfied with the financial arrangements."

Mick grins. On most people a grin looks good, but with Mick's eye patch and scar the effect is chilling. "Come on, Axel," I say. "Glove up; let's move. It's nearly ten o'clock."

"Where'd you get the truck?"

We're driving uptown on dark, quiet Tenth Avenue. Without taking his eyes off the road, Mick gestures out his side window. "On Twenty-fifth, between Eighth and Ninth. People are careless, y'know? Driver's window open a crack; I didn't even need the Slim-Jim. Coathangered the door handle, popped the hood, hotwired the ignition—I was off and moving inside of two minutes."

"Anyone see you?"

"Probably. But so what, with me made up like this? I just checked to be sure there weren't any cops on the block; after that all I saw was the truck. Looking back over your shoulder's a bad habit, Doc. Good way to get nailed."

"Too true." I point left. "Go in there."

"Huh?"

"Gas station. Go on in."

He squints at the dashboard. "But we still got almost half a tank—"

"Mick—where the hell're your manners? Borrow somebody's truck, you fill the tank."

We leave the truck in a parking space, a legal one no less, on East 60th between Fifth and Madison. I tell Mick to lock the door. "And be sure the window's shut. Damn city's full of car thieves."

Off come our gloves, into our pockets. On the other side of the dark street a man and a woman walk by. Mick yanks off the eye patch. "Whew! Nice to be able to see with both eyes."

"Would've been nice while you were driving."

"Hey, not my fault. You said I had to look like that—in case a cop stopped us or something."

"Just kidding, Mick. Your driving was great." I take the eye patch from him, lean forward, wipe with my handkerchief at the side of his face. "There—no more scar. And no more limping now, either."

At the corner of Fifth and 58th I drop back, let Mick go ahead, then watch him saunter past the doorman into the Regency Tower. I hang back until I see three couples approach the door. As the doorman bows and pulls the door open for them I sweep into the lobby, making sure to keep the couples between the doorman's eyes and myself. Straight on I go, into the elevator, up to the 32nd Floor.

25

Cleveland Gackle sits in a roundbacked chair, feet up on the table in front of him, face buried in a newspaper. Mick perches on a kitchen stool in the middle of the room, Edna leaning from behind, making him over into his new persona. Without looking around, she calls out, "Thomas?"

"Yo."

She glances up just long enough to make sure I'm properly withered. "Jesus, Thomas. 'Yo.' Listen, we may have a problem."

I shuck off my white shirt. "What kind of a problem?"

"Right after Gackle got back—goddamn it, Mick, *will* you hold still—Dassidario called. He said about the time you were leaving LoPriore's, things started to get sticky at the restaurant. LoPriore got impatient, wanted to go get the bird-temple right that minute. Sarah tried putting him off but no dice. They went outside, got a cab, and then Dassidario heard a loud noise."

Mick scambles off the stool, goes for his clothes. I sit down. "What *kind* of loud noise—ow, ouch! Hey, take it easy." The LoPriore hairpiece, ripped from my scalp along with an ounce or two of skin, dangles like a dead animal from her fingers.

"Stop being a sissy, Thomas. I don't know what kind of loud noise; neither did Dassidario. He just said it practically blew out his ears."

"Wasn't a shot, was it?"

Edna restrains my head with her left hand, rubs cold cream over my face with the other. "Thomas, how the hell am I supposed to know? Loud noise: that's all Dassidario could say. Stop wiggling, for Christ's sake."

"It's the cold cream. It feels disgusting."

"You're acting disgusting." Edna stops torturing me long enough to give Mick an approving look. "You're fine—go on, now. Get down to the lobby."

If Jesse James had had a mother like Edna he'd have retired rich and respectable. She studies my face like Picasso regarding a canvas.

"So what happened after the big noise?" I ask.

"Nothing." As Edna reshapes my left eyebrow her face doesn't change expression. "It was as if the bug went dead."

"I hope it was only the bug."

Edna nods.

She finishes her work in silence while I give myself a private licking with the rough side of my tongue. I must have been crazy to let Sarah dress up as The Whoopee Wench to go play big-stakes games with the likes of Vincent LoPriore. For that matter how about Trudy, sweet guileless little Trudy? Did she trip over herself and throw Schwartz out of kilter? Maybe we should have let Soapy Sandy show up with her black eye and swollen nose, take a chance she could tough out the evening ...

"You're Earl de Pinza again, Thomas. Go get dressed. Pete!"

Across the room, Gackle—silent since Mick and I came into the room—drops his newspaper and damn near jumps to attention.

"Put that silly paper away, Pete. Sit up and look worried."

"If you're having trouble doing that," I add, "just think about what we're going to do if LoPriore comes in here aiming a gun at us."

Gackle frowns, draws his brows together in thought. "Is that bird temple still back there in the closet?"

I shake my head. "Not on a bet."

"Where is it?"

"Frank's shop safe; Al'll take if from there. Safest arrangement I could think of. I'll face LoPriore with or without a gun every day for a year before I'd want to explain to Al why his friend's bird-temple is missing."

Gackle starts toward the bedroom. "Maybe I oughta go sit inside. That way if there's trouble I can call Dassidario."

"What the hell is he going to do?" I snap. "Better to call down to the lobby. Maybe Edna ought to go in there, not you."

Two birds put straight with one look from The Doll Lady. "I'm waiting here," she snaps. "Just like in the plan. Pete can go if he wants."

Gackle goes. It's the most decisive move I've ever seen him make.

Gackle's in the bedroom, probably having an emergency jam session with Mary Jane. Edna, looking marginally vacant, sits in an armchair. Me? I'd never get a job in a restaurant; I'm a lousy waiter. I pace up and down, march back and forth. Up again and down again; back again and forth again.

Fortunately our vigil is short. Ten or fifteen minutes after Edna finished making me over, I hear Sarah's voice outside in the hall. Harsher than usual, heavier on the New York intonation, but definitely Sarah—hallelujah. She's all right. Schwartz and Trudy? I hope.

"Well, hold on a sec, would you please, Mr. Hurryup. It's in my bag here somewhere—no, get your hand out of my purse. If you'd just leave me alone for a minute I could find it."

I clasp my hands behind my back, look in the mirror, put on the nastiest look I can manage. Edna's expression, perfect for the occasion, probably takes no effort on *her* part. She looks worried sick.

The door flies open; in with Sarah rushes our fool. Sarah waits until the door closes, then lets out a little scream. "Earl!" Quick hand to her mouth. "I thought ... you're back. Sally said you were going to be out late ... And Evelyn—"

"We couldn't get theater tickets, Dear," Edna says. "Right at the last minute and all that. So we just had dinner and came back to the room."

LoPriore looks ready to detonate. His white shirt and pants are covered with black smudge; his eyes are swollen, discolored. Strange. But I can't stop to think about it.

"I didn't need to stay out late," I snarl. "I work fast ... like some other people I know."

"Oh, Earl." Sarah rests her hand on my arm. "Mr. LoPriore has just been *so* nice. He came by after all of you left ... and I happened to be here, picking up a few things Sally wanted at the hospital. Well! He told me who he was and said he wanted to talk to you about buying some kind of bird-temple thing; then he took me over to the hospital to see Sally. After that he offered to take me to dinner—and we had just the most scrumptious meal at Mindy Roberts. Now we're back here 'cause he wants to make you an absolutely unreal offer on that bird-whatever-it-is of yours. I can't imagine how you'd ever say no to him."

Quavering voice; the hand on my arm is shaking. LoPriore's trying to look pleasant, an unreasonable self-demand if there ever was one. He can get only as far as a crooked-mouth simper.

"You can't imagine?" I shout at Sarah. "No! How's that? Ought to be clear enough even for you, you retarded bimbo."

I make the question line rhetorical by whipping my arm free from Sarah's hand, glaring at Edna, and pointing toward the bedroom. "Get in there, Mother."

"Earl ..."

"In the bedroom, Mother."

I grab Edna's arm, walk her as far as the bedroom door, yank it open. As I give her a little push inside I catch a glimpse of Gackle, sitting on the edge of the bed, hand poised for a quick snatch at the telephone. Not quite as laid back as you'd like us to think, eh, Pete? I slam the door shut.

LoPriore makes a last attempt to turn the conversational tide. "Hey, Mr. de Pinza, whyn'tcha just calm down, okay? At least let me make my offer." He hefts the briefcase in his right hand, flashes a sly smile.

"You garlic-stinking oilhead!" I shout, then ratchet the volume up a notch. "You really thought you could get your greasy hands on my bird-temple by pimping my idiot sister-in-law around the city? You must be as dumb as she is. Listen, Low-Priority: Number One, I don't like you. Number Two, I don't need your money. Now stick your offer up your ass and get out of my room."

Sarah rushes up to me. "Oh, Earl—at least you ought to listen to his—"

She never gets out the word "offer" because I hit her. Just the way Big Al showed me, open palm to the cheek, with Sarah moving off ever so slightly the instant I connect. Lots of noise, little pain. Her hand flies up to cover her assaulted face as she takes a near-somersault to the floor. "Oh, Earl," she whines. "What're you getting crazy like that for? I was just—"

"I don't care *what* you were just." I wave a fist down in front of her face. "One more word, your next stop's at the dentist's. Got that?"

She whimpers again, nods, sinks down crying. She's good, very good. It's all I can do to keep from kneeling down next to her and apologizing.

LoPriore watches the scene as if mesmerized. Maybe he's trying to pick up a few pointers for his next date. I turn to give him my full attention. "What, you're still here?" I yell, then add *fortissimo con brio*, "You're next, Butter-hair."

Have I ever felt more frightened? LoPriore's got advantages in weight, muscle mass, biceps girth, and fighting experience both clean and dirty. What's more, I know I've provoked him beyond any restraint he once might have shown. I stand up straight, extend my fists, try to see myself as one of those cigarette card pictures of bareknuckle-era pugilists with their physiognomies of dignified and determined manliness. Gentleman Jim Corbett. Ruby Bob Fitzsimmons. John L. (I-can-lick-any-man-in-the-house) Sullivan. Tough Thomas (Fake-him-out-of-his-pants) Purdue.

LoPriore, obviously no reader or respecter of history, drops the briefcase, lowers his head, charges forward like a thoroughly pissed-off warthog. As he comes up on me he tilts his head ever so slightly, cocks his right fist, and launches it sharply to my face.

His intended target is my chin: break the china with one shot, then get Sarah to show him where the bird-temple is. What he intends to do about Edna—and Gackle, when he sees Gackle is also there—I have no idea, nor do I want one. I sidestep; the blow lands against my left ear. My own punch ricochets harmlessly off LoPriore's shoulder. I hear bells; the room vibrates like a Magic Fingers bed.

Then I hear another sound, one far more welcome. Loud knocking at the door. LoPriore, jaw set, has his fist back for a second shot, but the knock makes him pause. I take the opportunity to deliver a nice left, straight to his gizzard. His convulsive "Oooph" as I hit him gives me as much satisfaction as I can remember feeling for a long time. Not that I stop to savor it. I skip lightly around my opponent to the door.

"Hey," comes through from the hallway. "Open up in there."

I pull the door open, restrain myself from embracing Mick, who now—thanks to Edna's skilled hand—is every inch Mick the Dick. He shuts the door firmly behind himself, glares at the two of us. "Okay," he growls. "What the hell's going on here?"

I can't fault LoPriore for gawking at Mick. Instantly, his every pugilistic advantage is not only gone but reversed. From intimidator to intimidatee in one swing of a door. Still I've got to hand it to the bastard; he doesn't fold. He gives Mick as nasty a bent eye as I've ever seen, then says, "Who the hell are you?"

"House detective," Mick growls back. "Lady next door called—said it sounded like there was a fight going on in here. Is this your room?"

"No," I holler, right on cue. "It's mine."

"What's your name, Mister?" Mick walks over to Sarah, still on the floor behind us.

"De Pinza," I say. "Earl de Pinza. I'm staying here with my wife and her parents."

Mick gives me a backward nod, bends over to help Sarah up. "You're—"

"Shirley McCoy," she says, with an impressive bat of her long eyelashes. "His sister-in-law."

"What happened to you, Ms. McCoy?"

Sarah looks at LoPriore, then at me. A marvelous mask of fear spreads over her face. "He hit me," she whispers, but with her eyes she indicates LoPriore.

I point at my throbbing ear, which has to be the color of a stop light. "He was coming after me," I say. "Would you please get him out of here?"

LoPriore's on the point of vaporizing. "Now, wait just one goddamn minute," he yells, but Mick has him by the right arm. Mick is a pro. If LoPriore is carrying, no way can he go for his heat. Mick moves him roughly toward the door. "*I* didn't hit her— I—"

"He came up here to steal a piece of my property," I say. LoPriore wrenches, tries to pull free of Mick's grip, but ends up flopping around like a fish being landed in a boat. Mick angrily jerks him forward. "You want to come quietly or do I have to make you quiet?" Mick folds his fist. "That's what you want, I can do it."

LoPriore tries a new tack, pulls himself upright, suddenly very dignified. "I want to speak to the manager."

I open the door as Mick and LoPriore approach it. "Manager'll be here at eight in the morning," Mick says. "You want to talk to him, come in then."

LoPriore wriggles; a sharp look from Mick stops that. "The night manager, then."

"Night manager only handles emergencies. He's got enough stuff to do as it is."

"But—"

"You don't like our arrangement, complain about that to the manager, too," Mick says, as they go out into the hallway. "In the morning. After eight."

As Mick and LoPriore dance toward the door, LoPriore suddenly lunges back. "My briefcase!" he shouts.

An extra half-million is enticing but I remember Sammy Shapiro's reward for being greedy. I pick up the briefcase, thrust it at LoPriore, give him a shove doorward. "Get him out of here," I growl. "With his goddamn briefcase and the horse he rode in on."

I watch the two men walk the length of the hall and disappear through the emergency exit door. Only then do I go back inside. I lean on the bedroom door, push it open. "All clear."

Gackle's face suggests it's one minute to midnight and the governor just called. He pulls a cigarette box from his pocket, then looks my way. "Go ahead," I tell him. "Give Mary Jane a kiss. Give her two—one from me."

Edna shakes her head, chuckles. "You're all right, Dear?" she asks Sarah.

"Oh, sure." Sarah grins. "He's a real powderpuff. Couldn't hurt me if he tried."

Another little laugh from Edna. "That LoPriore really *is* one mean son of a bitch."

"Not for much longer," I say.

26

Five minutes later the room door bangs open. Mick sails in, Schwartz and Trudy riding his backwash. "Jeez all man." Mick slumps against the inside of the door, wipes at his face with a handkerchief. "I hope I don't have to see that bird again. Ever."

"You shouldn't," I say. "Everything go all right?"

A nod. "I hustled him out the back way, told him if he sets a foot back in the hotel before eight tomorrow morning, he'll be talking to the cops, not the manager. Then I watched and made sure he went off down the street."

And what does Sarah do? My wife takes one look at Schwartz and Trudy, runs over, throws an arm around each of them. Then they stand in the middle of the room, yukking and high-fiving. Gackle and Edna watch the scene from the bedroom doorway. Ma and Pa Kettle and the Young'uns Go A-Scamming in New York.

"Nice to see everybody so cheerful," I say. "I'm just happy you're all alive and in one piece."

"Well, of course we're all right," Sarah says with a sly smile. "Why shouldn't we be?"

"Because Dassidario told Edna he heard a loud noise over your bug, then everything went quiet. He thought it might have been a shot."

Sarah reaches back, probes the thick tangle of hair above the nape of her neck. "Well, damn!" she says. "It *is* gone. Must have happened when—"

At which point she breaks down giggling. Sarah, giggling! I give her a quick up and down, and ask how much she's had to drink.

"Hey, she only had one drink, a cocktail," Schwartz chirps. "I was watchin'; I'll swear to it. We just had ourselves a little bit of an adventure, that's all. You want to tell him, Sarah? Or should I?"

Sarah wipes at her eyes, waves her hand. "Tell him, Broadway. Go ahead."

For close to twenty years they've been Mrs. Purdue and Mr. Schwartz to each other. Now all of a sudden they're Sarah and Broadway.

Schwartz coughs into his hand. "Well, our friend LoPriore got himself a little bit of the hots in the restaurant—"

Sarah was practically jiggling. "I strung it out and out and out—first I nursed that cocktail for more than half an hour. Then I had an appetizer, a salad, an entree, and ate them as slowly as a human being possibly could. But when I said, 'Now for the best part, Vincent, a great big sweet gooey dessert and a cappucino—that's Italian, like you'—"

"You said *that?*" She couldn't have; I can't believe it. "*That's* what you said?"

"Word for word. And right there something snapped, I saw it in his eyes. He leaned over the table, right in my face, and started talking like a madman, soft, very controlled, rumbly ..." She drew in a deep breath, swallowed hard. "Just remembering starts me shaking. He said it was past nine-thirty and we were going back to the Regency Tower *now* because he wasn't about to lose his bird-temple while I was ... Oh, Thomas ... While I was finger-fucking myself over a piece of Boston Cream Pie.

Then his hand started sliding like a snake across his chest, inside his jacket, and said, 'Let's go, bitch. Up. Dinner's over. Game time.'"

"He wouldn't have ... fired a gun *there*," I said. "In the middle of a crowded restaurant."

"*You* didn't see his eyes," Sarah barked. I saw her eyes and shut up in a hurry. "I didn't really think he would either," she said, considerably more quietly. "But I wouldn't have bet money on it. All I knew was I had to do something, so I said, '*Okay*, fine, whatever you say. Just let me go powder my nose first.' He said, 'Forget it, you nose looks fine, but it ain't gonna look so hot if you don't quit fuckin' with me.' 'Hey, look,' I told him. 'I'm *sorry*, but if I don't go pee I'm gonna do it all over the goddamn cab. You gotta pay the check anyway, right?' Oh, you'd have been proud of me, Thomas."

"Fortunately, Trudy picked up and met me in the Ladies' and we put a plan together."

Trudy turns full-beam admiration onto Schwartz. "Actually, Broadway picked up," she says. "He sent me in."

Schwartz, no shrinking violet, seems to grow three inches. "Well, it was up to us to make sure LoPriore didn't get back here too soon, right? So the noise Dassidario heard? That was our cab—Trudy's and mine—hittin' the one with Sarah and LoPriore in it. About a block and a half down from the restaurant."

"Well, talk about luck—" And plunk! drops the penny. "Luck," I repeat lamely. Which sends Sarah into another giggle-fit.

"Person's got to make his own luck," Schwartz says brightly. "We, uh ... persuaded our cabbie to hit the other guy."

"You, uh, persuaded him. Just how did you manage to do that?"

"Hey, Doc—money talks. For a couple of fistfuls of

frogskins, our cabbie was only too happy to do a clip on the other cab. Right rear fender, bang."

"Bang is right." Sarah is highly amused. "If I don't have whiplash now, I never will. The hit knocked me off the seat onto the floor; I'm sure that's where I lost the bug. "

"Their cab was this little Dodge thing." Live-wire Schwartz, current always running. "Ours was a Checker. You shoulda seen that fender—like hittin' a ladybug with a sledge hammer. The cabbie was an Indian guy, and talk about pissed? Whew! Jumping up and down, yelling, 'Look, look, you have drove right into me, you ruin my cab.' And *our* cabbie, he just says, 'You cut me off, raghead motherfucker.' Idea was for our guy to argue and shout all he could, keep things on hold as long as possible. But then all of a sudden LoPriore takes a look at me and says, 'Hey, wait a minute. I've seen you before.' I try playin' dumb, but it's no good. 'You were in the hallway outside my apartment, just a few days ago. With that doctor. Left with a pretty sore hand, didn't you? And wait ... wait a minute ... More'n a year ago, that estate on the West Side ... where I bought a bird. Son of a bitch, you were there, *too*, weren't you?'"

"Oh, no," is all I can mutter.

"You ain't whistlin' Dixie, Doc. LoPriore grabs me by the front of my shirt, twists me right up into his face. 'Start talking, you scummy little kike,' he yells. 'I want to know what's going on here.' And meanwhile, his other hand starts movin' towards his pants pocket."

Schwartz, the conquering hero, pauses for effect.

"I'm all ears," I say. "How did you get out of that in one piece? And what happened to LoPriore—all that grease on his ice-cream suit. Like he was down under the cab fixing the transmission. And his eyeballs—looked like somebody used them for pencil sharpeners."

Will wonders never cease? Effect is not what Schwartz is pausing for. He licks his lips, glances at Trudy.

"It's all right, Broadway," she says quietly. "They're friends. Go ahead, tell them."

Schwartz swallows. Trudy lays a hand on his forearm, "Really, it's okay. I don't mind."

Schwartz looks back to his audience with pain in his eyes I've never seen before. "Okay," he says, drawing out the word to three syllables. "LoPriore's ready to make hamburgers out of me when up walks Trudy, face on her like death, and she says, '*What* was that you called him?' LoPriore goes like a statue. 'A kike,' he says. 'I called him a scummy little kike, which is what he is. That okay with you, Lady?' Last word wasn't even out his mouth when Trudy brings down her foot on top of his. I mean, those white booties he wears look nice and pretty, but we're talking a three-inch stiletto heel on Trudy. LoPriore cuts loose some kind of a yell; Trudy gives him the one-two: knee in the crotch, fingers in both eyes."

I look from Schwartz to Trudy and back. Is he putting me on?

"LoPriore drops me in the street, and Trudy's all over him. Gives him a crumpler right under the ribs and a chop in the throat with the side of her hand. Now LoPriore's down in the gutter, choking and puking. I quick-grab Trudy and stop her, then I slip LoPriore's gun outa his pocket, tell him this was a message from Weepin' Willie—"

"Weepin' Willie? Who the hell's Weepin—"

Schwartz shrugs. "Name came to me, I used it. 'Stay the hell outa Weepin' Willie's way,' I say. 'Otherwise, next time no one's gonna stop her 'til she's done.' That Indian cab driver's scared positively shitless, figures he's seen a gang score and now he's a dead man. I stick out my hand, he screams like I goosed him. But then he sees the hand's fulla money.

'Enough to fix your cab?' I ask. 'Oh, yes, Sir,' he says. 'More than sufficient—' I slam the bills in his hand, tell him, 'Outa here—anyone asks, you found your cab like this after you came out from supper. Say anything else, *you* get a call from Willie.' Guy's gone before you can blink your eyes. Then I hustle Trudy back in our cab and we're gone."

Schwartz looks at Sarah, says, "I'm sorry—I didn't want to leave you there with LoPriore—"

Sarah waves him off. "You had to," she says. "But thanks for taking his gun. You should've seen his face when he realized he'd left his briefcase in the first cab. Lying there in the gutter, supporting himself on one elbow on the curb. 'Relax,' I told him; then I showed him *I* had the briefcase. 'What'd you think, I was going to let Sally's half-million bucks just go riding off down the street?' He laughed, actually laughed, and told me maybe I wasn't such a dumb twat as I sounded."

"Sweets from the sweet," I say.

"I asked him who *were* those people? And who was Weeping Willie? He said he didn't have a goddamn clue. He just lay in the street there, blinking at me and wondering out loud if he was ever going to be able to see straight again. I didn't hurry him. By the time he was on his feet and ready to find another cab, we were back on schedule."

White noise of crowd talk. "Wait a minute," I say. "There's one link missing."

Silence. I look at Trudy, whose face flares red as her suit and hat. "Cinnamon rolls, gefilte fish, chicken and dumplings .... no one in their right mind would take you on in the kitchen. But—"

"She was one of them German kids," says Schwartz, in a voice so uncharacteristically subdued I wouldn't have recognized it as his. "Parents got her out at the last minute. She went to Spain, bounced around Scotland and England, finally ended up over here. After the war she went back to Germany, looked for her parents, but she could only trace them *into* Theresienstadt. Right there by the camp, she said to herself, 'Never again,' and when she came back to New York she was into the movement with both feet from day one. She can use a gun if she's got to, or a knife or a rope, just as nice as Sarah saw her use her hands and feet. Anyone who says kike anywhere near her is a goner."

As fast as the color came into Trudy's cheeks it fades to a chalky white. Her little hands are clenched at her sides. Schwartz puts a solicitous arm around her.

"Like pullin' a fuse on a grenade," he says.

Little coughs all around. Sarah—of course—marches over and once again embraces Trudy and Schwartz. Trudy—of course—starts to smile.

Edna hoists herself to her feet. "We'd better get back to The Regina," she says. "Dassidario'll be disappointed if we miss the performance over his radio."

Mick grabs Edna's suitcase full of clothing and makeup; out we all go, into the hallway, onto different elevators.

27

Crowded around Dassidario in the back room at the Regina, we wait. And wait. I'm beginning to get nervous when over the receiver comes the sound of a key in a lock. "From the transmitter in the vestibule," Dassidario whispers. "I put it into the pocket behind the light switch panel."

"It's takin' him a while." Schwartz chuckles. "His hands must be shakin' so bad he can hardly hold the key."

Footsteps, four beeps of an alarm panel being deactivated, slam of door closing. Then something unexpected: LoPriore's voice. "Son of a bitch, Rover! Right now I oughta be holding that asshole de Pinza's bird-temple, and all I got to show for the night is a four-hundred-dollar tab from Mindy Roberts Yuppie Hash House plus the two sorest eyes this side of Guy Lombardo. Shit, who the hell *was* that hammered-down twat in the red hat, put me away with her two hands before I could even get a hand on my heat? And that little kike, all of a sudden there he is again? No coincidence, no way. And *Weepin' Willie?* Who in fuck is Weepin' Willie? Somebody new in town trying to move on me?"

"Never heard of no Weepin' Willie, Vin. Morning, you're gonna have to make you some calls."

All around Dassidario, blank looks. This is a voice none

of us has heard before. Schwartz shrugs. "Rover?" Dassidario, finger to lips, hushes him.

"Yeah. I'll say." LoPriore again. "I ain't gonna forget about the bird-temple, either—or Earl de Pinza, that snotnose fucker. You ain't just gonna ice him for me—you're gonna bring me his balls, I'll hang 'em in my collection room. Right next to the bird-temple. Show 'em off to my guests, like they did with Napoleon's cock." We hear liquor pouring, glasses clink. "Be just like with Billy Brezhnowski."

"Billy who, Vin?"

"Brezhnowski. Great big Polack kid in my seventh grade class, duck's ass hairdo, face full of zits. Got hair around his dick two years before anybody else, which was a problem for all the rest of the kids. One day it was me got sent home with a bloody nose, my clothes all ripped, and when the son of a bitch finished workin' me over he started laughin'. 'Hey dago, go on home and stick it to your sister. That's what guineas do, ain' it? That's why you're all a bunch of retards.' I run like hell, get myself home, and what does my Mamma do? Hauls off and gives me a slap in my face, yells 'You let that pimpleface do this to you, call you dago and beat you up? You want to be my son, you're gonna go back and fix Pimpleface so he never touches you again. You understand me, Vinnie? Never! Now go sit in your room.'

"So I'm sittin' in my room, and I'm thinkin': is my Mamma nuts or something? Billy Brezhnowski's a head and a half taller than me and he outweighs me two to one. Maybe after I take care of him I'll go a couple rounds with Rocky Marciano, like just for the fun of it. And then I look across the room and there's my Joe DiMaggio baseball bat, standing in the corner. Big fuckin' heavy wooden bat."

"Jesus, Vin!"

"Half an hour later there I am, scrunched behind the fence

next to the school ballfield. On the other side of the fence is
right field; behind me there's woods goin' down into a valley.
Billy Brezhnowski lives down the hill, through the trees, and
back up on the other side. After the game he's gonna come
around the end of the fence to cut through the woods on his
way home. But today he's gonna get a little surprise.

"So here comes Bad Billy around the fence, twirlin' his
catcher's mitt on one of his fingers and whistlin'. He sees me
and freezes–but that's all he has time to do. I'm already swingin',
and I was a super hitter when I was a kid, knew just how to time
a curve ball, could always bash the high heat. Bam! I go with
the bat on the side of Billy's head, and I'm tellin' you, Rover,
Joe D himself never got one better on the sweet part. That big
Polack cocksucker goes straight down in the dirt. He's twitchin'
all over, then he starts havin' epileptic-type fits. I watch him for
a couple of minutes. 'That's for the bloody nose and the ripped
shirt,' I tell him. 'Also for callin' me dago.' I never did find out
where my Mamma dumped the bat but inside of an hour there
was a new, clean, Joe D bat in the corner of my room. And
when the cops came by, you should have heard Mamma. 'Oh
no, my Vincent's a good boy, he was home all afternoon, lying
in his room after that bad Billy Brezhnowski beat him up. One
of Billy's friends told the police maybe it was Vincent? Well,
maybe it was him, Mr. Policeman. Maybe you should ask him
did *he* do it and try to blame it on my Vincent.' Mrs.
Brezhnowski, she got the same thing. Oh sure, Mamma was
sorry, it's a terrible thing, a boy in a coma, the doctors say he's
never going to wake up. But he got what was coming to him,
always picking on the little boys like he did.'

"'And,' Mamma told me that night, 'that wasn't just Billy
you took care of. No one in that school is ever going to try and
beat you up again. You'll see.' She was right, Rover, fuckin'-A
right. From that day on, not a lot of people ever talked wise to

Vincent LoPriore, and when they did they only did it once—
wait a minute, what the hell is that, on the floor ... huh! Piece
of plastic bubble wrap. I must've dropped it when I brought in
Asshole Curtis's snuff boxes the other day. Goddamn maid's
gettin' careless. Moron knows how to hold her hand out for
money, but do an honest day's work for it? But, hey, Rover—*you*
know what happens to a guy says no to Vincent LoPriore. You're
gonna help me give de Pinza double what Curtis got, triple
maybe. Come on inside—I'll show you Curtis's collection."

We move in closer to Dassidario and his briefcase; the little
man, methodically twisting dials and turning knobs, seems not
to notice the suddenly increased possibility of contamination.

Footsteps, click of light switch; then a momentary silence
explodes into, "Jesus fucking immaculate *Christ!*"

As if by mass reflex we move back from the receiver.

Man Med Neurology's a major referral center, and with
our huge affiliated Psych service we get a lot of patients with
brain disorders that make them more than a little difficult to
live with. The unchecked rage of amygdaloid tumors, the incredible coprolalia of Tourette syndrome, the fiercely aggressive behavior associated with some epileptic equivalents, the
horrifying delusions of severe paranoid schizophrenia ... I've
seen and heard my share. But never anything to come close to
the savage, naked fury of LoPriore's scream.

Rover's response is a harsh whisper, and no wonder. I'm
impressed he can even speak. "Vin ... they cleaned you out.
Locks ... all over the goddamn floor ..."

Thunder of pounding hoofbeats: LoPriore must be charging back into the living room or the vestibule. Dassidario
fiddles with his dials. "Swerdlow!" LoPriore screeches. "This
is Mr. LoPriore. I've been robbed ... Yes, you dumb son of a
bitch, robbed! Wiped clean. Call the cops and get the hell up
here. Now! Right away!"

A group cheer rises from the Regina Gang. "Got 'eem ... We *got* 'eem," crows Espinoza, his smile more brilliant than his purple satin shirt and grass-green pants. As LoPriore slams down the phone we push at our ear canals like passengers on a rapidly-descending aircraft.

"Ska-wawk! Oh, I say, Buddy," Edna Reynolds chants. "*Very* nice singing! Jolly good, eh wot?"

What the dig lacks in accuracy it more than makes up in spirit. Everyone laughs. Dassidario, the good soldier, reproves us. "Quiet ... but ... but ... *shush*! Everybody. Listen."

We hear scraping and thumping, interspersed with loud curses, mostly in the form of single-word ejaculations that if taken as commands in some sort of parlor game would produce a scene beyond imagination. After a momentary silence a door opens. "What the hell took you so long?" screams the Master of the House.

"I'm sorry, Sir."

That's Swerdlow, the evening-shift concierge at the Carroll Parkside, a lean man in his mid-sixties with a face like a horse that hasn't finished in the money in his last twelve starts. His collar button's probably open against the heat, red tie hanging loose. "I had to get Petrovich to relieve me at the desk," he says laconically.

"Relieve you, hell," LoPriore bellows. "As if it mattered if *anyone's* sitting at that useless goddamn desk. What did you do—let them walk right by you with all my stuff?"

"Stuff, Sir?"

Poor Swerdlow has to be trying frantically to remember whether there was any time all evening he'd left the desk unattended. "What did they take, Mr. LoPriore?"

"Look around in here, you idiot," LoPriore screams.

Silence. Then, "Well ... I don't see anything."

"Of course you don't, you shitbrain. That's what I'm telling you. All my birds are gone; my whole collection. They walked right past you with it."

"Mr. LoPriore, I beg your pardon." Swerdlow's voice drops an octave, indicating that whatever their relative positions, he's perilously close to his limit of politeness. "I was off the desk only once tonight, a little after nine, coffee and ... crapper break. While I was gone, Petrovich covered me. That desk was attended all night, every minute. Nobody could have gotten past me or Petrovich without us seeing them. Besides—how did they get inside in the first place?"

Behind me, Schwartz snickers, punches Gackle's arm lightly. Gackle chuckles. "Wasn't much of a problem a'tall."

"Goddamn it," LoPriore shouts. "That's right—how the hell did they get in here? Door was locked, both locks; alarm was set. I had to turn it off ... wait. Fire escape?" Hoofbeats again, running away from the transmitter. "No—no way. Window's locked tight. Jesus Christ on a pogo stick! How in hell ... Swerdlow, why are you looking at me like that?"

"Like what, Sir?"

"Don't diddle around with me. You look like you think I'm nuts or something."

"Sorry, Mr. LoPriore. I'm just trying to figure out how a thief managed to get in here without leaving any signs of a break-in, then got all your things down and away without being seen."

Maybe Swerdlow just remembered how the doorman came running in, saying he'd seen Mr. LoPriore and some gimp loading cartons into a panel truck. And what would Swerdlow have said to that? "Fine," he would have told the doorman. "Mr. LoPriore wants to load cartons, let him load cartons. *I* didn't see anything—did you?" Definitely not, the doorman would've agreed.

The irony in Swerdlow's voice hits a clunker in LoPriore's ear. Just a "Hmph" for reply.

Doorbell rings. LoPriore's going to exhaust himself, galloping from one end of his apartment to the other. The door slams open. "Is one of you Vincent LoPriore?"

"That's me," LoPriore rumbles. "My, uh, friend, Mr. Zatella—"

"I was just leavin', actually—check back with you tomorrow, Vin, okay?"

"Little allergy to blue uniforms, Rover?" Edna snickers.

Brief pause. Then, "I'm Lieutenant Corum; this is my partner, Lieutenant Wesley. We're responding to a burglary call; is this the place?"

"Goddamn right it is."

More footsteps, scraping of furniture. For the next ten minutes, LoPriore tells the cops his story. While he was out to dinner with a young lady and then having a nightcap with his friend Mr. Zatella, somebody cleaned out his extensive collection of valuable mechanical and musical birds. Without forcing locks, disturbing the alarm, or coming in through the window.

Swerdlow insists—politely but with unshakeable firmness—there was no other possible entry to the apartment.

Corum says he'll check the windows; he finds them all securely locked and with no evidence of replaced glass or putty. Wesley asks LoPriore to run through exactly what he did when he returned, including just how he opened the two door locks and shut down the alarm. Corum walks through the collection room while Wesley goes out to check the service entrance. Corum finds nothing. On his return Wesley reports the service door is securely closed and locked; all *he* found were a few plastic peanuts. "Could be from anything, sitting there forever."

"That area is vacuumed daily." Swerdlow's tone is icy.

"All right," Wesley says. "All day, then."

"Do you have any idea who it might have been, Mr. LoPriore?" Corum asks, almost off-handedly. "Any other collectors who might have wanted to get your things for themselves? Or to sell to other collectors?"

In the silence I have no trouble seeing LoPriore shake his head.

"He can't imagine who could be a bigger crook than him," Mick stage-whispers.

"All right." Corum says. "We'll make a report. Get the right people on the case; they'll be back to you in the morning. Meanwhile, you better alert your insurance company. They're not going to be very happy, but—"

"*I'm* not so friggin' happy myself," snaps LoPriore.

Door slams. "Concierges, cops," LoPriore mutters savagely. "Useless bastards. Might as well hang up a sign outside: Come right on in, help yourself." A few odd sounds, banging, scraping; then LoPriore screams, "David! Get your ass over here ... Yes, I mean now."

"David Mulgrew, Mulgrew Insurance Agency," I murmur. "The name on the policy in the safe. How'd LoPriore get hold of him at this hour?"

"Somebody can get a personal policy the size of this one, you better believe he can put a finger on his agent twenty-four hours a day," Gackle drawls. "You also better believe that agent's gonna be over there before LoPriore hangs up the phone."

He nearly is. I'm with Corum: David Mulgrew cannot be a happy man. Long enough in the business to have engineered an eight-figure policy for Vincent LoPriore, he knows he'll never live through the heat if the company has to pay off. I can just see him: out of bed in a bounce, wife pissing and moaning how the phone woke her up, throw on shirt and pants, forget the goddamn underwear. Socks, shoes, let the hair flop over his forehead. Downstairs to the street, hey, cab—cab! All the way

over, seeing LoPriore on one hand, the insurance company on
the other. Talk about rocks and hard places.

By the time he's inside LoPriore's apartment Mulgrew is
probably thinking about a quick flight to Brazil and plastic
surgery. Again, we hear LoPriore tell his story. Mulgrew asks
him to demonstrate the two birds in the hanging cage, the only
piece left in the room. We hear the birds go chirp-chirp-chirp
as they move their heads, flip their tails, flap their wings.

Toys for overfinanced grownups; that's what these things
were a hundred and fifty years ago when they were made;
that's what they still are. Every day, Mulgrew has to deal with
people who've lost a home, lost a spouse, had their mother's
necklace and earrings ripped off. People you can't help feeling sorry for, even while you're trying to dope out how to
deny their claims, or at least delay payment as long as possible. But here's LoPriore, crying like a man with a paper
asshole about how some nasty people stole his play pretties.
Even to me—as hardcore a collector as they come—it's revolt-
ing. *Mulgrew* is who Mulgrew's got to be feeling sorry for
now: unless they can track this stuff down and fast, it's *his* ass.
Between the company and LoPriore, he's charcoaled meat.

"Nothing else to do tonight," Mulgrew says. "I'll check
with the police first thing in the morning; then I'll be getting
back to you."

"What do you mean?" LoPriore sounds on the verge of
losing it one more time. "'Check with the police and then get
back to me'?"

"I can't do anything without a police report," Mulgrew
says with excessive patience. "Soon as I can get one, I'll start
investigating."

LoPriore mumbles something indecipherable, then says,
"You *better* get moving, David. Bad enough coming home and
finding the world's greatest collection of mechanical birds

gone, poof, kaput. I better not find myself getting screwed over by my insurance company. Know what I mean?"

Whatever he means, Mulgrew assures him—more than a little huffily—insurance companies are not in the business of screwing over their customers, a remark that draws a mighty clearing of the throat from Gackle. "Hope if a shot of lightning hits, it don't come through that speaker of yours," he says to Dassidario.

Dassidario's brow corrugates, jaw jerks convulsively. "Oh, no ... no ... Mr. Gackle. That can't happen. You see, those men are nowhere near the bug ... but ... but even if lightning did hit the bug ... even a direct hit ... it still wouldn't ... couldn't—"

"Dassidario!"

The little man looks at me popeyed, equal measures of hope and fear playing rapidly over his face like a laser light show.

"It's okay," I say, ever so gently. "Relax. He was making a funny."

A very tentative smile struggles its painful way across Dassidario's features. "Oh, oh, but ... oh, yes! I see. A joke. Oh. Ha-ha, yes. That *is* funny. Lightning—"

I pick up the phone, punch the numbers for Wind Me Up. Frank the Crank answers on the first ring, high as a blimp towing a Quaalude ad. "Sure, whaddaya think, Doc? Of course everything's under control. You don't have to worry, not for a minute, not with old Frank on the job. I got Al packed up, out of the shop by ten-thirty, drove him to Kennedy to catch the twelve-oh-one red-eye to Amsterdam. I gotta say, though, I don't know how in hell he's gonna get it all past Customs on the other side. Six boxes full? Whew!"

"Cool it, Frank. He won't have any problem; he's got ten thousand dollars from the expense money, converted into Dutch guilders. Customs there tends to be understanding in any case, and on top of that, a couple of the agents are long-term business acquaintances of Al's. One'll be on duty when he comes through with the boxes. Little clearer now?"

"Like ice water from the spring. Everything jake at your end?"

"Right on schedule. The cops and the insurance agent have been through LoPriore's. I'll see you in the morning; we'll take it from there."

"I'm rested, Doc. I'm ready. Corner of Seventh and Four-teenth, a quarter to ten, right?"

"Got it, Frank. See you there."

I hang up the phone, clap my hands. "Everything's right on schedule—now let's get some sleep. Dassidario, go back to the Regency Tower and don't leave that room, not for a second."

"Thomas, I ..."

A hanging introductory phrase from Edna takes prece-dence. We all stare at her.

"I was just wondering ... that Rover character. You don't think he's going to be looking for Earl de Pinza tonight, do you? At the Regency Tower, say?"

"Doubt it. I suspect whatever he and Vin-Boy have in mind is on hold 'til after the insurance investigation runs down. LoPriore's sore, but he's not stupid. He has to figure, a move on de Pinza and the bird-temple just hours after that scene tonight, the cops'd be right at his door. And not to investigate a burglary." I point to Mick. "He's not going to forget about the Regency Tower's house detective in a hurry."

Mick grins.

I don't want Dassidario getting nervous, certainly not at this point. "Don't open the door unless you can see damn clearly who it is," I say. "Anything happens you don't like, call Espinoza."

The little Puerto Rican's face lights up. "I be at my desk phone—you better believe it."

Dassidario's head bobs like an apple in a Hallowe'en water barrel. He gets up from his chair slowly, as if there were wires connecting him to his electronic apparatus and he needs to step carefully to avoid disrupting circuits. He looks at me expectantly.

"Don't worry," I say. "Mick'll stay at the receiver here, just in case LoPriore throws us a curve before morning. If there's any trouble he'll call you at the Regency Tower." I look at Mick. "Which room?"

"Thirty-Two-oh-One."

"Right. Now let's move. Edna, Gackle, Hugh, Schwartz, Trudy. Hang close to your phones; no grocery shopping or antique picking, no nothing 'til it's all over."

People edge toward the door. Soft chatter. A group of business executives talking calmly about their big collaborative project. Sarah gives me a look she's never given me before: then takes two steps toward me, rests her arms loosely around my neck and without disengaging her eyes from mine, moves her lips against mine. She kisses me, long, hard and hot. When we separate, her eyes are full of mischief.

Gackle pauses just long enough to roll his eyes. He shakes his hand as if it had suddenly caught on fire.

As the door closes behind him I take Sarah's hand, start for the door. Mick gives us a wave. "Your place or mine?" I ask Sarah.

More eye mischief. "Yours for you, mine for me."

I stare at her. I don't understand.

"Your rules," she says. "No talking, no drugs, no alcohol, no pretty women."

"But you're my wife—"

She holds up a hand. "Let's go, Caesar. It's been a long day."

I follow her quietly to the door.

28

Frank the Crank, looking rested and ready, is waiting for me on the corner of Seventh Avenue and 14th Street. It's a quarter to ten, beautiful morning, clear and warm. A day that tells you to enjoy what's left of summer.

Frank's foxy eyes glitter with eagerness. "Hey, here he is. Dr. Purdue, Fixer of Busted Phonographs."

I wave my black leather bag, actually an old doctor's bag, but full of tools and small parts for working on sick music machines. "Thomas Purdue, FBP. Emergency house call."

As we come up on 12th Street I nudge an elbow into my companion's ribs. "Look. Over by your shop door."

A man in a tan summer suit, holding a dark brown leather briefcase, is wearing grooves in the sidewalk in front of the Wind Me Up sign. He checks his watch twice within five steps. "Little anxious, are we?" I whisper.

Frank chuckles, a good ho-ho. "Think we got a live one."

Frank takes out his ring of keys, approaches the lock on the sliding metal barrier in front of the door and windows. The man stops pacing. "Mr. Maar?"

For an instant I think he's asking after the wrong man. I've never heard anyone address Frank the Crank by anything other than his Christian name, or variations thereon. But Frank doesn't miss a beat. "That's me," he says, extends a hand. "Frank Maar, owner and sole proprietor of Wind Me Up. What can I do for you, Friend? Interested in a nice music box? An antique phonograph? A clock?"

Frank in flying mode can filibuster Strom Thurmond all the way to South Carolina. The man smiles, a bit wanly, and retrieves his hand from Frank's unrelenting grip. He passes Frank a business card. Over Frank's shoulder I read: David Mulgrew, Mulgrew Insurance Agency.

"I'd appreciate a few minutes of your time, Mr. Maar," Mulgrew says. "About a very important matter."

Frank glances my way, then says, "Sure, sure, Mr. Mulgrew. Just let me open up. This here's my friend Thomas; he fixes machines for me. He came by this morning to look at a phonograph's not working right."

Brief handshake from Mulgrew, briefer inspection. The insurance agent is stocky, close to my age, with wavy reddish hair and a bumper crop of freckles. His eyes are red, the lines between his nose and mouth sag. He looks as if he didn't get much sleep last night.

"Nice'a'meetcha, Mr. Mulgrew," I say, then add, "No problem, Frank. Just give me the machine. Bet I have it playing by the time you're done talking."

Inside the shop Frank turns off the alarm, switches on the lights. He leads me to the rear, hands me a little Edison Gem phonograph. "Just doesn't want to go." Frank moves the start/ stop knob rapidly back and forth several times.

I set the machine down on the counter top. "I'll see what I can do."

"Great." Frank turns back to Mulgrew. "Okay, Mr. Mulgrew. Come on back of the counter and have a seat. See what *I* can do for *you*."

In his eagerness Mulgrew trips on his own feet, almost falls. In Frank's small shop, a near disaster.

I lift the phonograph bedplate and see that Frank disabled the machine by screwing down the speed-regulating arm on the governor so tightly as to bind the governor against any degree of spring pressure. A ten-second fix, but I'll take a lot more time than that. I open my doctor's bag, pull out a dental pick and a small pair of pliers, pretend to be deep in diagnosis over the little phonograph.

"Mr. Maar, let me come right to the point," I hear Mulgrew say. "You made a purchase last evening. A lot of very nice, very expensive mechanical birds."

I nearly knock the Gem off the counter.

"Huh!" Frank rubs his chin as if that might make it easier for him to visualize his prior evening's activity. "Yes, that's right. I did. But can I ask why—"

Mulgrew scans the room as if his head were on a swivel post. "May I see the pieces, please, Mr. Maar." No question mark at the end of the sentence.

"Well, no," Frank says calmly. "Actually, you can't."

"And why not?" Mulgrew sounds ready to scream for a cop. Come on, Frank, I think. Don't be too cute.

"Because they're gone. Not here any more."

"Where are they?" Mulgrew is on his feet, standing over Frank, fists clenched.

"Europe, I think." Frank makes a show of studying the agitated insurance agent. "Hey, now, Mr. Mulgrew—I don't know what's going on here, but why don't you just sit back down for a minute." He gestures at the chair but Mulgrew doesn't budge. "Go on, sit down," Frank repeats. "I'll tell you what I know. Then you can ask me whatever else questions you got."

The expression on Mulgrew's face as he lowers himself into the chair suggests he's afraid there might be a string between the chair and Frank's hand, and at any instant Frank's going to give that string a pull.

"Okay," Frank says. "Here's the deal. A couple, few days

ago, this guy comes in my shop. He looks like a pretty tough customer so at first I hang close to my panic alarm button here." Frank points under the counter, below where I'm pretending to work on the phonograph. "Guy said his name's Axel Moncrief and he's got a collection of bird machines he wants to sell. They sound interesting. Then he names his price, and for what he's got it's reasonable. But it's still more jack than I can put my hands on in a hurry. So I start thinking about brokering. This Moncrief is in one big hurry to sell, says he's got a tax problem, and a quick ten percent sounds better to me than a slow zero. So I get on the horn and call this guy"—Frank fumbles at his desk, pulls a business card from beneath the corner guard on the blotter pad, hands the card to Mulgrew—"this Alfred Roosenboom—he's from Holland, and whenever he's over here he comes into my shop. He always says if I get my hands on something *really* super I should call him, he'll come right over. So that's what I did. He said he'd get right on it, be over in two days with the money—"

"How much money, Mr. Maar?"

Foxy Frank rubs his chin again. "Well, I don't know I really ought to be saying, Mr. Mulgrew. I mean, my customers have a right to their confidentiality—"

"Mr. Maar, I don't know who your Axel Moncrief is but I'd certainly like to find him. A very serious crime has been committed over these items, which, by the way, were insured by our company. You don't have to tell me, of course, but I think before long you'll be compelled to. I'm sure you get my drift."

Frank licks his lips. "A crime? Like what kind of crime?"

"I'm really not at liberty to say right now." Prissy David Mulgrew. "But I still think you'd be wise to share your information with me. Voluntarily."

Dutch Uncle Frank beams benevolence. "Oh well. Hey, no problem, Mr. Mulgrew. I run a clean business, totally legit." Frank holds up his right hand. "You want to know, okay. The price was a million-two. Plus one hundred twenty thou for me."

Mulgrew looks like a willow tree in that instant between the logger's last blow with the ax and his cry of "Tim-*ber.*" Frank reaches forward to stabilize him in his chair. "Hey, well—I told you it was a lot, Mr. Mulgrew."

"A ... a ... *lot?*" Mulgrew is spluttering, apoplectic. "Mr. Maar ... do you know ... are you *aware* ... you let those irreplaceable items out of your hands for roughly ten cents on the dollar?"

"No shit?" The Soul of Honesty's wide eyes brim with shock and horror. "That much difference, huh? I figured they were worth more than I brokered them for, but how are you going to sell a whole big collection like that, and get market rate? Anyway, this Moncrief came back the next day like I told him to, and I said fine, we got a deal, bring the things in tomorrow afternoon—that would've been yesterday—and I'll have your dough for you. But about one o'clock Moncrief calls and tells me his friend with the truck can't get off from work until six, can I give 'em 'til nine or ten, say, to get the things packed and loaded? I said for that kind of dough, sure I'll be here at nine or ten at night, but Mr. Roosenboom—he's sitting right here, came all the way from Holland—I really hope you're not planning to send him home with nothing for his trouble. Moncrief says no sweat, he'll be there by ten o'clock. And he was. His friend and him unloaded the stuff, let Roosenboom look it over. And hey, let me tell you. Roosenboom was thrilled."

"I'll bet he was." Mulgrew looks as if Frank might have just backfired a bit of particularly rotten cheese.

Frank takes no apparent notice. "Yeah. Well. Roosenboom gave Moncrief the mill-two, and me the one hundred twenty-

K. Then after Moncrief left I got a big Checker cab for Roosenboom, we loaded his stuff and off he went. Maybe he's still in the city, maybe he ain't. Not my business."

"Is it your business to be certain you're not buying stolen merchandise, Mr. Maar?"

"Hey, Mr. Mulgrew!" The Highly Insulted Soul of Honesty half rises in indignant protest. "Twenty-six years I've had this shop, and you know how many counts of hot merchandise I've had? None, for your information. I do everything by the book, straight according to Hoyle." He pulls some materials out of his desk drawer, lays them on the desk between Mulgrew and himself. "Take a look," he snaps. "Here's my ledger with the transaction. And here's a copy I made of Moncrief's driver's license—"

Mulgrew, gone popeyed, makes a grab with both hands at the paper. "May I have ... could you make me a copy of this?"

"Sure." Frank shrugs. "But I got something you're going to like even better." He passes two photographs across to Mulgrew, then points toward the counter again. "Hidden camera, see? I always get my sellers on Candid Camera, 'cause like you say, you never can know for sure. But this's the first time I've ever had to actually use a picture."

I hope Mulgrew's had a recent treadmill test and passed it. He dog-eyes the shots Frank took of Mick and me the evening before, jabs a finger at my image once, twice, three times. "This man," he shouts. "This man ..."

"No, no." Frank exudes gentle patience. "That's not Moncrief, this is." He points at Mick. "This other guy, all in the white, he was the friend. You know, the guy with the truck."

Not an instant longer can Mulgrew's chair contain him. The insurance man levitates, faces Frank. "Mr. Maar, I need these pictures. I'll give you a receipt—"

"Uh ... no, I don't think so." Gently but firmly Frank

takes the photographs out of Mulgrew's shaking hand. "I mean, if you're sayin' these were hot goods I sold—by mistake, of course —then I'd really hate it if my pictures got lost."

"All right. Mr. Maar." Mulgrew swabs a handkerchief over his now-soaking forehead. "Let me be open with you. These pictures are not of thieves, exactly: the crime here is attempted insurance fraud. This man"—another jab at my image—"is the owner of the goods. I don't know the identity of the other man. I suspect he hired 'Mr. Moncrief' to pose as the seller but then he did something foolish, tried to buy off his accomplice with less money than he'd originally promised. Which made the accomplice angry enough to call my office this morning. He didn't give *his* name, of course, but he told me everything else, including the fact they'd left one item behind because it was the owner's very first purchase, not a valuable piece, but one with considerable sentimental value. And I've seen for myself that piece is still in the owner's apartment."

Mulgrew, buddy-buddy smile on his glistening face, looks like a chicken trying to slip the con to a fox. "We're really not concerned about you, Mr. Maar; you clearly did everything right. Even better, you've provided us with the evidence we need to tie up this case once and for all. And just for the record, we're not concerned about your customer, Mr. Roosenboom, either."

Which hardly matters. If anyone should take it into his head to check out the Amsterdam phone number on Alfred Roosenboom's business card, they'll find it's the office of Mr. Hendrik Willem Ten Bosch, a respected attorney. Mr. Ten Bosch will tell the inquirer he serves as contact person for his friend and client Mr. Roosenboom, who is understandably anxious about having the whereabouts of his fabulous collection known. Mr. Ten Bosch will further make it clear he's bound to silence by the rules of attorney-client privilege. Of course he won't mention his longstanding quiet business association with Mr. Roosenboom, a.k.a. Mr. Al Resford, in the acquisition, receipt and passage of liberated art goods and antiques.

"The only crime committed seems to have been the act of our client." Mulgrew drones on, a fly in late summer heat. "We have evidence from other quarters which at the least strongly suggests he arranged to steal his own things and sell them in order to collect on his insurance policy—a very sizable policy, I assure you, Mr. Maar."

The Soul of Honesty's eyes widen again, this time with innocent amazement. He lets out a low whistle.

"So you see why I'm so eager to have your photographs." Mulgrew extends his hand slowly, like a snake advancing over Frank's desk top. "They'd serve as absolute confirmation; we could send the perpetrator straight to prison and close our case." He sounds like an ad for Dr. Ophidian's Soothing Unguent for Achy-Breaky Joints and Muscles. "Why don't you let me take them now? After all, you'll still have the negatives."

Frank eases the photos out of Mulgrew's reach. "No negatives. It's a Polaroid kind of camera, just takes straight pictures."

Amiability and generosity are spread across Mulgrew's face like jelly from a two-year-old's sandwich. "I'm certain the insurance company will be inclined to show its gratitude in a ... material way, Mr. Maar."

"Well, I guess that's great, Mr. Mulgrew—but I got to tell you something." Frank taps a little chorus on the photos with the tips of his fingers. "Insurance companies are funny people. They're real grateful, but once they get their hands on whatever it is they're after, all of a sudden they're not so grateful any more. Kinda like a guy when he finally gets his girl friend in the sack. Now, I got to think anything under a ten percent reward'd be pretty chintzy, wouldn't you say that? And if what you're tellin' me is true, I'll be saving your company something like ten million dollars—"

Mulgrew's cheeks flame into splotchy scarlet. This man will be fortunate indeed if he manages to survive his morning with Frank the Crank. "Why, you can't be serious—"

"I sure can when I want." Frank suddenly looks very much like someone wanting to be serious. "These are your own numbers I'm talking; now, tell you what. Go check with your insurance company; let's see just how grateful they want to be. If *I* think they're being grateful enough, you can write out a receipt, saying exactly who it is who's on these pictures and I'm turning them over to you voluntarily. How's that?"

Mulgrew, voiceless, chokes on his spleen.

"And in the meantime I'll do the best I can not to lose them—hey, they're valuable pictures. Sad thing is, though, I *am* gettin' older and you know how that goes. I put something down, then damn if I can remember where it is." Frank slides the photographs into his pocket, extends his hand toward Mulgrew. "See you soon as possible, right, Mr. Mulgrew? That's the best thing for both of us."

Mulgrew shakes Frank's hand as though he's under anesthesia. As he shuffles past me to the door I make sure I look fully occupied with the Edison phonograph. Not that I think he's likely to take any notice of what I'm doing.

The door slams. I raise my eyes to Frank. The foxy eyes glitter a dark, deep happiness. Frank chuckles. "You can take it easy, Doc. He's up the stairs, down the street. In an hour, maybe less, he'll be back."

I straighten up. "With a check."

"Sure with a check. Why not?"

"Why not is it wasn't in the script."

Frank extends his arms full length, throws back his head, a preacher entreating the Lord to bring understanding to his dull, stubborn congregation. "So I improvised. Another million, give or take. Are we supposed to just toss away that kind of dough?"

Delicate moment. Frank in hypermotion, uncontrolled lithium bait. One off-handed, careless remark from him to Mulgrew and our whole operation goes flying down the tube. On the other hand if I start an argument I may send him careening into one of his bottomless depressions. Mulgrew comes back with his check, Frank tells him to shove it up his ass, and we're all packing for a quick run to Rio.

I force myself to grin at Frank. "'Are we supposed to just toss away that kind of dough,' huh? That means you're sharing the check?"

"Hey, what do you think? I'm on the bus, I pay my fare. Share and share alike." Up goes the hand; only the Bible is missing. "You know me, Doc. Soul of honesty. Hey, you fix my phonograph?"

If I didn't know Frank as well as I do I'd swear he was serious. I nod. "Plays just fine now."

"Oh yeah? Let's see." Frank reaches past me, pushes the start lever. As the 90-year-old wax cylinder starts to rotate I hear the unmistakable voice of Billy Murray, a popular singer in the early years of the century but now remembered only by those crazy people who fill their houses with silly, antiquated sound reproduction systems:

> *He goes to church on Sunday.*
> *He passes round the contribution box*
> *But meet him in the office on a Monday,*
> *He's as crooked and as cunning as a fox*
> *On Tuesday, Wednesday, Thursday, Friday, Saturday,*
> *He's robbing everybody that he can*
> *But he goes to church on Sunday,*
> *So they say that he's an honest man.*

Frank starts to laugh, at first just a chuckle but rapidly building until his whole body shakes. Tears run down his cheeks. He points at the phonograph, just in case I might somehow have missed the joke.

"Could've been a little embarrassing if I'd started that record playing with Mulgrew sitting there," I say.

Frank waves my concern out the door, into the street. "Ah, Doc. You worry too much. You ever meet an insurance guy with a sense of humor? By one o'clock that check's gonna be in the bank."

29

Frank's estimate is off by not much more than an hour: a little after two, he's got Tall Oaks's check in the bank, and if it's only for $250,000 well, better in our pockets than theirs, as Frank puts it.

Three o'clock, we're all in the back room of the suite at the Regina, crowded around Mick at the monitor. By Mick's account, the morning brought LoPriore even less joy than the prior evening. Mick recorded endless phone inquiries about Weepin' Willie and some grubby little kike, works for him. But nobody'd heard of any Weepin' Willie, not in the Apple, not anywhere. Nobody'd heard word one about a plan to put the hit on a big-time collection of antique mechanical birds. About ten-thirty LoPriore's pal Zatella dropped by. "One thing I know," Mick heard LoPriore grouse, "is that little kike's the key to this whole business—has to be. First at the estate sale, then out in the hallway, then that shit with the cabs. Step one, I got to find him. Green paper does good things for peoples' memories, you could use it to cure Alzheimer's. My insurance guy, this Mulgrew turd, he's gonna be here at three, bringin' his boss with him. Says he thinks we can get everything all taken care of. So the bundle I'm gonna get off Mulgrew — well, it ain't gonna *replace* my birds ... but I bet it helps find them. I figure I'll have that half-pint jew-bastard here inside of a day, and you better believe how fast I'm gonna find out who his friends are. Another day, maybe two, all the birds'll be back. Then we go after de Pinza."

"Your call, Vin. When you want me to move you know how to find me."

Doorbell.

LoPriore's hall door opens to silence. No hello, no nothing. Finally Mulgrew's voice comes through the speaker: tight, clipped. "Mr. LoPriore, this is Roger Zoller, Chief of Tall Oaks' Insurance Division of Fraud Investigation. These two other gentlemen are with the NYPD Fraud Department. Inspectors Marshall and Prothro."

"Fraud investigation?" LoPriore snarls. "What the hell you telling me? Somebody's tryin' to pull a fast one with my birds?"

Mulgrew clears his throat. "Can we step inside, please, Mr. LoPriore?"

Shuffling of feet, then the door slams. "I'll come right to the point, Mr. LoPriore," Mulgrew says. "We are in the possession of evidence—strong evidence, I have to say—to show you participated in a plan to steal your own collection, sell it, and file a claim for the insurance."

"Yes!" Schwartz high-fives my right hand, Frank the Crank my left.

After no more than a second, LoPriore explodes. "Mulgrew, what— Are you freakin' crazy?"

Little round Espinoza chortles. The discoloration around his eye is almost gone now. "I theenk eez more like *you* freakin' dead in the water."

"Please sit down, Mr. LoPriore." Bass rumble: Zoller, Marshall, Prothro? "I think you ought to hear Mr. Mulgrew out. I think we all should."

Chairs scrape. They're sitting down around the little table in the middle of the room, under the crystal chandelier. "Okay, Mulgrew, I'm listening." LoPriore's voice. "I sure as hell hope for your sake you got yourself a good story."

I think I actually hear Mulgrew gulp, can picture him glancing around the circle, slurping moxie from the containers to his right and left. "First of all, Mr. LoPriore, we have sworn testimony from the doorman and concierge saying you left the premises a little before seven o'clock last evening. Then you returned perhaps forty-five minutes later. And—"

"'Perhaps forty-five minutes later'..?" Someone—probably LoPriore—pounds the table. "What're you talkin' about, you little putz? I didn't come back here 'til eleven o'clock, when I found my birds missing. And called your piss-ant company."

"Wait—wait just a minute, Mr. LoPriore." I hope Mulgrew's got a major supply of Xanax in his briefcase. "Let me finish. Both the doorman and the concierge said you came back through the lobby at just about seven forty-five. They said you seemed very nervous, distracted. You went upstairs in the elevator. A little while later a man came to see you; he had a British accent, said he was a doctor. You told the concierge you had indigestion—"

"A doctor with a British accent— Hey, wait just a goddamn minute. I'm gettin' indigestion just listenin' to this shit. I bet you're gonna tell me this doctor's a big guy, right? Shaped like a pear? Kind of beady eyes, light brown ..."

LoPriore's voice peters out. He must've picked up on little nods and tight smiles all around the table.

"Good job, asshole," Gackle crows. "Way to go! Help 'em out all you can."

"Mr. LoPriore, please. A little after nine o'clock the doorman saw you and another man loading boxes out of the service alley into a panel truck. Which is interesting, considering how dirty and greasy your clothing was when you called me over last night to report the 'theft.' Well, that truck was reported stolen early this morning from a West Side address; it was found later, parked just a few blocks from here, undamaged. Mr. LoPriore, do you know a man named Axel Moncrief?"

"Axel Mon— Oh, come on, you shit-face catlicker. No, I *don't* know any Axel Moncrief. What the hell are you getting at?"

"That's the name your associate used. Maybe it's his real name, maybe not. But the shopkeeper you sold your collection to made a copy of Moncrief's driver's license."

"What?" LoPriore revs to go airborne. "This is just not fuckin' *real.* A shopkeeper got Moncrief's driver's license? Great! Go chase Moncrief. Find out what the hell really happened last night."

"We thought we'd talk with you first, Mr. LoPriore. You see, not only did the shop owner give us a perfect description of you, his description of Moncrief squares precisely with the doorman's. And—although you didn't realize it—the shopkeeper had a hidden camera. Here, let me show you."

Sound of papers rustling; a short pause. Then Mulgrew says, "We have other copies, Mr. LoPriore."

"Good for you, Pigshit," LoPriore sneers. "I can see you're gonna go far in Twin Oaks. Got yourself covered just in case I decide to eat your pictures for lunch, before one of your gorillas can grab my hands. Sure, those're my birds—but what'd you do? Decide to make it look like I'm selling my own stuff? Doctor up a couple of pictures to show me with some yahoo I never heard of or set eyes on? You pricks'll do anything to not pay off on a claim." His voice rises. "Well, you're gonna see—"

"Mr. LoPriore, please take a close look there." Mulgrew sounds like Aunt Polly telling Tom Sawyer she saw him with her very own eyes sling the spitball. "These are Polaroid pictures; you can't doctor a Polaroid. And while we're on the subject of photographs, do you recognize this one?"

Moment of truth. All around the receiver, open mouths. Silence heavy as clotted cream.

"Where did you get this?" LoPriore half chokes, half whispers.

No shouting now, no profanity, but LoPriore's voice is appalling. A block away, on the safe side of a speaker-box, I feel in mortal danger. The faces around me make it clear I'm neither alone nor crazy.

"When the doorman saw you loading the truck, he ran over to see what was going on," Mulgrew says. "You and your associate jumped inside and sped off. You were in such a hurry you dropped this into the street. You—"

The rest of Mulgrew's speech is cut off by a howl as if from a skewered animal. "You little shiteater! Cocksucker son of a bitch bastard—you threw my *mother* in the gutter! I'm gonna *kill* you—"

Squeal of fear and pain from Mulgrew, followed by a loud thump. Then the *basso profundo* of Zoller/Marshall/Prothro. "Mr. LoPriore—don't try that again."

A moment of heavy breathing; then when LoPriore speaks, it's in an odd, strangulated voice. "You two-bit bean-counter pricks. You bags of chicken shit. You're gonna hear plenty from my lawyer. When he's done with you, you're gonna be on the street, selling pencils out of a cup."

"I think calling your lawyer would be an excellent idea, Mr. LoPriore." Mulgrew, back in business. "I'm sure he'll be interested in seeing these pictures. Not to mention the receipt from the shopkeeper who bought your goods from you."

"Receipt?" LoPriore snarls. "What receipt?"

Crinkly sound, paper being passed. "The one the police found in the back of your desk drawer," Mulgrew says laconically. "While they were looking around last night. After the 'robbery.'"

No one could miss the sarcasm wrapped around that last word. Off to the side of our group, his feet up on the table, Gackle guffaws. "Where I left it with the door key," he crows. "Woulda been hard for even a cop to miss it."

"I ... *we* would like you to come down to the station with us," Mulgrew goes on. "You can call your lawyer from there—or if you'd rather, do it now. In any case, you don't have to say any more until he arrives."

"Fuck you *and* your Miranda shit," LoPriore snarls. "Let's just make sure I understand this. You're saying I came back here before eight o'clock last night, emptied my own place out, sold the stuff to some shopkeeper, then came back again about eleven. That's it?"

"That's about it, yes," says Mulgrew.

"Well, what if I can prove I was *with* somebody all that time? From a few minutes after seven 'til damn close to eleven?"

"Then we'd definitely want to speak with that person. But I think if I were you, Mr. LoPriore, I'd call my lawyer before—"

"Fuck my lawyer!" LoPriore rages. "I don't need any shyster, the thing's so obvious. Walk over to the Regency Tower on Fifty-Eighth with me and I'll *show* you who I was with. *Then* I'll call my lawyer. And then you can go back to your pissy little office and try and figure your way around the lawsuit I'm going to slap on you. On top of the regular insurance payment."

A string of mumbled sounds. "All right, Mr. LoPriore," Mulgrew finally says. "We can do that."

"Here it comes," I say. "Better get Dassidario on the line, quick."

30

The Regency Tower operator says he'll connect me to Room 3201. The phone rings. And rings and rings and rings. I shift from one foot to the other. "Come on, Dassidario," I mutter. "You're not supposed to be anywhere else."

The operator cuts in. "I'm sorry, Sir, but the occupant of the room you are trying to reach—"

"Is there!" I snap. "He moves slowly. Keep ringing—please."

On the ninth ring, Dassidario picks up.

"Where the hell *were* you?" I shout.

Everyone in the room looks at me.

"Well, I ... but ..."

Probably in the john, I tell myself. Had to wash his hands, dry them, spray them with Lysol, dry them again, put on new gloves ... "Forget it—just listen. LoPriore's on his way over with the insurance adjuster and the Head of Tall Oaks' Fraud Division. Plus two cops from the city's Fraud Unit. You ready?"

"Well, but ... but ... *yes*! That *is* what I'm here for, isn't it?"

"It is," I say, very softly. "Just wanted to give you a little warning."

"Oh, I've been ready all day."

"Good. No problem then." I come within a mental millimeter of telling Dassidario to knock 'em dead. "Give them a few minutes to leave," I say, very carefully. "Then call us."

I hang up. The room is quiet. Schwartz and Trudy are off getting sandwiches at the deli a few doors south on Madison. Espinoza, Sandy, and Mick are sitting on the sofa. Edna's parked in an overstuffed chair to their right. On their left, Gackle and Hugh sit like bookends on a love seat. Frank the Crank wanders into the bathroom.

Sarah pats my arm, smiles. "We're almost there."

It occurs to me to tell her we're not playing horseshoes, but a smile from my wife, particularly one that mischievous, is not to be discouraged. "We're close," I say. "But Dassidario's still got to do his bit."

The transmitter fills the air with crackles. A moment later, Schwartz and Trudy burst through the door, each carrying a bulging brown paper bag. Bouquet of delicatessen instantly fills the room. Schwartz looks around. "Hey, what the hell *is* this? I made a wrong turn and ended up in the City Morgue?"

"I'll get some plates and glasses." Sarah disappears into the kitchen. A gang of soon-to-be tax-free millionaires eating sandwiches off waxed-paper wrappings and drinking cream soda out of bottles? Not if my wife has anything to say about it.

We sit and eat, balancing our fragrant platefuls on our laps. Everyone eyes the transmitter.

Firm knock.

Hands all around the room freeze halfway to mouths. Even Gackle has crisp tension lines between his mouth and eyes.

"Here we go," says Schwartz.

It's make or break time, and whether we're made or broken is entirely up to Fenton Dassidario. If I had a choice it wouldn't be, but I don't and it is. Dassidario is the only gang member who's stayed strictly off-stage; LoPriore hasn't seen him, neither has Mulgrew. For better or worse he's our secret weapon. Please, please: don't any of his visitors sneeze on him.

Sound of door opening.

"Yes?" says a familiar, prim voice. "What can I do for you gentlemen?"

Was any pause ever so pregnant? LoPriore finally swallows, loud enough to be heard through the speaker at the Regina. "*What* the—" he begins, but the bass voice interrupts. "Are you the occupant of this room?"

"Why ... yes," Dassidario says. "Yes, yes I am. What is ... the matter?"

"That's what *I* want to know." LoPriore smashes through the conversational line. "Where the hell are the people who were here last night and the day before?"

"I ... I don't understand. Who *are* you gentlemen, anyway?"

Schwartz fetches me a solid elbow in the ribs. "Jeez, Doc, that Dassidario! He's fantastic. Doesn't even have to act."

"Mr. LoPriore, please." Bass Voice, back in control. "We'll handle the questions if you don't mind."

I have no trouble seeing Dassidario turn that popeyed stare onto his visitors, then wring his white-gloved hands as if he'd slept on them and is trying to work out a severe case of pins and needles.

"I'm sorry, Sir," says Bass Voice, oh so gently. "I'm Detective Buck Marshall; this is Sergeant William Prothro. NYPD." Little slapping sound, badge-holder being opened. Dassidario must be leaning forward at the waist to inspect it from a safe distance.

"Oh, yes ... yes. Police, of course. But ... but—"

"We're from the City Fraud Investigation Unit—"

"Oh dear ... Well, but ... but ... I haven't done anything fraudulent. What do you want ... with *me?*"

"Take it easy, Sir. You've nothing to be concerned about. We just want to ask a few questions about a case we're investigating. May we come in?"

"Certainly. But ... but *certainly.* Of course."

It's hard not to smile. By this point LoPriore must look like a Rottweiler on a leash, ready to tear into the bedroom, slashing at anyone or anything in his way.

"Nice suite you have here, Mr ..?" Marshall ventures.

"Dassidario. Fenton Dassidario. Yes. But ... *yes*. I mean, yes ... it *is* very nice, isn't it? That's why I come here in August. The good hotels have such low rates I can afford to stay in a suite like this."

"You're here on vacation, then, Sir?"

"Yes—yes. I take my vacation in August, at the end of summer. That way I can look forward to it all through the hot weather. And when everyone else is back home, I still have *my* vacation ahead of me. And the rates are so low—"

Marshall coughs politely. "Yes, Mr. Dassi ..."

"Dario. Dassidario. *Fenton* Dassidario, Officer."

"Where do you come from?"

"Akron. That's in Ohio."

"Yes, fine. And when did you get here?"

"Well, let me see. This is my third day ... yes. Yes, that's right. I checked in three days ago."

"Hey, wait a fuckin' min—"

"Mr. LoPriore!" Marshall booms. "I've told you to please let *us* handle the questioning. Break in one more time, you and Prothro will go outside and wait there 'til the insurance people and I are done. Understand?"

Silence. LoPriore understands but doesn't like it. I doubt Marshall cares.

"Insurance people?" asks Dassidario.

"Yes. These two gentlemen are Mr. Mulgrew and Mr. Zoller, of the Tall Oaks Insurance Company. We're helping them look into a case of insurance fraud. Mr. Dassidario: have you ever seen this man before?"

"The one in white, Officer?"

"Yes, Sir."

A pause, then, "No ... no ... but ... *no*. I don't think so ... no! No, I'm sure I never have."

"And you've been here three days, you said? You've occupied this room all that time?"

"Well, yes. Yes, of course. I came straight from the airport and checked in. But maybe ... well, maybe not ... not *exactly* straight, I suppose. It took forever to get my bags, and then I had a terrible taxi driver: he took me all around and finally just *shoved* me out of the cab down around Greenwich Village somewhere. He said that was where I belonged; what do you suppose he meant by that? I had to find my way up here, and on the way I got hungry, so I stopped and had some dinner. Yes. Yes, that was what happened."

"What do you do in Akron, Mr. Dassidario?"

Marshall's voice sounds weary. Dassidario is wearing him down. I know the feeling.

"Oh. Well. I own Dassidario's Party and Sickroom Equipment. Sales, rental, the biggest place of its kind in Akron. Here, Detective Marshall. Let me give you my card."

"Thanks." Marshall pauses—probably scrutinizing the card—then asks off-handedly, "Traveling alone, are you?"

"Oh, yes. Yes."

"Not married?"

"No ... *no*! Absolutely not."

"I'm sorry, Sir, but I have to ask you this. At any time—any time at all—since you've been here, have you had a woman in this room?"

"A woman?" Dassidario's tone suggests Marshall might have asked whether he'd been entertaining serial killers in his suite. "No, Detective, I most certainly have not! I ... I don't care *what* he may have told you, Detective; I've never seen him in my life."

"You lousy little pansy!" LoPriore's voice is chilling. "I'll give you—"

"Don't!" One quick word from Marshall, as if to a naughty puppy.

"Did he ... did he tell you he ... he ... *rented* me a woman?" Dassidario shrills. "If he did, he ... he's a liar ... besides being a pimp."

"Uh, Mr. Dassidario—"

Whatever Marshall might have been going to say to Dassidario is cut off by a howl, followed by a rapid series of thuds, bangs, and thumps. "Hope he didn't nail the fruit-cake," Hugh grumbles. "Somebody *touches* him, he could go bananas and we're all dead."

Dassidario's made of sterner stuff than that, I'm about to say, when we hear Marshall growl, "Get cuffs on him."

"I'm *tryin'* ... hold *still*, you fucker or you're gonna go out of here feet first." A voice grunty with effort: Prothro, I guess.

Heavy clicking sound.

"Get up," Marshall says. "Slowly. Try anything else, Mr. LoPriore, and you *will* go out of here on a stretcher. Mr. Dassidario, you okay?"

"Oh, yes. Yes. You stopped him before he could hit me."

"Good. I think you misunderstood what I was driving at, asking about a woman. It's not—"

"Detective, do you have any idea how many dangerous bacteria there are in a woman's vagina? And I'm not talking about prostitutes. Even respectable married women—why, even nuns in the Catholic Church, Detective—have an average of six point four different species of culturable vaginal bacteria. Streptococcus, staphylococcus, mycoplasmas ... they cause fatal pneumonia, you know. And oh, yes, yes. I almost forgot. E. coli. The vagina is so close to the rectum. Why, you'd be safer with a chunk of raw hamburger, Detective."

Frank the Crank is down on the rug in front of the sofa, rolling back and forth, snorting gales of frenzied laughter. Schwartz snickers, sees Trudy give him the fish eye, tries to hold it back, can't. Gackle and Edna look at each other, start to chuckle. Sandy giggles; Mick guffaws. Sarah's face could heat the workshop. Hugh Curtis is just as red, but the corners of his mouth are turned down into a tight scowl.

"All right, all right, all right. Mr. Dassidario!" Marshall sounds as close to hysteria as I imagine a police officer ever gets. "That's enough."

"But who *is* this man, Detective?" asks Dassidario.

"Person of interest in the case. He told us he was with a woman all last evening, and that they were up here about ten-thirty. The woman's sister, the sister's husband, and his parents were supposed to have been staying in this suite."

"Oh, no, no; they couldn't have been. No, definitely not. I was sound asleep in here by ten-thirty last night. That's after my bedtime."

"Yes, I'm sure. And the name de Pinza doesn't mean anything to you, Mr. Dassidario? Earl or Sally de Pinza? Or Shirley McCoy?"

"No, no. Definitely. Is that the lady this man was with?"

"So he says."

"I *was*, goddamn it to hell!" LoPriore's down but not finished.

"Maybe he has the room wrong," Dassidario says. "This is Thirty-Two-oh-One."

"We'll ask at the front desk on our way out," says Marshall. "Thank you, Mr. Dassidario. I'm sorry to have bothered you."

"Oh, well. No problem, Detective."

"Wait—the hospital!" LoPriore refuses to stay down for the count. "We can check out the goddamn hospital. Where the doctor took Mrs. de Pinza after her husband beat her up.

See, that's why I went out with the McCoy broad. I was supposed to be going with Mrs. de Pinza, but ..."

LoPriore's speech slows to a halt like an old 78 record on a wound-down phonograph. The more he says, the more idiotic he sounds. *What* doctor? *What* hospital? Some story. This same tubby Brit, this Dr. Alberts who the concierge is going to swear came to LoPriore's apartment about eight the night before, was here in this room just a few hours earlier, ready to take Sally de Pinza to the hospital. *What* hospital? Doc Alberts never did say, did he; just said to "the hospital." Sure. Good luck, LoPriore!

"Yes?" Marshall packs more impatience into one word than I'd ever have thought possible.

"Forget it," LoPriore mumbles, then shouts, "Wait ... wait a minute. "The restaurant. The McCoy broad and I were at Mindy Roberts last night for more than two goddamn hours. You can check with the headwaiter there. And our waiter."

"Oh, shit!" I hadn't thought of that.

Sarah bats her lashes, flashes me the brightest of smiles. "They can check all they want but I don't think anyone'll remember me—or him. Mindy Roberts is a big place and crowded; on my way back from powdering my nose it was a cinch to slip a few hundred to the headwaiter and the table-waiter, and tell them what a big shame and a bigger mess it'd be if my ugly, nasty, jealous husband found out about this particular hot date."

"You did that?" I can't believe it. "How the hell did you think to do that?"

"Somebody had to. You didn't."

"Hey, way to go, Sarah!" Leave it to Schwartz to keep order. "And if they check out Dassidario's business card, they *will* find out he's got a legit business in Akron. Party and Sickroom, just like he said. It's a great coverup, lets him travel around, do a big-money job here and there when he wants. And you better believe his employees'll tell the cops what a weird guy their boss is."

"Check and mate," I say.

"Dollar bills ..." Frank croons. "I got a million of 'em ..."

"Almost," I say. "Gackle and Dassidario have to get back into LoPriore's place one more time tonight. Shouldn't be a guard posted, not for an insurance fraud case. You've still got the duplicate key, Pete?"

Gackle makes no attempt to veil his contempt. "What the hell you think, I'm gonna lose it?"

"Rhetorical question, excuse me. We need to get the bugs out of the phones, the bird cage and everywhere else Dassidario stuck them; we don't want anyone stumbling on them, not next week or two months from now. Then we'll meet here tomorrow afternoon, four o'clock. Al'll be back with numbered Swiss accounts for each of us. 'Til then, remember: we're still in operation. No drinking, no talking, no picking pockets."

"Yeah, but we're made in the shade," crows Frank the Crank. It's a wrap. I can hear the fat lady."

"Not quite," I say softly.

31

"What did you mean, 'not quite'?"

Sarah and I are walking downtown on Madison. A public forum, my advantage. "What do you mean, 'what did I mean'?" I flip back at her.

Right in the middle of the sidewalk she stops. Hands fly to hips, a classic old-time Sarah hot-eye. "Thomas, don't play games with me."

'Bye-'bye Shirley McCoy. My wife is back.

"I know you. You said, 'Not quite,' and you weren't talking about what Gackle and Dassidario still need to do. You also weren't talking about getting together with Al tomorrow. There's a part of this caper still going on, and I want to know what it is."

I make a face.

"I'm waiting." Tap-tap-tap with the foot. Sarah and Thomas do the quick-step on the Sidewalks of New York. People dodge around us.

"Well ... all right. It's a small thing, I guess, but it bothers me. I counted the expense money this morning."

"And?"

"There was a shortage. Five thousand dollars' worth."

"Exactly five thousand dollars? Are you sure your arithmetic was right?"

"Yes, Sarah, I'm sure. Exactly five thousand dollars is missing from the suitcase."

Sarah starts walking again, slowly; I swing into step. "Look at it this way," she muses. "By tomorrow afternoon we should all have more than a million dollars safely tucked away and you're worrying about five thousand dollars. It seems ... well, a little disproportionate."

"I know. But it means someone in the gang stole it and I've got trouble with that."

The red light changes. We cross the street, hand swinging in hand. "Funny thing," Sarah says. "I'm sounding like you in this conversation, and you're sounding like me."

"I thought of that."

"Well, then." She smiles. "Let me talk to you in your own language, as you're so fond of saying. You hired a bunch of thieves to carry out a theft. Which worked—beautifully. But one of the thieves couldn't resist that suitcase full of money, and when he got his chance he grabbed a handful. Now he's going to be five thousand dollars richer than the rest of us. Big deal. Why don't you just forget it?"

"I know you're right, but it still bothers me. Maybe I'm getting a little overcooked. Tell you what. Let's get a cab, go home. I'll rest my eyeballs for a while, then maybe go out for a walk."

"I'll be glad to go walking with you if you'd like."

I kiss her lightly on the cheek. "Thanks, but I think I'll do better on my own. A couple of hours, a few antiques shops, I should be back to good old Thomas again."

Sarah rolls her eyes but she's still smiling. "Maybe we could all use a couple of hours of peace and quiet."

"I think so."

Back at our place, a kiss, then Sarah goes into her pad and I scoot into mine. But not to rest my eyeballs or any other part of me. I open my top dresser drawer, feel around under piled socks, pull out Hugh Curtis's gun and the little bag full of bullets. Then I take my black leather doctor's bag out of the closet, drop the gun and ammunition in on top of the stethoscope and otoscope.

I grab the phone, punch numbers. "Got to talk to you," I say. "I'll be right over."

32

Compared to New York on a late-August afternoon, Calcutta's a resort spa. Below his great Japanese warrior-lord's robe Hugh Curtis slouches on the sofa, drips perspiration, speaks in a weary undertone. "I sure wouldn't mind being a fly on the wall down at the cop shop. Bet LoPriore's doing a little sweating himself right now."

"Satisfied with how it went, then?"

Little shrug, a sigh. "Yeah ... I guess so. Son of a bitch is crowbait; he'll get ten to twenty, then wise off one day to a two-hundred-fifty-pound lifer and they'll find him with a sharpened spoon handle in his heart. But part of me still wishes I'd shot him full of holes ... or hell! Even just given him a good punch in the snoot."

Hugh looks past me, out the window, as if his next thought might be hanging in the soggy air, waiting to fly in and onto his tongue. His eyes are haunted. "What I really like is he lost his collection and knows it. That's perfect."

"We made the punishment fit the crime."

Hugh's grin is like a crack across the bottom of a ceramic pot. "Wish he could know it was me who did it to him."

"Life's a funny proposition. Maybe someday he will. But is that really so important?"

Hugh's cracked-pot grin fades. "There's something else. LoPriore gave eye for eye: his collection for mine. But there's no tooth. He didn't get nailed for killing Maddy."

"Why should he?" I watch Hugh closely. "He didn't kill Maddy."

Hugh moves as if to get up from the sofa, then sits back, rubs his chin, runs eye tape over me. "Thomas, you've got a loopy sense of humor—but be a little careful right now, okay? I'm not in a joking mood."

"Neither am I. It's not easy to tell a good friend you know he killed his wife."

Now Hugh does get up and in a hurry. He marches to the door, opens it, gestures toward the street. "Out, Thomas. Come back when you've got your head on straight."

I lean back in my chair. "Before I go I've got some things to tell you. Shut the door; sit back down."

For a moment Hugh stands, stares, tries to figure. Slowly, he swings the door closed. As if moving through molasses, eyes fixed on me, he walks back to the sofa, lowers himself by degrees, sits rigid, watches, waits.

"It almost worked, Hugh—everyone in the ER thought Maddy had heat stroke. Lying out in the sun, drinking wine ... got herself a pretty good sunburn. But her chest, shoulders, and abdomen were as red as her face. How'd she get sunburned under her dress?"

Hugh's eyes get very big.

"That's right—she wasn't sunburned, was she? The blood vessels to her skin were dilated because the nerves to them were paralyzed right along with all her other nerves. She had *fugu*—Japanese pufferfish poisoning. A classic case, in fact."

Hugh grips the arms of his chair, then relaxes. "I'm telling you for the last time, Thomas. This is not funny."

"No argument. But why did you do a dumb thing like that? You worse-than-wasted your big chance."

Hugh's mouth is an ugly, crooked gash. "What do you mean .... 'worse-than-wasted'?"

"Can the tripe, Hugh. I mean you not only let Maddy off the hook, you put yourself on. No wonder you don't really feel satisfied. No fun winning a game you know is fixed."

Hugh breathes in deeply, blows it out. "You really think I killed Maddy? With tetraodontoxin?"

"I know you did. For starters, how many people who've lived all their lives in New York even know the word tetraodontoxin, let alone that it's the poison in the Japanese pufferfish? I do, because it's a nerve toxin, and nerves are my business. You do because ..." I let my eyes wander up to the robe on the wall behind Hugh. He follows my gaze.

"Both of us also know pufferfish is a great delicacy in Japan; the tiny bit of toxin in the flesh of the fish gives a rush. You get warm, a little tingly in your tongue and lips, feel a nice euphoria—like having a couple of stiff drinks in a hurry. But the toxin's concentrated in the ovaries so you've got to do a perfect gutting job—otherwise whoever eats that fish is dead. Isn't that right?"

Hugh just nods. Which could mean "yes, that's right," or "go on, I'm listening." It could mean "I'm thinking as hard as I can."

"When I came over here the other night to get your toothbrush and razor and fresh clothes, I did a little snooping for a bottle with a bit of white powder in it. Dried pufferfish ovaries—LoPriore's dose."

Hugh's eyes narrow; his face goes crafty. "You find the bottle?"

I shake my head. "Didn't have time to really toss the place. Besides, I didn't want to leave a mess, maybe get you to thinking."

"Well, then." Hugh's face relaxes, his arms extend expansively. "All this is just a little guessing game."

"I didn't say that."

"You didn't find any toxin here."

"No."

"So you have no proof."

"I didn't say that, either. I'm betting it was here and I'll bet it still is." I point toward the hallway. "You've got a shelf full of Oriental AirWays blankets in the linen closet there—the same kind of blanket Maddy was lying on when they found her in Central Park. An airlines blanket would've been just about the last thing she'd have taken along when she ran out of here. Some way or other you got her to meet you in Central Park and slipped her a good slug of toxin. She got euphoric, then paralyzed. Couldn't scream, couldn't make a fuss. You left. Maddy'd be found dead, no obvious cause. It would've worked, too, if she really had died out there in the Park; who in hell would have thought to look for tetraodontoxin? But when they brought her in to Man Med paralyzed but alert—right after she'd copped out with your snuffboxes—I had to wonder. Guess what those samples I took of her stomach fluid and blood were loaded with? Autopsy showed her skin vessels were only dilated, not ruptured the way they'd be from sunburn. Game's over, Hugh. Where's the rest of that toxin?"

Hugh's smile says he's going to bear with my indiscretion. "There *is* no toxin, Thomas; there never was any. Your imagination's always been part of your charm, but your judgement could stand a little overhauling. Telling me that cockamie story at a time like this ..." He punctuates his expression of dismay with a sad shake of his head.

"Sammy Shapiro didn't think it was cockamamie."

"Sammy Sha— Oh, Thomas, please. Time to quit. Way past, in fact."

"In fact, Sammy confirmed the cockamamie story."

"He did, huh? What, did he talk to you before—"

"You shot him? No, it wasn't me he talked to. Big Al was keeping an eye on Sammy, saw you go into his place and come right out again. When Al went up he found Sammy, fresh meat on the floor."

Hugh seems to find something interesting about his shoes. "He was already dead when I got there, Thomas."

"He was? What are you telling me—you picked the lock, found Sammy laid out and didn't call nine-one-one, just ran out and locked the door behind you?"

"I'm saying I assumed he was dead. I knocked and knocked; he didn't answer. So I left."

I stare at Hugh; he doesn't blink. "Why'd you go over there, Hugh?"

"He called. Wanted to talk to me."

"About?"

Shrug. "Not a clue."

"Hugh," I say as gently as I can, "we had a bug on Sammy's phone. Dassidario picked up your whole conversation with him."

Hugh chews at the corner of his mouth. "I suppose you've got it on tape."

"With Dassidario at the console? What do you think?"

Both of us smile reluctantly.

"Only thing I don't know is how Sammy tumbled," I say. "Want to tell me?"

Hugh looks like a patient getting back a bad biopsy report. "Right before I went to Japan, Sammy called. He had the snuffbox of the century to sell me, and yes, he'd hold it until I got back. Which was actually two days earlier than I told you. When I saw what Maddy and LoPriore did to me I hopped right back on a plane, flew to Tokyo, bought a pile of pufferfish, took them to my hotel room. I gutted them in the sink, put the ovaries into the little microwave in the room—the toxin's not destroyed by heat—and then ground the dried-up ovaries into a powder. On my flight back I figured how I was going to kill the two of them. Maddy, I wanted first. I called her, told her Russell had phoned to say he was coming up from DC with a girl he wanted us to meet, and that Maddy could either be civilized, sit down with me and work something out, or I'd just have to tell Russell and his girl exactly why Mom wasn't there."

"Hugh, that's good. Very good, in fact. And you talk about *my* imagination."

"Huh! Well, Maddy agreed to meet me but said it had to be somewhere out in the open. Central Park was her idea. I was just about ready to go when the doorbell rang and there was Sammy. I forgot all about the damn appointment we'd made for him to show me the snuffbox."

I've never seen a sadder smile.

"I know I should've played it cooler, especially with a sleazeball like Sammy. 'Hey, my man, what's *up*?' Thought I'd never get rid of the bastard. Finally I just pushed him out of the way and went charging up to Central Park with my blanket and wine. The rest you know—it's all on your tape. Maddy and I drank the wine—easy enough to hide a little white powder at the bottom of one white paper cup—and when she began to get weak I told her she was being emotional, she should lie down for a few minutes. That took care of that. As soon as she couldn't possibly yell for help I told her what was the matter with her. I wanted her to know ... and she did. When I left, she was barely breathing. I never thought she'd last until somebody found her, let alone got her to a hospital. That's the story. But if you knew everything right from the get-go, Thomas, why haven't you said anything 'til now?"

"Because I'm your friend."

Up goes the light in Hugh's eyes. "Meaning you're not going to tell anyone else?"

"That depends on you."

"Thomas, you're not talking about blackmail—"

I shake my head. "You just don't get it, do you? You had every right to give Maddy exactly what we gave LoPriore, but instead you did the one thing you're not allowed to do—you took her out. You cheated, Hugh, don't you see? If you want to send someone to hell you've got to do it in this life."

Hugh looks thoughtful. "Who knows about this?" He clicks off names on his fingers. "Dassidario for one, Al Resford for two. They couldn't care less. Hmm ... Sarah know?"

Hugh's question is casual, almost off-handed, but every muscle in his body is tense.

I shake my head. "Just you, me, Al, and Dassidario. Whether it stays that way's up to you. Remember the physical I gave you? After you got dizzy ... because I put a little propranol into your coffee cup. Propranol does a nice job of lowering blood pressure, doesn't it?"

"Oh, you bastard—" Hugh is half-out of his seat.

"My chart note on that visit shows high blood pressure. Alarmingly high, in fact. It also shows I let you know you were at risk for a stroke, told you to see a cardiologist and get on some proper medication. You said you'd do it as soon as you could fit it into your schedule ... but maybe time ran out. I'm still betting you've got some toxin stashed away. Swallow it tonight, the whole supply. Get rid of the bottle before you go under. I'll drop by tomorrow and find you. Sign you out as a stroke."

Hugh takes a moment to study me. Am I serious? "You can't let it go that I killed Maddy," he ventures. "But it's all right for you to force me to kill myself?"

"I'm not forcing you. I'm giving you a choice. Partly because we're friends. Partly because Maddy stealing your collection was an extenuating circumstance if there ever was one. Partly because your kids don't need to know what their mother did or that their father killed their mother. They'll get your full share of the proceeds from LoPrior's stuff, plus every nickel your collection broght. Money's already in a Swiss account; I'll make sure it gets to your kids. Oh, and by the way, none of LoPriore's birds were forgeries; they all brought gold. Couple of million-plus tax-free dollars for Russell and Lucy; that'll give them a real leg up on the world."

"My kids are not dumb." Hugh's tone is oddly flat. "They're going to wonder why I decided to liquidate my collection and set up a Swiss account for them."

"No problem. I'll tell them between losing Maddy and learning about your own health problems, you decided to open that account just in case. If your health straightened out, you'd go back into collecting. If not, you figured you'd be saving them a pile of trouble and a heap of taxes. Don't you think I can convince them? Me with a million bucks in each hand?"

Hugh laughs softly. "Play along, the kids never know. Refuse, they find out their mother was a betrayer and a thief, and their father a murderer."

"Your choice, Hugh. Sometimes a forfeit's better than a blowout. Here." I reach into my pocket, pull out a pistol, toss it to Hugh. He ducks, then recovers himself and catches the gun with his right hand. He looks at it curiously.

"You left it at my place, remember? Last week?"

It feels like last year.

Hugh grips the handle of the pistol. A look of cunning comes into his eyes, then fades. "It's empty, isn't it?"

I toss him a little lead slug. "I got rid of all the bullets but one, just in case I'm wrong and you don't have more toxin hidden away. Not quite as neat as a stroke, but a grief-stricken suicide would work, too."

While I'm talking Hugh cracks the gun, slips the bullet into one of the chambers. He waves the barrel roughly in my direction. "Aren't you afraid I'll use it on you?"

"Only a little."

The gun zeroes in on my chest. "What's going to stop me?"

"I hope the decency I still think you've got."

Without moving the gun off target Hugh leans back against the seat of the sofa. His red mustache bristles. Eyes shot through with red lines and blotches, hair a mess. I try to look away from that black circle pointed at my chest.

"Decency!" Hugh sounds as if he's going to spit on his own living room floor. "Goddamn, Thomas, some bloody friend you are! My wife steals my snuffboxes and hops in the sack with a greaseball gangster, goes off with my heart and my soul, damn her straight to hell! If you were really my friend you'd have put real bullets in that gun you gave me to shoot LoPriore with. And signed Maddy out as a heat stroke. Who'd have known the difference?"

"You for one, me for two. And excuse me, Hugh, but let me remind you that you didn't rush over to ask me to help cover up the fact you killed Maddy. You came flying into my workshop, frantic husband with a dying wife. 'Save her, Thomas, save her.'"

That squeezes a wry smile out of Hugh. "Have it your way." He levels the gun. "I think there's going to be an unfortunate accident. I was showing you my gun, there was a bullet in the chamber, it went off. Sorry about that. I may spend a couple of years out of circulation, but as you've been telling me, consider the alternative."

"The tape, Hugh. You're forgetting about the tape."

"Hell I am. It's you who's forgetting something. Who do

you think is going to go public with that tape? Your English friend? Dassidario? And kiss their million bucks goodbye, not to mention their freedom? The only one I'd worry about is Sarah—but you just told me she doesn't know about the tape."

"Hugh, you're making a big mistake—"

His finger tightens on the trigger.

"Don't do that, Hugh." My voice sounds thin, strained. "Please. For both our sakes."

"Both our sakes?" Hugh's face is scarlet, his mouth twisted in fury. "I'm doing it for *me*. Fuck *you*, Thomas."

He pulls the trigger. The gun goes click. A second pull, a second click. "Shit!" he whispers. "Son of a bitch!"

He's up off the sofa, moving toward me, the gun raised over his head, ready to bring it down squarely on mine. Just as quickly, I'm on my feet. "Hold it, Hugh."

Now *he's* looking down a gun barrel.

"This one's real," I say. "Real and loaded and legal. Sit down."

He just stands, gawking.

"Sit down, Hugh. If you make me shoot you now, you lose it all. I've got live bullets in my pocket for your gun there; after you're dead they'll go into the chambers. Self-defense. I confronted you about my toxicology studies on Maddy; you told me you'd opened a Swiss account, you were getting out of the country, and I wasn't going to stop you. You pulled a gun; I shot first. There'll be a paper on your desk with an account number in a Swiss bank. The IRS'll get every nickel. In the process your kids and the world will find out all about Maddy and LoPriore—but nothing about any kind of big-time scam. Just a revenge murder by a pissed-off husband. Now sit the hell *down!*"

The gun falls from Hugh's hand, crashes to the floor. He lowers himself onto the sofa, looks up at me as if suddenly there were light-years separating us.

"You bastard," I say softly. "After as long as we've been

friends. Besides, how dumb do you think I am? I never would've come here without leaving at least one note to be opened in the event of my untimely death."

Hugh's face goes slack. Game's over; he's lost.

"Take the toxin, Hugh. Go out euphoric; exit smiling. Plenty worse ways to die. And don't try anything silly. Think about your kids."

He studies me, eyes leaden with regret.

"Be back in the morning," I say quietly as I walk across the room and open the door.

Hugh clears his throat. "You didn't know it was me until I nailed Sammy?"

"Wrong, Hugh. I did know it was you; I just couldn't prove it. But I also knew if I kept playing the game the proof would come."

"Sarah doesn't know about this, does she? What you're doing now? She'd have a shit hemorrhage."

I shake my head, then close the door behind myself, put the gun back into my pocket, and walk across the courtyard, out of Hugh Curtis's life.

No, Sarah doesn't know what I'm doing, and yes, she would have a shit hemorrhage if she did. But she'd probably be less disturbed than Hugh thinks because although my gun is in fact real, it's neither legal nor loaded. When a person points a loaded gun at someone, he has to be willing to pull the trigger, and Hugh didn't understand I never *would* be willing to do that. He only knew what *he* would have done in my place. Never mind I'd already faked him out twice with nonworking guns. Never mind I'd told him it's absolutely against the rules to take out your opponent. He'd have been wise to test me as I'd tested him, giving him that jammed pistol to use on LoPriore. A man betrays his character no more clearly than when he's playing a game.

33

Two days later, a break in the weather. Sarah and I sit in her living room, sipping at glasses of ginger ale, watching rain splatter windows. She grins crookedly in my direction, then shakes her head. "You look so different with no hair. How're you going to explain when you're back at work?"

"No problem. I'll say I did it on a bet."

Big sigh. "Right. Anyone who knows you won't give it a second thought. Maybe you don't look like Thomas Purdue but the minute you open your mouth, you're unmistakable."

"I did all right with LoPriore. He never caught on."

"I can't argue that—fortunately." Sarah leans back in her chair, stretches lazily. "Hard to believe it's over. I feel like I ought to be doing something."

"Want me to think up another scam?"

Sarah's pained smile is just this side of tolerance. "No, Thomas, thank you. This one will hold me for a while."

A flash of lightning brightens the room; thunder follows closely. Sarah looks out the window. I know what's on her mind. "We did good," I say. "Good and well."

Sarah makes a show of looking past the far end of the sofa, where Oscar the Parrot sits on his perch. "It won't be so good and well if some collector comes visiting and happens to recognize that bird."

"No sweat. He's rare, but not unique. While we were casing LoPrior's apartment, Edna made a slip, had to cover herself by saying she'd seen a parrot just like Oscar in a shop in Paris. LoPriore didn't bat an eye, and neither will any collector who sees Oscar here. Besides, Phalibois didn't stamp these guys with serial numbers."

"Mmph." She's convinced, but she doesn't like it. "I should have known you'd come out of this with a toy—wait, what am I saying, 'should have'? I did know. I just didn't know which toy."

"Nothing wrong with that. Why not get paid when you can in your own coin?"

"Everyone else seemed happy enough with coins of the realm." In the unnatural twilight, Sarah's face is suddenly solemn. "Except for poor Hugh, of course."

"Yeah."

Sarah looks at me over the top of her glass. "Thomas ..."

"What?"

"Yeah, what?"

"What do you mean, 'yeah, what?'"

"Stop it, Thomas! Why do we always have to play these games? The way you said that 'yeah.' You practically tied yourself in knots trying to talk me out of going along to Hugh's yesterday morning. And when we got there you came within an inch of knocking me over so I didn't go in before you. You've got very good manners; you always hold a door open for me—but not this time. You knew what we were going to find, didn't you?"

"Not exactly."

True enough. I figured Hugh would be lying in bed, a peaceful look on his face, and he was. But there were two other possibilities. He might have been slumped in a chair, gun barrel in mouth, the top of his head sprayed across the wall behind him. Worse, he could've been crouched some-where, aiming his gun at the first person to come through the door, figuring that person would be Thomas Purdue. when you put money on the counter, you're foolish to ignore your horse's track record. Besides, this bet was mine: it was for me to take the risk, not Sarah. Besides, I was wearing the Kevlar vest Schwartz had gotten for me along with the unloaded gun I'd pulled on Hugh the day before. Which Sarah still doesn't know. And never will.

Sarah's glass is on the table. She's glaring. "All right, Tho-mas—talk and talk straight. What *did* happen to Hugh? And how were you involved?"

"How was I involved? I knew LoPriore didn't kill Maddy. I knew Hugh did."

Little gasp, hand to mouth.

"Sorry, but you asked. He poisoned her. She was supposed to die before anyone found her but she didn't, and when I was examining her I tumbled. I gave Hugh his choice. Either do what he did, or go through the conventional sequence."

"The 'conventional sequence.'" Sarah in default mode, righ-teous indignation running roughshod over shock. "My God, Thomas! I keep thinking nothing you say or do will surprise me, but I keep coming up wrong. What on earth gave you the right to give him that choice?"

"I knew what he'd done and I didn't think he should get away with it. Simple."

"Simple, nothing!" Mrs. Grundy is on her feet, standing over me in the gloom. "It was your obligation to report him to the police. Right then, as soon as you found out."

"That would've been just ducky. Maddy'd still be dead, the kids would've had to deal with knowing their mother was a thief and their father a killer. LoPriore, that bum, would've gotten away free and clear, and next week poor Espinoza would be out on the street. And—"

"And you wouldn't have come away with Oscar there. Don't try to sound noble, Thomas. You're the most self-centered person I know—never think of anyone but yourself."

"Hugh, Russell, Lucy," I intone slowly, like a prayer. "Espinoza, Schwartz, Al, Edna, Frank—"

"Sammy Shapiro!" Sarah's voice rings triumphant. "Are you going to tell me how well he came off? What you did for him?"

"Sure. I gave him the same opportunity the rest of us had. If he'd played the same game as you and I and everyone else, he'd be alive today, rolling in money. Problem was, Sammy was greedy."

"He tried to make a separate deal with LoPriore?"

"Uh-uh. With Hugh. Sammy came by to show him a rare snuffbox just as he was going up to Central Park to meet Maddy. When he practically pitched Sammy out of his house, Sammy began to wonder what was up—especially since there were no snuffboxes on Hugh's living room shelves. So Sammy followed Hugh to Central Park, watched him and Maddy, then ran over after Hugh left to try to pump Maddy. When he saw the shape she was in he took off in a hurry, stopped just long enough to tell a cop there was a lady on an OAW blanket who looked to be in a bad way. That's why she didn't die in the park. Sammy loused up Hugh's whole plan; if she *had* died in Central Park, who would've thought of testing her for Japanese pufferfish toxin? After the call from Man Med ER Hugh had nothing to do but go tear-assing over there, satisfy himself she was past help, then charge over to good old Thomas's place to play the grief-struck husband. Meanwhile, Sammy saw his chance. He'd let Hugh keep his snuff boxes in exchange for Hugh's payoff from the caper. That was his game, Sarah, not mine. I'm sorry he got killed, but I don't feel responsible."

"But if you'd never started this business, Sammy never would have ..." Her voice trails into silence.

"That's right," I say softly. "Sammy didn't need my game to try to shake Hugh down. He'd have done that anyway."

"Thomas, you're blowing smoke in my face. Any way you put it, what you did to Hugh was wrong. There are laws—"

"Written by people just like you and me. And they're pretty reasonable general guidelines—"

"Come on! Who gives you the right to decide which cases are the exceptions?"

"I do. Listen, Sarah, tell you what. You know the truth now, the whole truth and nothing but. Go call the police."

She doesn't say a word, just glares at me.

I point at the phone. "Go ahead. Call the cops; tell them the whole story. The rest of Hugh's bottle of poison is in my bureau drawer, under my socks. I found it next to his bed when I went in there; guess it was his way of confessing. I'm going to get rid of it tonight."

She looks as if she might throttle her glass of ginger ale. "You've really got that bottle?"

"Yup."

"If that's true and I call the police, you're in trouble up to your chin. They'll—"

"Don't worry about consequences," I say lightly. "Go on, call the cops. Rules are rules. No exceptions."

"Thomas, you ..." The glass of ginger ale whizzes past my left ear as I duck to the floor. It crashes against the wall behind me, sending chunks of glass and ice sailing in every direction.

"Bad sport." I straighten up, duck past Oscar on his perch. "Cool it, Sarah. Neither one of us wants to give anyone unnecessary pain. The only difference between us is I include myself in my group of beneficiaries."

She sits back, takes my measure. Her face softens. "Thomas, you really can charm birds out of trees, and that worries me. I don't think I'm up for a career as a thief's accomplice."

"That's good. I'm not up for a career as a thief."

"I wish I could believe what you tell me."

"Take it at face value—we had an exceptional situation; our caper was the best way to deal with it. But I'm not about to go around snatching things that belong to other people simply because I want them, or for the money they'd bring. Call it the Collector's Golden Rule, if you'd like."

"I say, Buddy, *nice* singing," screeches Oscar the Parrot. "*Very* good, what-what?"

Sarah tries to look stern but can't carry it off. "I never saw you turn him on."

"When I got up from the floor a minute ago. While evading dangerous flying objects."

Sarah smoothes back her hair. "I'm sorry, Thomas. I shouldn't have done that."

"No you really shouldn't have. But it's all right. You—"

"Let me finish. I shouldn't have thrown that glass because I had no right to get sore at you and I knew it—but that made me even more angry." A grin spreads over her face. "Remember that missing five thousand dollars from the expense money? *I* took it."

"You? What do you mean, you took it?"

"Just what I said. I figured if I was going out for a night on the town with LoPriore and your friend Schwartz, I'd better have some cab money handy."

"Cab money? Five thousand dollars? That's one hell of an expensive cab ride. Sarah, you've got to be kidding."

She laughs out loud. "Where did you think the money to bribe those cabdrivers—and the waiters, for that matter—came from? You never thought of it, did you? But while Edna was making me up it occurred to me I might need some cash in a hurry. So I went into the bedroom, pulled the suitcase out of the closet, and counted out five grand. Oh, you were so smug, Thomas. You figured you'd engineered that whole fancy plan, and I was just a convenient middle-aged woman to hang on Schwartz's arm to make him look halfway respectable. But when Sandy got hurt, who figured out what to do? Who stepped in and took her place? Who thought about the emergency money?"

"You, you, and you. Shirley McCoy, the Whore of Babylon, with five thousand dollars' worth of mad money. I'll bet you could've picked a pocket if you'd had to."

"Thomas—"

Up go my hands. "Just kidding."

I'm not, though.

"You'd better be. But you really didn't think I could handle LoPriore the way I did, did you? Honestly?"

"Honestly ..? No. I was scared silly for you."

Her eyes fill; she fights it off. "Well, it wasn't all that hard. It had to be done; I did it. Not that I like pretending I'm someone or something I'm not."

Someone or something she's not, huh? Who's the real Trudy: the stove-bound dumpling or the loaded ethnic grenade? A woman betrays her character no more clearly than when she's playing a game. That kiss back at the Regency Tower ... happiness expands like a bubble in my chest. But I keep my eyes and face bland. Just wait for Sarah to go on.

"I used only about half the money, though, Thomas—and it just doesn't seem right that I should keep the rest."

"Nothing else to do." I shrug. "Game's over. Al's already put the suitcase money into the account for Hugh's kids. Besides—didn't you say with millions of dollars involved, it was silly to worry about a couple of thousand? Isn't that what you said?"

"Hmmph." That's what she said, all right, but now it applies to her, she's not happy about it. "Okay, Thomas ... I suppose it really was a cheap insurance policy. If I hadn't taken it out, everybody, us included, would have lost a lot of money ... Thomas, why are you looking at me like that?"

It was the "us included." "*We're* not coming out of this with any money, Sarah. I took my share in toys."

Sarah jabs a finger at Oscar. She can't seem to speak.

"Not just him—he was only fifteen thousand. I also took the best pieces from Hugh's collection, including the Napoleon-and-Josephine double-bird snuffbox, the one that started all the trouble."

"Nice little souvenir."

If words really could cut I'd have bled to death before I was two words into my reply. "Altogether they came out to just short of a million. Which would have been our share." Sarah hurls wild glances around the room. "Al's got them in his hotel room," I add quickly. "I asked him to hold onto them until I could ... tell you."

"Thomas ... you slugtrail!" Eyes bulging, sizzling with anger; fists clenched at her side. Damn good she doesn't have another glass to throw at me; this time she wouldn't miss. "Just how do you figure you're going to explain Hugh's snuffboxes to your NYMBCA buddies who come here and see them?"

"Maddy died, Hugh was despondent, he sold me what I wanted from his collection, then dumped the rest on the international market. Then he died."

"And the gang? How about the *gang?* Schwartz comes here, Frank does. Won't they wonder how you happened to end up with Hugh's little treasures?"

"No way. Aside from you and me, the only people who know what really happened to Hugh are Al and Dassidario. Can you see either of *them* asking a question? Even if they do, though, there's still no problem. While we were packing up at LoPriore's Hugh took me aside, told me he wanted Al to sell his stuff along with the bird collection. Looking at them there, he realized he could never enjoy them again. Said if I wanted anything, I should go ahead and buy it with part of my share. So in the truck on the way to Frank's, I talked to Al. After we took the photographs, while Frank and Al were repacking, Al made sure to get Oscar and the snuffs I wanted into one separate box; then he checked it in a long-term security locker at the airport. On his way back from Amsterdam he picked it up, took it to his hotel room. Piece of cake."

Sarah cradles her forehead in her hands, a living ad for Bromo-Seltzer. "Piece of ... oh, Thomas, I just can't ... *Damn* you. You don't think for *minute* I'm just going to believe ..."

"And you know the best part? When Russell and Lucy were here for Maddy's funeral—of course they noticed Hugh's snuff boxes were gone. So he told the kids he'd sold them. And the kids just shrugged okay. They figured Dad finally grew up. Is that perfect?"

Fingers move apart just far enough to launch eyeball missiles. "And of *course* no one else heard about your little arrangement with Hugh, did they?" A hand flutters in my general direction. "Don't answer; I don't want to hear it. Oh, you *are* good, Thomas—even that bit about Hugh not being able to enjoy his snuff boxes anymore. Anyone could understand that. But what I *can't* understand is how *you* could ever enjoy them."

"I look at it a little differently from the way Hugh did," I say quietly. "All those years we were friends, all the good times we had, there were always his snuff boxes. The one lousy week of bad times only began after the snuff boxes were gone. When I see the snuff boxes, when I listen to them, I'll remember the good times."

Sarah looks as if she's going to burst into tears. She's right, I *am* good. "So if I throw sixes before you do, don't forget, I paid what we'd have gotten from Al's contact in Amsterdam, less than open-market value. Call it an investment; we can afford it. Are we hurting?"

"Only when we cry." Tears roll down Sarah's cheeks but she's smiling. "I said you could charm birds out of trees, didn't I?"

"I did have a little trouble keeping a straight face when you said that."

"*Damn* you, again." The words were there but her heart's not in them. "Bad enough I let your little game make a thief out of me. But the worst part is, I enjoyed it."

"I say, Buddy," Oscar squawks. "*Nice* singing. *Very* good, what-what?"

"Oh, turn off that silly bird." Sarah tries not to laugh but it's hopeless. She puts here arms around my neck, pulls me down onto the sofa. "And while you're at it, turn off the phone and clip the wires to the doorbell." She starts unbuttoning my shirt.

"This is suspicious behavior," I say. "I think you might be plotting to expose me to six point four different species of highly dangerous bacteria."

"Well, now, I might just be," Sarah sounds more like Cleveland Gackle than Gackle himself, "but then again, I might not." She unhooks my belt, pulls at the zipper. "Are you interested?"

Water pounds the window. Tomorrow's September. Days shortening, night coming on. So much pain, why? I stand up, walk slowly across the room, push the start lever of the fine cylinder music box I restored and gave Sarah for our twentieth anniversay. The room fills with the aching loveliness of the trio "*Protegga, il giusto cielo*" from *Don Giovanni*. In the music I hear Maddy Curtis's plaintive appeal trembling between Hugh's ominous baritone and the *basso* thunder of Vincent LoPriore. But there's Edna too, maintaining a precarious harmony with Cleveland Gackle and Big Al. Soapy Sandy and Mick the Dick, one voice blending with Espinoza's cheerful counterpoint. Trudy, Schwartz, and Frank, a breezy air of optimistic good nature. And through them all, Sarah's clear, sweet tones, like the sun low on the western sky, its glow made redder, ever more gorgeous, by the clouds lying across its face.

All this and heaven, too? Maybe not that. Eternal perfection, every game fixed, the win in the bag before play even starts? Sounds like LoPrioreville to me. Boring as harp concerts, tedious as monochrome.

But every day on earth, a whole new ball game.

I shake free of my shirt as I rush back, grab Sarah. "Yes, of course I'm interested. Yes! But ... *yes!*"